REIGN

OF

BLOOD

AND

SHADOWS

First published in Great Britain in 2023 by INKED ARROW BOOKS.

Copyright ©2023 Rhian Edwards.

Published by INKED ARROW BOOKS

Contact: rhian@rhianedwardsauthor.com

www.rhianedwardsauthor.com

ISBN:

Paperback: 978-1-915719-07-2

Ebook: 978-1-915719-06-5

Cover by 'Get covers'

RHIAN EDWARDS

REIGN OF BLOOD AND SHADOWS

KINGDOM OF DRUIDS
BOOK ONE

STORY CONTENT

This is a new adult romance with spicy and steamy scenes which will increase as the series progresses.

There is violence and death and characters who curse. If you want a more detailed list, please don't hesitate to contact me.

If you love women who drop the 'f' word fairly regular, dark and broody men, a lil of bit spice, and some fantasy sword fights, then go right on ahead. Our heroine has a long journey ahead of her, but she isn't a shrinking violet.

ALSO BY

SOUL BOUND SERIES
(YA urban fantasy)

Ascending in Chaos
Avenged by Fate
Alliance of Enemies

The Alliance (prequel short story)

KINGDOM OF DRUIDS
(NA fantasy romance)

Reign of Blood and Shadows
Throne of Lies and Ruin
Realm of Kings and Curses

For those who need to escape, I've got you covered.

ONE

DARKNESS DESCENDED UPON THE capital of Balmore Kingdom. I gazed up at the wide eye of the moon and pursed my lips. Its taunting gleam dared me to make a wrong move in the bright glare as I moved through the streets. While the lunar light eased the strain on my eyes, I would have preferred to not be so...exposed. I slid to my right, into the alleys at the heart of the district—a shortcut to where the fair had already begun and where less brightness would find me.

Tunnelling wind caught my hood, almost taking it down with my speed, but I yanked it back in place. The off-black, well-used cape concealed the icy-blonde hair I'd roughly twisted together into a plait—a signature style down in the common city area. It was one of my many practised efforts to blend in.

"Of course," I sighed when I rounded the corner, leaving the alley I had gone down and stepping into the bright light of the blasted moon. I swore the Gods hated me.

I pulled up my hood and walked through the market street, merchants smiling and waving as I went by. My heart squeezed. It wasn't recognition for why they smiled at me; it was their trusting and warm nature. Upon a quick glance, many wouldn't guess my true identity, but I didn't want to chance it. A polite nod was the only interaction they got from me.

As I hurried by my favourite bakery, glorious scents of warm bread embraced my senses, and I fought the urge to stop and go inside. I had no coin on me for a start. Granted, I could alert them to who I was and have some for free, but then my nightly adventures would get back to the palace, or worse, my mother. An expected shiver tore through me and I somewhat reluctantly marched on ahead. She was the reason I snuck out anyway.

Usually, I headed to the most popular tavern after daylight hours because it was the only time I got to really see Fox. My best friend for years, he worked at the tavern and enjoyed my illicit company and palace gossip almost as much as he protested he didn't.

But today, I made my way to the city's night fair. Celebrating the return of the guard trials for the first time in twenty-five years, the fair was all anyone could talk about. People were annoyingly excited.

Fighting another sigh, I refocused on who I was going to meet: Fox. The tavern had secured a spot at the fair, and Fox claimed he'd be working in the temporary tent pitch. A smile spread over my face as I remembered what else he'd said: stalls from all over the kingdom would sell their wares and services. I'd never travelled beyond the city, so I was determined to get the most out of every second of tonight's festivities. It would be the closest to travelling I'd ever get—outside of my royal duties, of course.

Lights from a thousand candles and lanterns lit the path ahead as merry chatter and music drifted closer to me. I joined the back of a group walking towards the centre of the open-air arena, tension leaving my body now that I was one of many rather than on my own. It always surprised me how much more invisible I could be within a crowd.

Large, pitched tents sat around the edge of the field where I imagined the larger establishments like the tavern were based. Rows of back-to-back stalls took over the middle of the area. People interacted with sellers, their faces free, joyous.

I wandered towards one of the nearest stalls, my eyes widening in glee at the exquisite, colourful silks when someone barged into my shoulder. I frowned after him. Not even an apology came from him as he stalked away. And then it hit me: he hadn't known who I was. I smiled and moved closer to a rack of silks, testing them between my fingers. They were by far some of the smoothest silks I'd ever felt. And that was saying something. The vendor talked with a friendly-looking couple, so I nodded in appreciation at him before walking further down the row, taking my time to admire a silver trinket stall and a home-made fudge company.

My breath misted in front of me as I headed towards a sign for the tavern, weaving in and out of the slowly meandering crowds. A child squealed as he was pulled on a small cart around a track, his hair going wild and his reddened, round cheeks stretched wide by his grin. I couldn't help but smile at the carefree joy on his face.

Smoothing my cloak before I pushed through the tent flaps to the bar, I took a deep breath at tonight's temporary freedom.

The potent scent of beer and testosterone greeted me when I stepped inside. By the looks of some of the men in here, many were likely taking part in the trials themselves. Unmarried soldiers and warriors, including those who just considered themselves good fighters, all desired to enter the trials, and some even ventured from beyond Balmore.

So tonight, I wanted to scope out some candidates. While they would first be protecting me, as soon as I took the crown, they would officially protect the queen, so only the finest and strongest men could win. I had grown up under the current guards' protection, and they were the best men I knew.

I fought down a heavy groan. I snuck out to forget about my duties as princess, the ones my mother always insinuated I wasn't good enough for, and I swore to God that if Fox even dared to call me a princess tonight, I'd have him hanging upside down by a part he wished he no longer had.

Speaking of, the guy popped up from behind the wooden bar where he helped Sadie, the tavern owner. With Sadie being the only other person who knew about my true identity—and labelling me the 'granddaughter she never had'—she always kept a close eye on any palace soldiers entering who could easily identify me. Luckily for tonight, most who could recognise me even in my common clothes would be patrolling the outskirts of the fair, and thanks to my mother's paranoia, I was rarely outside the palace as Princess Rayleigh.

Streaked with grey, Sadie's short white hair escaped in tendrils and stuck out in curly wires around her crinkled face. From my guess, she was in her mid-eighties and still a formidable woman who worked at the tavern every day. It always impressed me when

I saw her, and I would absolutely never dare ask her actual age unless I wanted a quick slap to my head, royalty or not. Sadie's chestnut-coloured eyes sparkled with recognition when she faced the tent opening. She waved me over and finished drying a glass, but then roughly elbowed an unobservant Fox in the ribs. He dramatically yelped, rubbing his side, and scowled at the woman who had taken pity on the orphan when he'd arrived in the capital looking for work many moons ago.

Fox's unruly dirty blonde hair and sullen blue eyes were a comforting sight, and I knew as I bounced over with a big smile plastered on my face that my joy at his 'injury' would only make his frown deeper. Served him right, to be honest.

"Take a break, Fox, our lady is here," Sadie's weathered voice cackled when I approached the busy bar. I reached into the folds of my inner pockets, taking hold of a small vial of pale blue liquid, and passed it over to her. She grasped my hands between her own and touched my cheek softly, tilting her head as she smiled. The action moved the creases around her eyes. "Bless you, child," she whispered, but then pursed her lips at Fox, who still rubbed his side. After shaking her head at him, she limped away; I made a mental note to ask if she had been resting like she promised she would. The medicine I could get for her only helped so much. Without it though—and I knew for a fact there was no way she had the extreme finance needed, or the means, to buy it safely her-self—she would become bound to a chair as her bones weakened with her illness.

"Man, that woman has a bonier elbow than a corpse!" Fox complained, hanging his washcloth on a rail above a large make-shift sink of water, rolling his sleeves before vaulting over the bar. It was a busy night, so no one paid any particular notice to the action, but when he jumped down next to me, I slugged him on the arm.

"Don't compare Sadie to a corpse!" I chastised, causing Fox to yelp again. "Oh my word. You are such a baby."

Fox rubbed his arm. "You know I bruise like a peach!"

I beamed at him. "What do I have to do to get a drink around here?"

Fox rolled his eyes and gestured to the other serving guy who had been recently hired. The young lad's gaze shifted to me. His nostrils flared and pupils dilated with cold calculation. I had no doubt it was because he had an eye for me as a woman, not because he suspected I was heir to the kingdom or had any value beyond what his dick wanted. Somehow, the thought didn't comfort me. Nope. No way. It was never going to happen with him. I failed to suppress a visible shudder.

"You sure Sadie can spare you? It's packed," I asked Fox, turning away from the guy.

Fox's eyes darted around, and then he shrugged. "People want Sadie's beer; they'll wait." He flashed me a huge grin as we grabbed our cool drinks and navigated our way to a small round table near the corner of the tent, slipping into newly vacated seats.

The tavern's tent was among the biggest at the fair. I had seen the peak climbing higher than all the others on my walk over. Sadie's tavern was definitely one of the most popular in the city—if you ignored some of the seedier establishments, that is. It made sense it was as sought after here, too.

Fox snapped his fingers in front of me, jerking me out of my daze. I tore my eyes away from scanning the sea of faces and focused on the drink I now put down on the handmade table. Scents of cedarwood drifted to my nose just as keenly as the notes of whatever stew Sadie had made earlier. They must have hauled most of the tables here from the tavern for the fair.

"Sorry, I was just thinking."

Fox raised his thick, dark brows. "About the would-be warriors here?"

Fuck. I should have been watching the warriors. That's what any normal person in my position would have been doing. The four champions who gained the guard position would swear an oath to forgo a life outside me, only serving me, never marrying, or having children. It was a massive dedication for only the bravest, strongest, and most loyal. I wanted to see who might fit that requirement. Who I might be stuck with, forever.

My shoulders rose again, and I took a sip of the tart liquid in front of me, scanning the men in the room. Some were giving too much attention to the ladies. Others were busy trying to be bigger or stronger than the other; I counted at least three arm wrestling matches. There were some throwing back beer almost faster than Sadie could pour them. I sniggered, thinking about the sore heads they were sure to be nursing come morning. My mother's personal guard rarely drank, and if they did, it wasn't the same volume some of these men were downing.

"What's so funny?" Fox questioned.

"Nothing, nothing. What have you noticed so far, then?" I asked. He wasn't always the most observant, but knowing him, he would have been scoping out what he could for me—even if he wasn't the most subtle while doing it.

"Well, there are a lot of guys. A lot. I've seen some older ones who have got to be thirty plus, which I find odd as surely this is a young man's game?"

"I suppose, but it's their skills that are important, not their age."

Fox scoffed. "I'll see if you're still saying that when you're being guarded by someone as old as Sadie!"

"Sadie can kick ass, so don't knock someone just because they're older." I kicked him under the table for insinuating Sadie as useless. "Anything else noticeable apart from the ancient ones?"

Fox pointed to a man in the darkest corner of the tent, hood up, concealing his face, shovelling stew. "He's been here two days already, boarding at the tavern. He came down here tonight, I guess to scope out the competition, but he doesn't interact with anyone and keeps to himself. Never seen his face."

"Ooh, now that's interesting," I mumbled, propping my chin on my fist, leaning forward on the table to try and catch a glimpse of him. Even in shadows, I could tell he was tall but slender.

"Yes. Yes, it is. I'm desperate to see his face. Maybe he has a scar or something?"

"You do like scars."

Fox grinned. "That I do. Means they've been doing anything but the boring shit I do."

"You like what you do."

"Correction, I like Sadie, not the job," he said, and I rolled my eyes. "He doesn't drink either."

"That's...odd."

"You're telling me. This is a *tavern*."

"He's probably just taking the trials seriously."

Fox's face fell. He stared into his glass.

"I'm not happy about all these strange men competing for the role of your protector. It's a stupid requirement that should have long gone. Look at these guys, most of them are a bunch of drunken idiots!" He cast weary eyes around the busy room, and I couldn't exactly argue his point. Testosterone led most of the contestants here, with many appearing to sport few brain cells. My mother's guards were intelligent men.

"I understand your worries, Fox. Do you not think I have them myself? They'll be by my side forever. No peace. No escape. They'll know where I am and what I'm doing for the rest of my life. I know it's required if I'm to rule, but I'm losing the only bit of freedom I have, the only thing my mother can't control."

Fox leaned across the table to cover my hand with his. "I hate that in a few short weeks you'll have to stop coming to see me."

I stared at my drink, unsure of what to say to my best friend. It wasn't long ago I had to explain to him that a personal guard would ensure I could never sneak out of the palace again. He had soured at the knowledge and, from then on, had nothing but negativity for the trials. It was tiring, but I shared his feelings. I was perfectly happy under the watchful eye of my mother's personal guard, who often left me alone to focus on the queen and their duties.

I drained the last dregs of my drink.

"Fox, we just have to make the most of it now. We can watch and survey the contestants before they even know who I am. That'll be fun! Especially with you. What better way to spend my last few weeks of freedom?!"

He huffed and downed his drink, too. "I suppose. I can be as nosey as I like, yeah?"

"Wouldn't expect any less. How else can we be sure the best people are being picked for the job?"

"Right," he said, slapping his hands together. "I've got a little more time before Sadie will need me back. Want to do something fun?"

"Always!" Fox grinned and grabbed my hand, pulling me out of my chair, quickly exiting the tent and hurrying past stalls. I laughed, dodging and darting around people, offering breathless apologies to anyone we cut up. "Where are we going?"

Fox glanced behind to look at me with a wicked grin. "You'll see."

He pulled me to a stop at the back of a crowd of people watching a trio of performers as they took to the small platform ahead of us. Their skin-tight clothing allowed them to leap through the air, tumble from long strips of material tied to wooden poles overhead, and when one of them spat fire, the crowd roared. I clapped with them, smiling when Fox leaned down to speak in my ear.

"Stay here. I'm getting us a pretzel."

"What's a pretzel?" I asked, but he'd already turned away and disappeared into the throng of people who'd gathered behind us.

I stayed where he left me, watching a slower performance, admiring their art even though some people left now the fast-paced action had died down.

Behind me, I caught snatches of a hushed conversation. The words 'Cilla' and 'brutal attack' reached me. I tucked some loose hair behind my ear and focused in, not wanting to let whoever was talking realise someone listened to them.

"It was brutal, man. Seriously. I was travelling through, hoping to sell my tools, but it was eery. Balmorian soldiers were there, blocking anyone from going in, but...I used to work at a butcher, and there ain't no mistaking the smell of blood." Blood? I frowned.

"Are you talking about the Dydairian attack?" another asked.

"Shh! Are you crazy saying that name out loud? Either shut up or talk bloody quietly, for pity's sake!" the original voice hissed.

"What?"

"Have you seen the number of unfamiliar faces here? Any of them could be one of them druid bastards."

I flinched, casting my eyes around the crowd in a new light. Dydairians? Here? It couldn't be the druids, they couldn't cross the mountain ash-lined wall bordering our kingdom, but their violent human population and the cursed creatures plaguing their land weren't affected by the magical boundary. It was why the wall was heavily guarded by soldiers from Balmore, Ashmeer, and Creed. Three kingdoms desperate to keep the darkness on the other side of the wall. And I knew extra units had been sent to the wall from all three kingdoms recently in answer to the increased attacks from the Dydairians.

"Oh please," one of them said, albeit quieter, "as if they've made it through the wall, a heavily guarded wall at that."

"Not yet."

"And what's that supposed to mean?"

I had to agree with the voice. What *was* that supposed to mean? Those not of druid blood couldn't find a way through with all the soldiers on the wall. Right?

Fox slid up next to me holding a large twisted-shaped dough in his hand.

"This is a pretzel," he said with a toothy smile, breaking off a bit and handing it to me.

The men behind me either stopped talking about the incident or had walked away.

"Ray?" He dipped his head slightly.

"Sorry. What?"

"Pretzel?"

"Oh," I mumbled, taking a bite. The salty flecks burst on my tongue, mixing in perfect harmony with the chewy savoury dough. "I like it."

"I thought you would," he replied around a mouthful, tearing off another piece for me.

My body shivered, so I wrapped my cloak tighter around me as I reached for the dough. We couldn't afford for the wall to fall. It not only stopped the Dydairian druids, but was also a physical barrier to keep out the cursed, born from the dark evil magic that festered there. I couldn't even imagine the death and destruction, the utter chaos, that would ensue if the druids and their cursed were able to run freely this side of the wall.

We started walking back towards the tavern's pitch, and I ignored what the men had said behind me. Now was not the time to work Fox up on what I'd just heard; I wanted to savour every moment of this night with him. And I knew, I categorically knew, druid magic couldn't cross the wall. We were safe from them, at least.

I repeated it in my head.

"Your mother been making you take any more lady lessons?" he asked.

I took a deep, calming breath. "Calling them lady lessons is ridiculous."

"But accurate."

"I suppose. And yes. Honestly, she will not give up. She makes me wear the most preposterous, impractical dresses and gets Yola to put my hair up and then forces me to walk with frigging books on my head. 'Princesses do not slouch, Rayleigh'," I mimicked in her tone.

"I really would pay money to watch these lessons, you know."

"You've told me. On multiple occasions. She's threatened me with a day at Lady Mila's again." I mocked throwing up, which made Fox bark with laughter.

"Lady Mila?! Gods, what did you do to elicit that threat?"

Not even the least bit annoyed he'd made another—correct—assumption, I smiled. "They caught me in the palace guardroom."

"Playing cards again?"

"Yeah, one of our generals spotted me when I left, but Fox, the new recruits are some of the only people willing to actually converse with me inside the palace! What's a girl got to do? Sit around and learn to sew?"

"That's exactly what she wants!"

I was quiet for a few moments, Fox's words stirring up long felt emotions when I thought about my mother. Groaning, I tucked my arm through Fox's and leaned my head against his arm as we ambled through the fair.

"I sometimes wish I was who she wants me to be."

"Nonsense."

"I mean it. If I was, maybe she'd actually...like me."

Fox tutted. "Seriously? If she doesn't like you as you are, she's not worth it."

"You know who she is, right?"

"You're hardly going to snitch on me," he said and smiled slyly to which I rolled my eyes.

"Why doesn't she like me or even just trust me that I'm capable? That I'd actually be half decent at ruling if she just gave me a chance? If she had another option for an heir, I'd be out of the picture."

Fox snorted. She may be the queen, but I know he didn't rate her as a mother. Can't say I did either.

"That's her problem, not yours."

"But it *is* my problem if she won't let me learn. She's keeping me from everything, and all I do is continue to disappoint her. As much as I want to prove her wrong, it doesn't matter what I do. I only ever appear a failure in her eyes." I angrily kicked at the dirt path.

"You're not a failure."

I pressed my lips in a tight line before I spoke. "I am. I don't know what I ever did to be so pathetic."

"You're starting to wallow," Fox said as he squeezed my arm. "The real Ray that I know wouldn't wallow. She's a sneaky little badass."

I laughed. "If she wasn't so controlling, I probably never would have snuck out the palace that first night, so I never would have met you. Maybe I can thank her for something after all!"

"I'll allow that." He pursed his lips in thought.

I eyed the path towards the fair's exit, and Fox said, "Time to go?"

"Unfortunately. I shouldn't risk it too much longer. I'd get more punishment than a day at Lady Mila's if she ever found out I came down here."

"You okay for getting back?"

"Always," I answered, the conversation I'd overheard about the Dydairians racing back into the forefront of my mind. What happened at Cilla? Had Dydairians really bypassed all the guards and attacked this side of the wall?

Popping back into the tent with Fox, I spotted Sadie who waved at me when I caught her eye. I left then, deciding to sneak between the larger pitches around the edge and take a shortcut through some alleys rather than the fair's main entrance and exit.

I navigated through the crowds outside, attempting to reach the edge of the tent. People either wanted to head inside for a drink or chatted happily with each other outside. Many of them would be candidates for the trials. I tried not to focus on them and pulled my hood further up in case a palace soldier wandered by here, but my thoughts now overran with the men I spied around me. Would the guy with the long scar running through his eyebrow become one of my guards? Or would the older man with streaky grey hair even survive the trials? And what did the young boy's mother, who looked younger than I did at nineteen, think about him taking part? What motivated these fit, healthy, mostly young men to give up a life of love, passion, children—normalcy—just for me? I didn't think I was even worth it.

I slipped between two of the larger tents, sighing a breath of relief as shadows washed over me. Fewer people were around the back, mainly drunken idiots taking a piss against the canvas and a few conspicuous ladies drawing the 'paid for' kind of attention.

A woman cried out. I spun, instinctively bringing my fists up, but my shoulders sagged almost as quickly. The woman sat on the edge of a beer barrel, a man between her thighs and skirts bunched around her waist. Heat rushed to my cheeks as I raced around the corner, not hearing the telltale sign someone was approaching. I turned the corner and bounced right off him.

TWO

FULL SPEED. I WALKED full speed into another body, slamming my bent head right into a muscular chest and ricocheting back a small step. A masculine scent wrapped around me as strong hands reached out to steady me from falling on my ass. His large, warm hands gripped my upper arms. I inhaled sharply on a startled gasp, causing me to do a horrid combination of a snort and a hiccup. More than a masculine scent worked its way into my senses: hay and woods settled around me, leaving an unnerving fluttering in my stomach. Before I could even register what that meant, a string of profanity left my unfiltered mouth that would have my mother ordering a day with Lady Mila quicker than I could have taken my next breath. There was barely an 'oof' from the guy. An 'oof' would have been polite.

I looked up at his face and holy fucking smokes. I had literally just walked into a god. Brown hair warmed his face and hung over his forehead in such a casual manner that begged my hands to run through it to see if it was as silky as it appeared. My hand twitched with the forbidden need. If I could have slapped my hand, I would have. His green eyes glinted with a trace of humour as a smirk twitched at the corners of his glorious mouth. My mind already started betting on how his lips would be confident but gentle as they kissed the sensitive areas of my body...wait. What the hell was I doing?

I blinked and stepped out of his hold—despite enjoying the delicious heat coming from his hands on my arms, even through my cloak. He didn't wear any armour, but he'd casually slung a scuffed chest plate over one shoulder. My eyes travelled down and a worn belt holstering a sword hung low on his hips, forcing my sight where they absolutely did not belong. Regaining some form of composure, I quickly raised my eyes, travelling back up his body. I gulped. The cream tunic he wore tucked down into his trousers didn't leave much to imagine about his tight figure. Damn. The guy clearly worked out. The thought made me shift uncomfortably as I started uncharacteristically fretting over how I appeared right now in my disguise, knowing my face was likely flushed and sweaty from my earlier speed walking.

I met his piercing eyes again, almost falling into the depths of them. His physique and the soft stubble around his lower face suggested more man than boy, so I guessed him to be in his mid-twenties. Pulling my lower lip in between my teeth so I wouldn't say any of these thoughts through my traitorous mouth, I froze. Oh hell, his smirk grew. Oh, double hell. I was staring.

Get a grip, Ray. You're behaving like a...oh gods no. I was behaving like the high-born girls my mother always wanted me to play nice with.

After that shock, I rolled my shoulders back and wiped imaginary dirt off my ragged clothes. I was heir to the kingdom, after all; I could act less of an idiot.

I cleared my throat to speak. "If you're entering the trials, you ought to be more aware of your surroundings." Well, swallow me whole and call it a day. *That's* what came out of my mouth?

The stranger raised one brow, which only made his face look more sculptured than it already was. "It would appear so. I wouldn't want to run the risk of being stabbed, would I?" His smooth, deep voice hummed in my ears, and I had to sharply tell my weak knees to pull it together. This reaction was ridiculous: I absolutely refused to literally swoon in front of a guy. How absurd. Absolutely not. "Are you okay? You just appeared out of the shadows with no warning," he asked, dipping his head to look level with me, and it would now appear I have lost my voice. Fuck.

"Mmm, yes," I mumbled. Drowning. I was drowning in his forest green eyes, now shining with a mix of concern and a hint of humour. I focused on the audacity of his humour, and thank the gods, it made me feel more like myself than the wet blanket I was at risk of becoming.

"Do you need any aid?"

"Oh heavens, we bumped heads—or rather, I hit your chest as you're so tall and...it doesn't matter. I don't require anything, thank you," I said, shaking my head just to emphasise the statement.

"Hmm."

"Did you just 'hmm' me?" I asked and took a small step back, folding my arms across my chest. His eyes swiftly dipped down my body when I moved, but quickly found my face again. His appraisal gave me strangely delightful goosebumps, a much different feeling to when the creep at the bar did it.

"Forgive me. Where are my manners? I'm Wrendor Netero, a hopeful competitor in the guard trials, and I was probably too occupied to notice where I was going. Again, forgive me, my lady." The guy, Wrendor, bowed his head, appearing sincere in his apology. But when he lifted his head back up, my eyes zeroed in on the full-blown smirk now plastered on his face. My mouth dropped open.

"Are you planning on winning with your humour, Wrendor?"

"Please, call me Wren. And oh, I plan on winning all right." Something flashed in his eyes. Something I couldn't quite name.

"Do you mind me asking why someone such as yourself would give up a normal life for the guard?"

"Someone such as myself?"

Crap. "I just mean someone who...someone who clearly, umm, well..."

Wren mirrored my pose, crossing his arms over his well-toned chest, his biceps bulging. I honestly had a hard time keeping my eyes glued to his. *Do not look at them, Ray.*

"I'm not quite sure what you mean, my lady. Could you enlighten me?"

"It's hardly my fault if you've got more brawn than brain." My comeback made even me grimace.

Wren nodded confidently. "I assure you my 'brawn' is equally, if not outmatched, by my brain, but you'll have to wait and see if that's true for yourself."

Was that an invitation? Was he inviting me to watch him in the trials? Was he flirting with me? No. He couldn't be. Not if he was serious about entering the trials.

"You assume I'll be watching," I said instead.

"Doesn't everyone?"

I tried to come across as nonchalant, but I was pretty sure, judging by the glint in his eye, that I wasn't pulling it off. "Only if nothing else interests me at the time." Such a lie. First, it was mandatory I was there given they were trials to find *me* a personal guard. Second, I was heavily invested in this: the four guards who won would be my shadows for the rest of my life. The thought sent a shiver through me.

"Are you sure you're all right, my lady?" he asked, mistaking what my shiver was for.

I coughed down the fear of how my life would become even more stifling than now.

"Yes, I am. I do, however, need to be going."

"I shall escort you to your home. It is the least I can do."

"Ahh, it's okay. I can manage."

"I can't let a woman walk home alone in the dark. Plus, there are dangers out there right now."

I almost asked if he was referring to the Dydairians but stopped myself. That was not a common conversation anyone should be having, let alone risking it getting out that someone was asking about Dydairians. It was a wild leap to presume he meant them, anyway. I shook my head to get rid of the words I'd heard earlier as they clearly lingered and thanked him inwardly. I wasn't some defenceless girl, and his assumption that I was, happened to be just the fuel I needed.

"Oh Wren, you couldn't keep up if you tried. I'm more than

capable of defending myself." If only my mother had such faith in me; I smiled brightly at him, though. He shifted uncomfortably, probably because he actually did think he ought to walk me home and well, he couldn't because I lived at the palace, and that would be a dead giveaway that I wasn't who I acted to be. I tilted my head to the side, studying him. "Off you go, then, and I'll be on my way too." I smiled sweetly.

Wren narrowed his eyes, obviously sensing I was up to something, but he relaxed a fraction when he realised there wasn't going to be a different outcome. He started walking backwards, in the direction I'd originally come from, and held his hands up in surrender.

"Okay, as you wish, my lady."

I twirled my finger at him so he'd turn around.

He shook his head in amusement, but begrudgingly turned and took two small steps forward. I quickly launched to the side of the first building, racing round it, and planted my back against the stone wall as I tried to control my racing breath.

His murmur of surprise lit a smile on my face.

"Well played, Little Shadow," he said out loud, and my body shivered at his teasing tone. I was so screwed.

THREE

I SLOWED MY PACE once I reached the palace walls along the section with the tall iron gates. It was an unused entrance to the palace gardens, as a more convenient route had been cleared closer to the stables, which had obviously proved more helpful for the groundsmen. The gates I stood at rarely got used and were always padlocked. But that didn't matter. I could scale them and drop down the other side thanks to a well-located oak tree on the opposite side.

It was trickier getting across the lawns. I often had to hide behind bushes to avoid detection by soldiers on duty. I kept to the darkest patches where possible, but I'd had many a close call.

I approached the exterior palace wall of the wing my room was in, three floors up. Ivy had been growing for years up this side providing me with the best way in and out of my room undetected. There was absolutely no way I would get in and out by travelling through the actual palace, far too many soldiers patrolling and people to pass.

The dry night made the ivy nice and easy to climb. At the top, I swung my leg over the window ledge and used my shoulder to shimmy up the thin windowpane I'd left slightly open so I could pull myself in. I very much looked forward to getting into bed clothes, feeding the fire because it was too damn cold in here, and then settling into bed. Even though I was trying not to think about him, imagining falling into bed conjured all sorts of thoughts about Wren, and my stomach did that clenching thing again. What was that about? I sighed, shutting the window behind me. Thinking of Wren, no matter how beautiful he was, would do nothing to change the fact he was out of bounds. For a multitude of reasons.

I dusted my hands on my trousers and the hairs on the nape of my neck stood alert. The room was dark, the fire I'd left now just embers, but something whispered to me that I wasn't alone. I froze, holding my breath.

"Really, Rayleigh? It took you that long to notice you weren't alone? My training must have been terrible," Markin's somewhat amused voice greeted me, and every tense muscle in my body immediately relaxed. The head of my mother's personal guard had been in charge of my physical training programme growing up. Like my grandfather had once said to my mother, Markin told me that no future queen should be left defenceless. Fifteen years I'd trained, but I wondered what the point was if my mother wouldn't even let me in on political discussions. She was hardly going to let me go fight should we start a war at the wall. I shuddered, thinking of the bloodbath we'd enter if the Dydairian druids found a way to break through.

The strike of a match hissed, and then the lantern beside my bed came to life. Markin moved to sit in the armchair by the small table in the middle of the room. Fear set in when I thought Markin might tell my mother about my adventures. My choices: grovel, or hope he didn't believe I had just been outside the gates.

I stiffly but casually made my way over to the very low-lit fire and fed it with some of the logs resting in the large basket beside it. It would soon chase away some of the frosty chill I would otherwise be forced to sleep in.

"I was just doing some strength workouts, climbing the ivy outside to build some upper arm muscles." His silence spoke volumes, and I gulped. "I wanted to see if it was safe to use the ivy should I ever need to escape, because you always said that I must ensure there was another way out of any given location." I turned around. His hands clasped together, and he raised one brow. His long grey hair now kissed the top of his collar; it still amused me he'd grown it out. Along with my mother's other three personal guards, they all wore fine clothes, even in the palace. Derril, the youngest guard, shared my discomfort with wearing fancy clothing, as he too felt like an imposter. Markin usually despaired when he saw me in dirtied, typically male clothing. His tight lips confirmed he had such thoughts now.

He gestured for me to continue and crossed one black boot-laden foot over his knee before folding his hands over the top of his deep-red velvet jacket. My eyes were drawn to his leather sword belt, and I couldn't help but compare it to Wren's well-worn one.

I gulped. "Are you going to make me continue my lies, or shall

I just accept you know I was out? Like, out-out."

"There we go. I know more about the goings on of this place than you could possibly imagine. Of course I knew you were 'out-out'." He sighed, and I nodded in reluctant agreement, relieved he hadn't sent a unit out to find me and march me back. "Do I need to remind you that it's dangerous going out alone, even as trained as you are?"

"No. I know it's a foolish thing to do."

"And yet you still did it. I know you've been craving some freedom from your mother, especially lately, but Rayleigh, the city is full of strangers coming in for the trials. You must be careful."

"I will be," I said, trying to hide the bubbling excitement that Markin wasn't running straight to my mother and that it sounded as though he wouldn't stop me going again.

"Although, I have a mind to refresh some defence training with you."

"Anything!"

Markin rose from his seat and stood next to me, placing a hand on my shoulder as he looked down, his sharp eyes softening slightly. His warm face began to show its age with creases around his mouth and eyes, but the corners of his lips turned up at my enthusiasm. His age became more observant when he smiled. Markin may have been a stoic and a somewhat formidable man, but growing up beside him meant he'd been a father figure to me. He'd been the one to teach me how to ride a horse, how to fight, how to get along with my mother. His rare smiles were only reserved for me when we weren't in the presence of others, like now. I had no doubt he'd taken pity on me when my father passed away at such a young age—I didn't even really remember the man. Markin's constant presence in my life left me feeling grateful beyond words. I couldn't imagine life without him in it. I raised my hand to squeeze his gently as it rested on my shoulder.

"Be careful, Rayleigh. These are tough times with the trials and the problems we've had at the borders."

Markin dropped his hand when he recognised my expression.

"What problems? I overheard people talking about some attacks. Is it the Dydairians? Have they crossed the wall?"

Markin narrowed his eyes on me. Just because I was one of the few people he smiled at, didn't mean I was exempt from his sterner expressions.

"And what, exactly, have you been spying?"

"Spying? People were speaking loudly. Hardly my fault."

"Rayleigh." He drew out the word, placing hands on his hips.

I tilted my head back and sagged against the wall.

"You're not going to tell me anything even after you drag out what I heard."

"At least we're on the same page."

"Fine," I grumbled, crossing my arms. "I overheard—not spied—on some traders it sounded like, talking about an attack on Cilla. I honestly wasn't paying much attention, but then a third joined them and asked if they were talking about the Dydairian attack. Why were Dydairians attacking villages in Balmore? They're not permitted to cross the kingdom's boundaries," I said, hoping to lure him into a conversation, but his eyes shone: he knew exactly what I was doing.

"Thank you for telling me. News does indeed travel fast."

I pursed my lips. "Not to me it doesn't."

"Rayleigh—"

"No, c'mon Markin. You know my mother should allow me in on this stuff!"

He cocked an eyebrow. "This stuff?"

"Ruling the kingdom."

"It doesn't concern you." My stomach churned. Something was wrong. Something was bothering him. What was so bad that both he and my mother had to hide it from me? It was bad enough my mother didn't believe in me, I couldn't have Markin doubt me too.

Spine steeled, I met his gaze, keeping my voice steady, "But it will. One day, it will, and I will be incredibly unprepared. You know it. Why does she keep me out?"

"You know I can't answer that. Your mother..."

"Doesn't think I'm capable of ruling this kingdom and is a controlling—"

Markin held up a hand. "Don't finish that sentence," he warned, and I huffed. "You need to clean up and get to bed before anyone else discovers your...new exercise regime." He walked over to the door and then paused. "And I mean it about the training. As soon as I have more time on my hands after the trials, I'll be topping up your defence skills. I'll ask if Loch can spare some strength and cardio training with you in the meantime. When your mother steps down, I want to ensure you're ready."

"Markin, about my mother discovering my...exercise regime?"

"She doesn't need to know from me."

I sagged in relief. "Thank you."

"Get some sleep. You've a busy few weeks ahead of you. I know what it may seem like, but you will make a good queen one day, you will." Light from the fire caught his face, his eyes full.

I cleared my throat. "Are you getting emotional?"

"Don't be ridiculous." He opened the door but paused again. "Night, Rayleigh."

"Night, Markin."

FOUR

KNOCKING ECHOED THROUGH MY mind and reverberated around the room; I groaned and pulled the pillow further over my head. The knocking rudely continued.

"Princess Rayleigh!" a high pitched and far too cheery a voice sounded from the other side of my bedroom door. A stark contrast to the 'not-a-morning-person' state of my sleepy mind.

Throwing back the covers, I let out a small huff of frustration and padded over to the door. Sheri, my mother's handmaid, smiled when I greeted her. The woman straightened the pinny that matched the length of her pale skirts and smoothed a stray strand of her dark hair back into the tidy bun she always kept it in. Only slightly older than myself, her time was usually split between me and my mother, but we were still quite friendly—when it wasn't early in the morning.

"I told you not to call me that," I grumbled, trying to make sense of the bright daylight behind her. Maybe I'd slept longer than I thought.

She curtseyed briefly. "I'm sorry, Rayleigh, but your mother has requested your presence this morning to discuss the meet and greet event with the warriors."

I grimaced. The meet and greet with the elite and rich of the kingdom spelled: boring, with a frigging capital 'b'. The only thing I had to be grateful for was that Fox said he was working the event as waiting staff. He often took on extra jobs for money in the palace, which suited me no end.

"Your Highness?"

While the prospect of meeting some contestants enticed me somewhat, even the high-born ones, I dreaded seeing my mother beforehand. 'How to be a proper lady' would be on the morning's agenda for sure. My eyes rolled involuntarily, and Sheri pursed her lips at me.

"Yes, yes. Tell her I'll be ready," I answered. Sheri held up her finger to say something when I tried to shut the door, but to no avail, thanks to her well-placed foot in the doorway. I groaned. "And I'll wear something suitable," I added on, anticipating Sheri's next message.

When I finally shut the door, I turned to my stupidly large wooden wardrobe and rifled through the frill and lace, my face scrunching at the fabrics as I searched for the least fancy dress I could possibly find, settling on a pale blue design. The long-sleeved, cotton dress's square-cut neckline was a modest number. The bodice was created from soft materials, not a corset, and moved gracefully with the skirt, providing plenty of flexibility. It was one of my favourites, but my mother hated the undecorated, jewel-less, plain dress. Perfect.

It wasn't that I wanted to annoy my mother…okay, I did, but that's only because everything was always about the kingdom, always about anything other than me, really. Not to mention I was never good enough as I am. Her attempts to change and control me were just one of the ways she showed she didn't care for me as a mother should a daughter, and I was lying if I said that didn't bother me. I didn't know what I ever did to insult her so much. *'You are the heir. You are going to be taking over one day'.* They were the important things, according to her. Not 'emotions' or 'pandering to a silly child'—her words, not mine.

Sighing, I slipped into some dark blue pumps to go with the dress and combed my waist long hair to leave it long and loose. No doubt Mother would send her hair stylist over to me before the event, anyway. We argued several years ago that I could dress and style myself on normal days, but I had to acquiesce and let her take charge for events. It was a compromise I'm glad she accepted.

I grabbed the delicately twisted, pale gold bangle my father had left for me after he passed away and threaded it onto my hand. Turning it on my wrist out of habit, I smiled at the piece of jewellery I always wore unless I was sneaking out of the palace. According to Markin, my father hand crafted the piece not long before he died. I smiled, thinking about what he would have been like had I been old enough to truly remember him. Some days guilt would eat away at me for how little I thought of him, but I'd barely been four when he succumbed to the bone sickness. It was that which ailed Sadie now. Since my father's passing, doctors had discovered a new and expensive medicine to help sufferers live longer and with fewer side effects. Saving my father wasn't possible, but I would prevent Sadie from wasting away at any cost.

I left my room and made quick haste through the palace—I wanted to annoy my mother slightly, not get a special 'lesson' of hers doled out. Staff rushed by me quickly, busy preparing for the traditional meet and greet. Cleaning, cooking, flower arranging, all happening as I sped past them. My mother no doubt asked them to make it suitably decorated even though I was nearly certain the event was being held on the lawns. As I hurried along the windowless corridor leading to the area of the palace my mother's throne room was in, I counted at least ten people working in the gardens; putting out chairs, last-minute pruning, and I'm pretty sure I spied someone dusting a statue. Figures.

When I approached her open door, I didn't knock, but I did wait inside the doorway while she finished a hushed conversation with one of her personal guards: Derril. The youngest of the four royal guards, Derril was the funniest—except I wasn't supposed to know that, or share that knowledge with anyone. Even now, the taste of the most delicious chocolates he always bought back from his yearly visits to his hometown lingered on my tongue's memory. I smiled at him from the doorway, despite him not looking over at me. With the chocolates came the stories he told me, stories from all over the continent—ones perhaps my mother wouldn't approve of for a young lady. If Markin were akin to my father, Derril was undoubtedly the fun uncle.

Derril ran a hand over his closely cropped dark hair, his eyes pinching in frustration. Where my mother was pale like me, Derril was dark—yin and yang stood together like they were.

The royal guard worked seamlessly with my mother, having been with her for twenty-five years. I swallowed a knot in my throat. As much as I loved her guard, the thought of four warriors being forever my shadows sent the butterflies flapping wildly in my stomach. I covered my midsection with an arm to keep them at bay.

They both ignored my presence and leaned back over a document I couldn't read from where I waited but spanned the length of the rectangular table—a map, maybe? My mother's eyes briefly flashed up to meet mine, her tight lips an obvious sign of her disapproval that I stood there gawking. I made a show of looking around the room, anywhere but the one place I wanted my eyes to stray.

She wasn't fooled.

My mother's plain throne sat upon a small podium, two steps high. Only a small cushion for comfort adorned the chair as this room was mostly used by herself and the guard where they plotted strategy and discussed other boring crap like finances. Finances involved math so normally I'd be happy to leave that to others. But I wasn't privy to anything relating to the kingdom recently, despite being the heir, so I'd actually take on finances if it meant some involvement. Anything to prove her wrong in that I *was* capable of leading someday.

Derril straightened and rolled up the document in his hands, nodding at my mother. The tense way they both held their shoulders made me wonder if they'd been discussing the Dydairian attack.

Derril bowed deeply and turned to leave, winking at me as he passed.

"Ah, Rayleigh, there you are," my mother said, like she hadn't seen me standing here for the last few minutes. I fought the urge to roll my eyes.

Queen Isla wore a similar blue dress to me except hers was darker and covered in a light material that shimmered when it caught sunlight streaming through the small slitted windows around the room. Unlike my ice-blonde hair, her light brown hair was already elegantly braided into a bun. If it were down, it would have been the same length as mine, which was about the only similarity between us. Even our eyes were different: mine an icy blue-grey and hers a light hazel. Based on paintings of my father's pale blue eyes, I assumed most of my looks came from his side. I wondered if more of my personality came from him, too, but it was hard to know. People rarely spoke about him upon my mother's insistence. A familiar ache settled in my chest for a man I never really knew.

I walked into the room while she tidied other papers on the table. "What were you discussing with Derril?" I asked as innocently as I could muster, pushing aside my long-standing grief.

"Nothing for you to worry about," my mother began. I curled my hands into fists to calm the anger that started brewing and a vicious pain stabbed at my temples.

If only one thing had been impressed upon me throughout my life, it was that the Dydairians—even the human ones—were a despicable, violent, and problematic kingdom. The dark magic that tainted their lands and infected their people created the cursed and it was a threat we needed to keep away from our people no matter the cost.

"But, mother, how am I meant to learn how to deal with the Dydairians if you never teach me?"

My mother froze. "There is nothing for *you* 'to deal with the

Dydairians'. Markin and Derril are coordinating patrols to address the problem. Right now, though, we must worry about the trials. Finding you your own personal guard is imperative." She finished tidying the table and stood tall with hands clasped before her, face slightly pinched. I refrained from rubbing at the growing pain at the sides of my head as her worried and pained eyes made me take a figurative step back.

I nodded, vowing to bring it up again. There clearly was a growing problem surrounding the Dydairians.

"Okay, then, what do we need to discuss regarding the meet and greet later?" The only sign she was relieved I stopped my questioning was the barely imperceptible relaxing of her shoulders. I couldn't let this go, but perhaps a hunt for Markin would be on my agenda. Maybe I could finally convince him to tell me something if I pleaded enough.

"The warriors you're meeting today are important, not necessarily for your guard, but their families support us in one way or another. Most, if not all, will end up in our ranks as soldiers, and so it is important you welcome them with warmth and grace. They need to see you as a leader, so they continue to pledge their loyalty to us."

"Got it. Be nice. Be a lady. Be nothing like I really am."

"That's...you know what? Yes. If you could pretend to be a high-born lady, heir to the Balmore Kingdom, and not the mannerless, self-absorbed, rough and tumble girl you act like most of the time, then I'd really appreciate it."

A little taken aback by her words and the tired way in which she spoke, I opened my mouth to argue, but nothing came out. She made me sound like some selfish brat. My head throbbed in answer, zapping some of the heat from my anger.

"Yeah, sure," I said.

I physically recoiled at her sharp glare. "Yola and Sheri will be in your rooms later to help you into a dress of my choice, and I will see you on the lawns prompt on time."

"Yes, ma'am."

"Remember your manners around those who help you prepare."

"Yes, ma'am."

I winced at another sharp twinge across my head.

"And try not to get into trouble between now and then."

"Yes, ma'am."

My mother raised her eyes heavenward and let out a long sigh. "You're dismissed."

I turned on my heel and marched out of the room, finally giving in to the need to put pressure to my temples. The headaches always, without fail, showed up when I argued with my mother. If she knew one was brewing now, she'd send me to my room in case anyone saw. I didn't think this one was going to end in a blackout, so I pushed on, aiming to find Markin in the hopes he'd tell me something.

He wasn't in his office, so I made my way back towards the throne room, being careful not to bump into my mother in case she noted the pain on my face. She always said my headaches were a weakness we couldn't afford to openly display. If word got out the heir to the throne suffered with debilitating headaches and needed special tonics every night to reduce their intensity and frequency, we may very well appear vulnerable.

I sneered. Of course, my mother used something I suffered with to control me and make her displeasure towards me well-known.

I'd only made it half-way back, when I ran into Loch who informed me I was on his list of jobs for the day. I groaned at the blonde-haired warrior.

"Now?"

Loch crossed his arms, his thin lips tightly pressed together, and his amber eyes narrowed on my face.

"Yes, Rayleigh. Now."

Without arguing, I went and changed my clothes, and then followed him into the courtyard around the back of the sunroom, knowing he was annoyed with me. At least the pain had subsided to a dull ache. That, I could deal with.

"Markin told me what you were doing last night," he announced when I rounded the corner.

"He said he wouldn't say anything!" I protested, now understanding why he acted so mad at me.

"To your mother, he never said anything about us."

"So you all know, great." I rolled my eyes, and Loch grabbed a long strip of grey material, winding it around my hands. He grabbed hand pads and took his usual stance before me.

"You know the drill."

FIVE

L OCH PUSHED ME FURTHER than I thought was fair given it had been a while since we'd trained together, but I didn't complain...much. I knew he'd been mad at me for sneaking out on fair night.

When Sheri came to fetch me for a bath, I made a show of acting grateful to Loch but was relieved to leave and soak my aching muscles in hot water.

Sheri stayed outside my bathroom, trying to tell me about some of the important names my mother told her about. I dried off and tucked the towel around my body to leave the bathroom, but now I was about to get ready, all I could think about was what Yola might do to me.

Yola, my mother's stylist, no doubt already had the dress, the hairstyle, and makeup all picked out and ready to go. She was probably one of my mother's closest 'friends', if I could even use that word to describe her. I weirdly felt sad for my mother, but that changed when Yola walked through my door.

Tall, willowy, and nearly fifty, the woman's stern face often matched her stern hands. She hadn't been afraid to chastise and knock me a few times growing up and all at the acknowledgement and encouragement of my mother. Yola was a harsh mistress, and if I wanted this to be as painless as possible, I needed to stand tall, sit straight, and zip my mouth shut. Fun.

"Ah, there you are." Her high and haughty voice pierced through me. I grimaced, which she took for a smile. "Undergarments, please."

Sheri helped me into the cotton underwear, and then Yola came at me with the dress. Yola manoeuvred me in front of the mirror so she could adjust and start doing the ties at the back of the floor-length, deep forest green dress. I tried not to gasp when she cinched the ties in more at my waist—I had some curves already, I didn't need Yola to carve them out for me.

Looking at the dress in the mirror, I ran my hand over the tiny 'v' cut out of the bustline and admired the sleeveless straps. Sheri secured a velvet belt of matching colour around my waist where it gathered, pinning a delicate gold buckle embellishment in the middle.

"This material on the top is thin. Thin," Yola warned before I'd even done anything. I tried not to roll my eyes as she smoothed out the folds and draped it down my legs, the dress flaring slightly at the waist. The embroidered, delicate looking vines down the length matched the gold buckle at my middle. I actually quite liked the dress. Not that I'd openly admit that.

Yola and Sheri excitedly discussed the event as they did my hair.

They left it long, giving a soft wave to my tresses, and pulled back two small front sections, twisting them around the back until they met in the middle. Yola finished it with a forest green ribbon which stood out against my ice-blonde hair.

"For the love of all that is holy, stop squirming!" Yola hissed at me as she attempted to put some colour on my cheeks and lips.

"You know, some would say natural beauty should shine."

She raised her eyebrows at me. "We tweak our appearance to appeal to those around us, and today, you will appear a youthful lady with an abundance of calm and grace."

I wasn't sure if I should take that as an insult, but she finished, stepping backwards to smile proudly. She clasped her hands together, and Sheri joined her in their inspection of me.

"I wonder how long it will last?" Yola pointedly asked. I took a deep breath knowing the dig aimed right at me and gave her my sweetest smile.

"Until mother says so."

"Exactly right, young lady!"

I followed them both to the sunroom where we met my mother, in a similar colour but more extravagant gown, and Markin. She no doubt deliberately co-ordinated our outfits as she had done for as long as I could remember. Derril and Loch would already be waiting outside. Floor to ceiling windows gave me a clear view of where our beautiful grounds were covered in well-dressed ladies and gentlemen; swords strapped to the sides of many. I guessed those carrying swords were warriors, trying to show off their impressive steel works.

"You look beautiful." My mother smiled approvingly; she clutched the top of my shoulders. While I believed she did indeed think I was beautiful, somehow, the fakeness of her voice made my stomach turn.

"Is everything okay?" I asked under my breath. Her eyes sparked with an unrecognisable emotion. She nodded, gently pushing back a lock of hair over my shoulder.

Abe, her final member of the royal guard, stalked into the room behind me. He nodded at my mother, his salt and pepper hair tied back into a low bun as usual. I smiled at him and got a small, tense one in return. Not even the small lines around his eyes moved. I opened my mouth to ask if he was okay when my mother spoke.

"Shall we? It is a very exciting time, meeting warriors who could become your personal guard." She looked to Markin, who smiled fondly back at her.

With no time to waste, Markin pushed open the sunroom doors and stepped out before us.

"Ladies and gentlemen," he bellowed deeply, turning all heads in our direction. "I present to you Queen Isla and her daughter, Princess Rayleigh." He stepped aside and I took my mother's arm, walking out, side by side. Abe followed us while everyone bowed or curtseyed, and I inclined my head delicately, as I had been taught to do. The smile plastered on my face became genuine when I spotted Derril to one side, winking at me conspiratorially while no one looked. I could always count on Derril to help smooth my nerves.

To cover my laugh, I took a glass of pale gold bubbly liquid and followed my mother around the crowd, smiling, laughing, and being 'impressed' at the stories told. The trials could not be bribed or bought, but some warriors and their families clearly thought they were achieving some form of political clout by being here.

I eyed Loch walking close by the tree line around the far side of the garden. He rubbed his chin, and just as I was about to look away, his hand snapped to the hilt of his sword. I took another sip of my drink to cover the nerves flooding through my body. Why was I so on edge? He spent several motionless seconds staring into the thick of trees before he walked away, returning to the crowd. He saw me looking and gave a curt nod, a slight smile ghosting the corner of his lips, and then he was back in guard mode. I breathed out deeply and suppressed a smile back at him, lest it unintentionally invite another unwanted story from a keen competitor trying to win some form of favour from me.

It already felt like I'd been here for hours when one of the lords of southern Balmore appeared in front of me; his thin greying hair and protruding nose matched the hideous moustache that ran across his top lip in a thick line.

"Princess Rayleigh, so good to see you!" he exclaimed, bowed, and then held his hand out for mine. I pressed my lips in a tight smile to stop them grimacing. He was often at palace events without his wife, and it hadn't escaped me he frequently had female company—company that he bought.

I placed my hand in his and dipped my head slightly, snatching my hand back as soon as I straightened. That was enough respect for this tool, thank you very much.

"Lord Allen."

Lord Allen beckoned over a man younger than him by about three decades. The man may not have had a moustache and grey hair, but he had the same protruding nose and sharp eyes I'd often caught lingering on the rears of many of the female serving staff.

I wasn't exactly thrilled when Lord Allen started bringing his son to events.

"Princess Rayleigh, this is my son, George. He'll be partaking in the trials," he said with a beaming smile. I tried not to puke as George bent into a bow.

"Oh, how wonderful. I do wish you luck," I replied, dipping my head in George's direction in preparation to finish the conversation and move away.

"It'll be an honour to be in your personal guard."

I pressed my lips together again so I didn't blurt out the first thing that came to mind which was: I'd rather bloody poke my eyes with knitting needles.

"I'm sure, but let's not get too ahead of ourselves. The trials are said to be very dangerous. No one would blame you for wanting to follow your father's impressive footsteps in lordship."

"My brother is all set to take over the lands, Your Highness, it would be an honour to my family to serve you in your personal guard."

I took a sip of my drink and nodded, knowing full well that he was not built for the action of a fight. He might have received training, but he was all talk and show. Fighting was not that.

"I really must see to the other guests, make sure you try the canapes—they're delicious." I turned on my heel and marched over to one of the serving girls to swap my glass. She smiled warmly which I reciprocated.

"Have you seen Fox?" I asked.

I had sworn he said he was going to be working the event; it was the only thing I looked forward to about it.

Her eyes widened and the tray she held wobbled. "Excuse me,

Your Highness?"

"He's not in trouble! I just want to talk to him, he's my friend," I hastily explained, and she relaxed. Slightly.

"I don't think he's on this event, Your Highness. A last-minute change; something about his grandmother."

"Sadie? Is she okay?" I grabbed the girl's arm and rushed to help steady the tray when it trembled under my sudden lurch.

"I'm sorry, I don't know."

My heart beat fast wondering if something was wrong with Sadie. Did the medicine not work? I noticed her limp last night, but I hadn't pushed to ensure she was doing okay on the new dosage I was able to get for her. The girl watched me with pinched brows. "That's okay, here, let me help you with that."

I re-centred some glasses that had slid around and bid the girl on. My mind scrambled for an excuse to leave early, but there was no way I could escape to the tavern in daylight hours. I'd have to wait for the cover of darkness.

A cold shrill shiver raced through my entire body, gripping it in ice. I lifted my arm; the hairs stood on high alert. I scanned the crowd trying to find the soldiers patrolling the event to see if they felt what I did, wondering why my senses were yelling at me to run. A scream pierced the once calm atmosphere, jarring pleasantries and shattering small talk. People started backing away as more and more screams followed. A sharp pain tore through my head and settled at the base of my skull, a constant, steady drum. I found Markin making his way towards my mother, a serious expression on his face and jaw clenched tight.

Derril appeared from behind me, taking hold of my arm, his other hand on his sword ready to draw at a moment's notice.

Everything happened so fast, I could barely keep up, my mind still reeling, pounding, trying to figure out the danger. My mother spun from Markin, her eyes searching the crowd for me as she gathered the bottom of her dress in her hands. Dread slithered in my veins as soon as her wide, green eyes landed on me.

She issued an order at Derril, "Take her inside, now."

While no tremor hid in her voice, the command was met with panic from the crowd closest to her. Aspiring warriors started pushing innocents aside, attempting to get to where the original scream had come from. People moved in disorganised chaos when the distinct clang of steel on steel penetrated the screams and shouts.

Derril's firm hand dragged me towards the doors, but I stumbled, straining to look behind me. I lifted my blasted dress off the floor.

"Derril, we need to help!" I squirmed in his grip, but his strength outmatched mine, and he continued to drag me through the chaotic crowd.

"Dydairians!" a woman shrieked behind me. I turned. Five men, clad in tight black armour, attacked the palace soldiers along the outskirts of the civilians. The ferocity and skill with which they fought sent a deep wave of fear through me: this was a well-oiled, co-ordinated unit. The realisation left me breathless; this was not a haphazard or fortuitous event.

Three more men in blackened armour caught my attention as they moved through the battle. No. The middle male wasn't in the same clothing. His dirtied, ragged clothing hung from his taut body as he fought against the chains the men flanking him held tightly. Matted hair covered his face while he tried and failed to fling himself against the two either side of him as they dragged him along. He screeched and roared, spittle flying from his mouth when he threw his head back.

I tripped over my feet. If it wasn't for Derril, I would have fallen to the ground. The man's pitch-black eyes swung from side to side, his mouth snapped open and shut erratically, flinging saliva and black blood everywhere. Black streaks lined his pale face and disappeared under his torn collar.

"It's the cursed!" a woman screamed. "The cursed are here!"

SIX

T HE CURSED WERE HERE? How the hell did a cursed get *here*? Through the wall and through our palace defences? It didn't make sense. It couldn't. But Derril froze with me, his hand tightening on my arm like an iron band.

"Shit," he cursed under his breath, and then drew his sword. He shoved me towards the doors. "Get inside, don't let it bite you."

I wanted to argue; I'd been trained—I could help. I knew I could. But instead, my heart leapt in my chest when Derril ran towards the two holding the cursed man. Before Derril could reach them, the men let the cursed go. The now free cursed man didn't hesitate and leapt toward the closest person. A woman in a fine lemon-yellow dress screamed as it landed on her, possessively clutching her body close to his, and then he buried his head in the crook of her neck. The woman screamed and flailed as Derril neared, but he was too late. The cursed man ripped his head away from the woman's neck, dropping the lifeless body, hot red blood pouring down his face. I froze, pressure squeezing my head as lights danced behind my eyes.

Loch grabbed my arm, shunting me from my still frozen steps.

"What are you still doing here?" he hissed, tightening his grip when I stumbled yet again. This goddess-forsaken bloody dress.

"Loch, that isn't really a cursed, is it?" I mumbled; pretty sure I was going into shock.

He met my eyes but said nothing. More screams echoed as one by one the crowd really understood the danger. Derril and Abe joined our palace soldiers, trying to subdue the cursed one. Markin yelled commands at the rest of his men, the grounds erupting in a fight with the Dydairians. Who else would risk bringing a cursed into the kingdoms, a cursed who came from Dydair in the first place? None of this made sense.

My head spun as Loch continued hauling me toward the sunroom, feet tripping over each other like the useless bystander I felt. If I was just allowed to move on my own, I may have already been inside. Up ahead, my mother approached the steps when one of the Dydairians rushed between our palace soldiers and threw a hessian bag at my mother's feet.

I'd never seen a head detached from a body before, but it wasn't something I could mistake for anything else. Three heads left bloody streaks as they rolled out of the bag and towards my mother, their decapitated faces frozen in shock with wide eyes and open mouths in silent screams.

Pain danced across my head and my stomach violently lurched, but I kept the contents down, keen to maintain my composure much like my mother was somehow currently doing. I couldn't black out now. I couldn't. I took a deep breath as the pain pulsed behind my eyes and my hands shook.

Loch and I rushed past the heads and up the steps. I couldn't hear my mother as we passed her, blood roaring in my ears. Her mouth moved quickly, pointing at the senior soldiers, issuing commands as though heads hadn't just rolled to a stop near her feet.

My mother turned on her heel and stalked in after me. Behind her, the cursed one fell to his knees, Derril's sword slammed through his chest. With steel deep in its body, Abe then swung his own sword straight through its neck. I quickly averted my eyes.

Soldiers brought the now bound remaining Dydairians toward us while others carefully laid cloths over the decapitated heads.

"Mother!" I breathed when she breezed past me, her face still as stone. Derril and Abe came through the doors panting.

"Follow!" she barked. Derril came back to my side and gently took my arm again, kick-starting my feet into moving. He pulled me slightly behind him as we trailed after the prisoners, each sneering and laughing at the queen. Derril's hand tightened around my arm once or twice at the vile language those men spat at her, but not even a flinch came from my mother.

We filed into the throne room where she quickly ordered all but the captured men and her guard out. The soldiers pushed the prisoners to their knees and left, closing the door behind us. Derril stood slightly in front me.

"You're not fit to run a kingdom!" one shouted.

"Whore!"

"Pathetic!"

"Enough." The calm, composed command was nothing like the venom I felt welling inside me. How dare they call her those names! "What are you here for?" my mother demanded, clasping her hands elegantly in front of her body, her face a marble mask.

"Did you like our gifts?" one man spoke, his hair long and straggly like the cursed man's had been. He tossed his head to one side, throwing hair out of his face. Thin lips puckered into a kiss, and the others beside him laughed. Derril stiffened beside me.

My mother swiftly turned to Markin. They did not speak as he handed her a sword. She tested the weight, and then let it hang down beside her, the tip resting on the stone floor.

"You killed my people," she stated, and I smothered down a gasp at her fact. I suspected the heads were Balmorian, but this confirmed it. An unexpected twinge of guilt ran through me. "You broke the rules about crossing boundaries. You scared my guests. And you bought a cursed here, risking us all."

One of the Dydairians huffed, "So what? What are you going to do about it in that pretty little dress of yours? Make us go through one of your pathetic little courts? Ones that pretend to give the people a 'fair chance'? Please. You're not fit to rule a kingdom the way it should."

"Oh? Do you recommend brute force?"

The man she spoke to raised a snake-like smile at her. "Power. *You* don't have any."

"I don't send my men out on suicide missions," my mother calmly said. "You will not receive a trial. You will not receive mercy."

"It's a privilege to be—"

My mother lifted her sword with surprising ease and swung it in an upward curve in one fluid motion across the neck of the man who spoke before her. The man jerked, a gurgling sound filling the room. Loch and Abe did the same with the last two men, mirroring her actions without question.

Three bodies fell to the stone floor, silently flapping around like fish out of water, and the ground quickly turned crimson. I knew my mouth fell open. I knew I gawked. Was I going to have to do that someday? My mother handed the sword back to Markin.

"Arrange for this to be cleared and ensure everyone else leaves safely. Find me later to discuss our perimeter. Derril? Check in with the border patrols. It seems our traitor has just upped their game."

Wait.

My head throbbed, and I wanted to rub at my temples again. Traitor? What was she on about?

She walked over to me, her shoulders back and head held high. A touch of colour drained from her cheeks: the only noticeable change.

I may have been sickened by the heads that rolled outside, shocked at seeing throats slashed, but neither of those held me as speechless as I was now. It was the knowledge we had a traitor among us, and no one had thought to tell me.

"Mother..." I breathed out. She paused by me, closing her eyes for a split second before opening them again.

"A ruler does what a ruler must."

"But...what even just happened? How did the Dydairians get here, past the wall and in the palace? Was it this traitor? Why didn't anyone tell me we were being betrayed? What did the Dydairians want? Have you done that before? Executed people without trial? How can you be so calm—" She held up her hand, effectively shutting my rambling mouth.

"Quiet. You will not share with anyone that you know about a leak in our defences. You are to go back to your room and stay there until I tell you otherwise."

Now my mouth dropped open for a different reason, and the pain in my head pulsed in response. I just witnessed the most graphic thing I had ever seen in my whole life, which she very well knew, and discovered someone was betraying us, but neither my mother nor her guard knew who. And they expected me to go to my room like a good little girl? I wanted to stay with her, learn from her, show her I could do this—that I didn't need protecting.

But I didn't get a chance to tell her my thoughts and wants because I was dismissed. I mumbled and stomped the entire way to my bedroom, slamming my door shut behind me, and then flopped down onto my wide bed. I closed my eyes even in the dim room, and my head thanked me for it. How the heck was I meant to process this?

Dydairians.

The cursed.

A traitor.

My mother.

SEVEN

DARK SKIES CONCEALED ME as I finally fled down the main cobblestone path towards the tavern. The moon goddess clearly took pity on me tonight.

With the fair over, business would be back in the old stone building. I held my hooded cloak with one hand to stop the breeze created from my speed pulling it down. While I was dressed in old, tattered trousers, a cream tunic, and a cloth wrapped around my chest and over my shoulders for warmth, I worried that after today's events, talk of the palace, and therefore me, would be on people's minds. I wasn't even out much dressed as Princess Rayleigh, but paranoia still clutched me in its grip.

Pushing open the familiar tavern door, I spotted Fox cleaning a table over in the far corner. He looked up after I entered and sagged in relief, leaving the dirty rag behind as he wound his way to me.

Arms banded around my waist, and he lifted me straight off my feet. "Thank heavens you're okay!" he whispered in my ear and set me down again, searching my face for a sign I wasn't. I grabbed at his sleeve and pulled him to the empty booth he'd been cleaning.

"Where were you? Is Sadie okay?" I asked, casting my eyes around the place one last time and then finally feeling safe enough to pull my hood down when nobody was staring.

"Yes, she was unsteady on her feet but adamant she was the only one who could cook tonight's stew. I had to stay and help her; I couldn't leave her."

"As long as she's okay, I was worried."

Fox raised an eyebrow. "You were worried? What about us? I heard there was an attack at the palace! Was there really a cursed there? Here? In Balmore?"

I leaned forward to cover my head in my hands, gently massaging at the fading ache.

"It was awful, Fox, just awful. I'm pretty sure I went into shock."

Fox's eyes softened as he squeezed my hand and then rolled up his sleeves before scanning the room, settling his gaze back on me.

"Is it true the Dydairians brought heads them with them? And that the cursed was..." he mimed sawing a hand over his neck "too?"

I nodded. Fox snapped his hands up to cover his mouth, dry heaving as he turned a pale shade of green.

"You okay there?"

"Yeah, just, um, you saw that?"

"Uh-huh."

"Please tell me you squealed or something? Just anything to

cover the fact I nearly threw up only hearing about it?"

"Sorry, but no. I felt queasy, I'll give you that."

"What about the queen? Nothing else has been said so I got really worried about you."

"She sent everyone home, so perhaps that's why." I leaned in closer. We were talking quietly anyway, but for some reason, I felt the need to whisper even lower. "Fox, she was ruthless."

He frowned. "What do you mean?"

"I've never seen her so stoic, so calm, so...like a warrior."

"Your mother can be cold I'll agree, but a warrior?"

I nodded, eager to share what I saw. "Yeah, she was all 'I'm the queen', and then she slit their throats. No trial. Nothing. They weren't even worth that after killing some of our people. Honestly, I've never seen her like that before."

"She executed them? Without trial?" Fox asked in disbelief, and my eyes widened in excitement that he'd shared my reaction.

"Yes!"

"I suppose I shouldn't be all that surprised."

"What do you mean?"

"The stories?"

"What stories?"

"The stories from when her father sent her into Dydair to establish a communication line with them? The whole convoy that went with her...apparently it turned bloody, and the survivors had to fight their way back. Your mother included. Few made it home."

"I knew she'd been trained like I have, but I didn't know that story. Why didn't she tell me?"

Fox gave me a pointed stare. "Notwithstanding how she holds

you back from everything already, I don't think she'd be fond of recounting that particular horror tale."

"Ok, yeah, I can get that to an extent. But not everything else, though. I'm getting sick and tired of being sent to my room while she deals with the kingdom."

"She sent you away? After this? Surely it would be a prime opportunity to let you in."

"She's keeping something from me. Her and Markin are, definitely. It's been more noticeable since the Dydairians upped their attacks on the wall. I don't know why she doesn't trust me or thinks I'm not capable enough to handle whatever secrets she's keeping."

"You could try speaking to Markin?"

I smiled, great minds thinking alike. "I tried that. He has a sixth sense for knowing I want something, so he sent Loch to do some further training with me."

"Dang, girl. You've been through the ringer today."

"You could say that again. Enough about the palace. What about here? How has it been with the warriors and such? Distract me."

Fox rolled his eyes. "I think I've come across some of the biggest, wimpiest, whiniest men I've ever known. Then there are the ones who think they single-handedly protected the queen today if they were at the meet and greet." I smirked, barely suppressing a laugh. "That's what I thought. Real warriors don't brag."

"No one caught your attention as a potential?"

Fox stilled. "None are good enough to protect you yet. Want a drink?"

"Please." I watched as he left to get us something, hating the pain in his eyes while he counted down the time we had left. I stared after him, already grieving our time together.

"Fancy seeing you here, Little Shadow." Wren's silky voice slid musically to my ears.

He slid into the empty booth seat opposite me. I knew he hadn't been at the meet and greet earlier, which meant he wasn't a high-born influential. I liked him better already.

"Little Shadow?"

He lifted his shoulders and then took a gulp from his beer. I was suddenly jealous of a glass.

"You leapt from the shadows at me last night. Seemed an apt name for you," he said, taking another sip of his drink. That damn glass. I shook my head but smiled. "You looked like somebody had died when I saw you sitting here. What's up?"

"What if somebody has died?" I questioned back with a playful smirk. Gods. What was wrong with me? People *had* actually died.

Wren rubbed his chin. "Then it was a terrible choice of words. Apologies."

"Surely you must have heard that Balmorians lost their lives after an attack at the palace?" I knew I responded with an air of annoyance, but the frozen faces of the heads flashed before my eyes again. I shivered. Wren's face softened.

"It was insensitive of me. I knew about that. I just wrongly assumed you wouldn't be so consumed with grief."

My brows drew together. "What does that mean?"

Wren shifted in his seat. "You don't strike me as someone who is particularly interested in political matters."

Something stirred in my chest; something close to how inadequate my mother made me feel. "Political matters? On people dying? You've met me once. Once. And you make that assumption?"

"I'm going about this all wrong. You seemed different from what I'm used to. It was a breath of fresh air. A distraction to what I have to do. I apologise, Little Shadow. I did not mean to insult."

The way he called me 'Little Shadow' made my insiders quiver, but I pursed my lips instead.

"Aren't you competing to be in the trials? Surely that makes you very much inclined to get involved in 'political matters'?"

"Yes. Well, no. I'd rather focus on physical dangers than polit-ical ones."

"If you make it through the trials, you'll become an advisor, too, not just a protector."

"I know, but the biggest threats are always physical. Especially right now."

My eyes narrowed. "Care to elaborate?"

"All the violent attacks, especially near to the borders, indi-cates Dydairians have crossed the wall. Anywhere could be danger. You should be careful coming out on your own." He frowned, running his finger up and down the condensation of his glass.

"Bold assumption."

"It's what everyone is saying. There's usually some truth in what the people talk about."

"What about all the border patrols? The wall is heavily guard-ed," I argued, but Wren just shrugged and crossed his arms. "What else have you heard about the Dydairians?"

He went quiet for a few moments. "Nothing much, just that they seem to be crossing the wall and being caught. The stories I've heard about the devastation they leave..."

"What stories?" I asked breathlessly, hooked on his words.

This was the closest I was getting to any sort of clue what was happening within my own kingdom. I couldn't believe I wasn't being told any of this. Did my mother not think I could handle it?

"Some of the smaller villages closer to the borders? They were ransacked. Men, women, and children slain or tortured."

My eyes widened before I had chance to school my features. Wren's eyes were hard, his face casually blank. I took a deep breath, channelling my mother's confidence. "Everyone has an opinion. What's yours? Why do you think they're torturing people?"

Wren glanced around him before he leaned over the table, his mesmerising eyes pulling me closer to him. "To find out information on Queen Isla and Princess Rayleigh." I recoiled faster than if he'd slapped me.

"What?!"

His face twisted to one of concern. "I didn't mean to worry you. I'm sorry. It's just I think they want to take the kingdom, break free of the wall. That's my guess, at least."

"But the queen is heavily protected, and so is the wall. They'll never take us," I mumbled. Numb. Why would my mother hide that the Dydairians wanted Balmore, and thus, our own heads? Bloody images from earlier popped into my head again and the contents of my stomach rolled. They'd brought a cursed in. Why risk this side of the wall if they wanted to take it?

Wren reached his hand across the table and encased one of mine, his eyes deep with concern. "Hey, don't worry. The trials are about to take place for the princess's guard, and then both of them will be heavily protected. Plus, there is literally an army of soldiers at the palace. It's part of the reason I'm taking part in the trials. To protect the people."

I nodded, overwhelmed by the Dydairians and the tingling sparks up my arm from Wren's touch. Probably both. Did that make me messed up? I decided to not focus on that.

My mouth opened to speak, my eyes focused on his when Fox appeared, slamming two drinks down on the table as he slid in beside me. I had to shift down the seat and let go of Wren's hand. I didn't miss Wren's quick frown when he snatched his hand back and briefly studied it. Maybe he'd felt the electric sparks too?

"So, what did I miss?" Fox asked, his voice tight. He glared at Wren as if he'd sprouted two horns and was about to eat us.

Wren shot his eyes towards mine, a question in them.

"This is Fox, my best friend," I introduced. "And this is Wren, a hopeful contestant in the guard trials. Be nice," I added to Fox when he continued to stare down Wren.

"Nice to meet you," Wren said.

"Guard trials, huh?"

"Yeah, starting tomorrow."

"And you're here, rather than resting? I would have thought dedicated warriors would be resting, taking it seriously."

"I'm sorry to disappoint," Wren snapped, his lips thinning.

Fox opened his mouth to retaliate, but I jumped in. "Okay there, boys. Fox, all the other soldiers are out right now. It's not that late."

Fox's slightly hurt face tugged on my heartstrings. I hadn't taken his side as I normally did, but I felt bad for Wren. He was just trying to be nice.

"Sorry," Fox began in a very unapologetic tone. "What makes you want to compete in the trials? You do know the oath you have to take, right?" I sighed, but Fox ignored me.

"Of course, and I'd be honoured if I made it into the princess's guard."

"But why?"

Now I groaned, leaning my head on my hands.

Wren took a deep breath in. "I think I should probably get some rest as after all, the first trials begin tomorrow, and I wouldn't want to be fatigued." Wren stood up and nodded at Fox. When he turned to me, pain flared in his eyes. I wasn't sure why. "Stay safe, please."

It surprised me that I missed the way he'd called me 'Little Shadow' when we'd been on our own. Wren turned and walked away, pausing to say goodnight to Sadie who smiled at him. I couldn't shake the haunted look he'd given me.

"I got you a—" Fox said, but I held up my hand, immediately reminding me of my mother.

"That wasn't very nice. He's competing for a position in my guard, Fox. I know you're upset, but he's a good guy."

Fox's eyes narrowed. "How do you know that he's a good guy?" he asked, and I quickly told him about bumping into him last night. "But still, you've met him twice. How could you possibly know he's good enough to become one of your guards?"

"How could I possibly know any of these men are good enough to be in my guard? I don't, but four of them will be. I have to be okay with this, Fox, even though it tears me up the thought of losing my freedom. Please don't make this harder than it needs to be." My voice broke, and his face crumpled.

"I'm sorry. You're right, you're right."

I launched my arms around his neck and squeezed tightly,

revelling in the deep scents of whisky, cedarwood, and iron—distinctly Fox.

"Promise me we're okay?"

"We are."

I leaned back and held up my little finger, plastering a smile on my face. "Pinky promise?"

Fox rolled his eyes but failed to hide the grin spreading slowly. "Pinky promise." He hooked his finger around mine, and my racing heart slowed. I didn't know what I'd do without Fox, and I didn't want to think about the end of the trials where I'd find out.

Setting a quick pace, I left the warmth of the tavern and made a move to head straight back to the palace, but I saw Wren quietly enter the stables to my left. Struck by a courage I probably shouldn't have had, I followed him in.

Scents of hay and horse boldly took over the lingering smell of beer, and I smiled at the soft whines and snores of the horses as they ate or slept. Wren's broad back stood in the distance, holding his hands up to stroke a beautiful grey horse.

"Why are you following me, Little Shadow?" he said without turning, and I grinned at the nickname again.

"Making sure you aren't stealing any horses," I replied, promptly moving over to stand near him and pet the horse who lowered his head towards me. "Is he yours?"

"Unfortunately not. I just come in and take care of them, part of the deal I have with the owners of the stables."

"Lucky deal," I muttered, knowing he had to have a connection here to have secured it. "What do you get in return?"

"Board and some meals," he replied, flashing me a big grin as he grabbed a brush and started brushing down the horse.

Watching him move and stretch made my stomach flip in ways it never had before, and a pressure built even lower than that, so I peppered him with questions, none of which he answered. After a few moments, he stopped brushing and sighed at me.

"How about anything you ask me, I'll answer, as long as you answer the same question. Fair?"

It was fair, but I'd have to be careful what I asked, obviously. I took a seat on an upturned metal bucket and huffed. I should be going back. I should be ignoring the delicious feeling I got when I was near Wren.

But I was far from sensible.

"How old are you?"

"Twenty-four."

"That's younger than I expected actually," I mused.

"I get that a lot," he chuckled. I bet.

"You do a lot of manual labour."

"That's not a question."

"It's an observation."

"How very perceptive of you." He turned around and flashed me a small grin, a dimple appearing on his left cheek. Hot. "Your turn," he said, far too joyfully. I made sure to make a dramatic roll of my eyes.

"Nineteen."

"And that's younger than I thought."

"Hey! You saying I look old?!"

"Not at all," he quickly said, watching me closely, the intensity making me fight my instinct to fidget. "You just seem to hold a...I don't know, a weight in your eyes? A burden of some kind. I tend to see it in those who have...been through things."

I quietened at his perceptive thoughts. Did I really carry the weight of my position in my eyes? Was I that obvious?

"That's not a question."

"It's an observation." Okay. Touché.

"All right, then, how about spilling what you did for fun as a kid?" Much safer territory.

"I had a brother and a sister growing up, so we spent a lot of time outdoors, exploring and making up games. That kind of thing." The thought of little Wren running around in mud with siblings had me smiling, but then the way he said 'had' filtered through my thoughts. "You?" he said, still brushing the horse's coat.

"No siblings, just me. I played a lot with other kids when allowed. I had a lot of lessons growing up, so I didn't get to play much," I answered, keeping out they were lessons on decorum, appearance, education, and how to run a country. Not the typical lessons one might expect. I couldn't ask him why he was here for the trials because he'd ask me the same thing, but I could ask him what he wanted in life. That seemed safe enough if I answered vaguely in return.

"What do you hope to achieve? Even without the trials."

He let out a quick, humourless laugh. "That's a question and a half, isn't it? But I want to serve my kingdom, for my family and the people who can't protect themselves," he added quietly, stroking the horse with his hand rather than the brush. The horse gently rested his head against Wren. "And yourself?"

I sighed. "The same. Very much the same."

Outside the stables, a loud chorus of drunken celebrations exploded in the night. I didn't want to leave. Something kept me rooted to the spot far longer than I should have stayed.

"I've got to get going, but it was nice chatting with you," I finally said and stood up, but I must have been closer to him than I thought because when he turned around, stepping forward to say goodbye we were practically nose to nose.

"Yeah, same," Wren muttered, clearly not expecting me to be as close as I was. I hadn't been expecting it either, but now that his body heat reached out towards me, his scent slowly wrapping itself around me, I didn't want to step back. Some twisted part of me, hidden deep inside, whispered a hint of what I really wanted him to do next. Heat rose on my cheeks at my newly discovered sordid thoughts. "I can walk you home?" he asked, his throat bobbing as he swallowed thickly.

I smiled up at him and his eyes darkened a little. "You know I'm good," I said and walked backwards towards the barn door, trying to dispel the thoughts I had. The corner of his mouth quirked up a fraction, and he nodded a farewell. I'm not sure why he didn't speak, but I guiltily drank in his appearance one last time before I walked out of the stables and left him behind.

EIGHT

I SECURED MY GRIP on the ivy, swinging my leg up and over the window ledge at the same time. It's as I was half in, half out, that I realised my room—yet again—had another presence.

"Markin?" I called out quietly. Hopefully.

"I'd guess again." A jolt of dread raced through my stomach. I was more worried at her calm, low tone than if she had shouted. The voice belonged to my mother. I pulled my other leg in, turning to shut the window behind me, and hurried to think of an excuse, any excuse. "I'd also refrain from lying to me."

I winced. Excuses poured through my mind like water from a tap—I couldn't grab onto any she wouldn't see right through. So I did the only thing I could: I told the truth.

My fingers trembled as I lit the lantern beside my bed and then fed the fire so warmth spread through my numb body. When I finished, I sat on the floor facing the fire, not yet daring to observe my mother.

She was quiet. So quiet.

"Rayleigh." Her soft voice surprised me; my eyebrows pinched together. "Just turn to look at me."

I did as she asked, and my jaw slackened. My mother raised her eyes heavenward before coming over to me. She knelt on the floor beside me and gently pushed my jaw closed.

"What are you wearing?!" I finally asked, and she half smiled at me, crossing her legs. Her legs. That I could see. Because she wore trousers and not a dress. Queen Isla wore dark, baggy trousers made from a roughly woven material, and a cream tunic tucked inside the waistband of her trousers. A thick fabric waistcoat cinched around her waist, wrapping around her torso to provide warmth, and in her arms she held a dark, hooded cloak.

"I'm a woman of many secrets. I used to sneak out of the palace, too, back in the day. Like mother, like daughter, so they say."

"But you're so...proper! You never break the rules!"

Her smile tucked up on one side of her mouth. "I did when I was younger."

"What about now?"

"Now? Now I just bend them, with a little help from Markin. There's much you don't know, and I do intend to share what I can with you, to help you be the best ruler you can be because one day, you will be queen. I need to keep reminding myself of that." She turned her head to study the crackling fire, but I couldn't take my eyes off her profile. My mother was a strikingly beautiful woman, but incredibly modest about it. It was my pale hair that made me stand out, and I really didn't need a helping hand in that, considering trouble always had a way of finding me. Mostly, though, I feared my mother sometimes thought I was too different to her, both in looks and attitude, that I'd never be good enough to take over from her.

I stayed quiet, worried she might suddenly clam up and become the mother I'd always known.

"Come, I want to show you something," she said, standing up to wrap the hooded cloak around her shoulders. I followed suit, repositioning my cloak to ensure I stayed warm.

Our footsteps echoed softly down the palace hallways, cushioned by our old leather boots.

We passed several soldiers who studied us intently but said nothing as we waltzed by; my mother may have been in civilian worker clothing, but the air around her as she walked still signalled confidence and authority. How on earth did she walk through the city with no one realising who she was? Without any protection? Although I didn't assume that I'd be attacked, I took precautions to protect myself. My mother—the actual queen—if something happened to her, who knew what chaos might ensue?

As we approached the side doors in the kitchens, I grabbed onto my mother's arm. "Wait! What about safety? Shouldn't we get Markin or Derril or someone?"

My mother raised one perfectly manicured eyebrow. "Do you not leave the castle without a soldier?"

"Um, well, I'm not, I...I can fight. I know how to defend myself," I finished lamely, but when I looked up to her face, all I saw was a wide smile.

"I know. I can defend myself just as well." My jaw dropped again. "Oh, for goodness sake, Rayleigh, stop gawking. You saw for yourself how capable I am. I train with Markin now and then to ensure I stay well prepared. We are not useless women. We are strong both physically and mentally. So, I, too, can defend myself if needed. Shall we go?" She gestured to the door, and I could only nod.

My head was ready to explode. It made sense. She wielded the sword that killed those Dydairians with ease. She was clearly used to holding and wielding a weapon with the strength to match.

We travelled around the edge of the palace, keeping to the darker shadows. I got the impression that my mother would rather keep our late-night amble to the city on the down low, but she didn't take as many precautions as I did; perhaps she was just gambling. She motioned for me to stay quiet before we marched across the grass and through a small gate in the walled gardens—it seemed like a much better exit than my own to be honest.

Before long, we were walking down the uneven cobblestone path of the main city roads. Merchants still passed us by despite the night and late hour. Others cleaned the market stalls down, and I spotted some scarcely dressed women loitering with what I assumed were questionable intentions as we slowly ambled by. My mother's face relaxed from her usual pinched expression, and her eyes closed on a deep inhale.

"You enjoy this, being out with the people," I stated.

"It brings me a sense of peace I can never quite achieve in the palace." Something about her voice, her words, made me inexplicably sad for her. "I know we've not had the best of relationships, my husband was always the child-centred one, but I do care for you, and because of that, I feel you should know the truth about being a ruler."

"The truth?" I repeated, hoping she'd tell me something about what had been happening with the Dydairians and ignoring the way my heart squeezed at the rare mention of my father.

Something whispered against my skin, and then a scream echoed into the night. Ahead of us, a woman and a heavily cloaked man tugged a basket of wares back and forth between them until the woman lost her grip and fell back. The man ran off down the nearest alley. I started forward, but my mother grabbed my arm and yanked me back. A dull ache took up residence at the base of my skull again.

"Help! He stole my money! That's all I have!" the woman wailed, struggling to her feet as another man ran out from a building and helped her up.

"Mother! Let me go, we can help, get her money back!"

She only stared at me with glistening eyes.

"My father wasn't very forthcoming about what it truly meant to lead, and I made some mistakes, stupid mistakes. I don't want you to do the same. You cannot focus on the individual when making big decisions, you must focus on the good for all. Sometimes that means making harsh choices, ones others wouldn't always agree with or understand. Laws are there for us to uphold; it creates boundaries, unity, a sense of right and wrong that the people must adhere to. I often find myself wanting to help the individual person, and I do what I can to help, but I do not care for one person. My duty of care is to an entire kingdom. I cannot show favouritism. I cannot show mercy in one situation and not another. I must be consistent. I must be fair to all. Am I making sense to you?"

"I guess, but what about that woman? Why can't we help her?

Give her the money she lost?"

"Because she is one woman. If people hear we helped her, others will beg for our help for the next issue and the next, and it will never end. We must be consistent even if it doesn't seem kind. We cannot rush in to help one when a whole kingdom relies on us."

Guilt wrapped me closer than my cloak did: I'd never seen, never imagined it like that.

I glimpsed a quick flash of turmoil across her face as she watched the crying woman being helped down the street empty handed.

"Being a ruler is about making those hard choices. That's what we have to do for the good of *all* the people. Making hard decisions is an essential part of being a ruler, which may not always be appreciated, but it's our responsibility to do so. Some things won't make us feel good, and they may not sit well with us, but they are necessary. I'm not a cold-hearted person, but I fear you may think me of one," she trailed off, still watching the woman.

"I...I don't think that." At least, I didn't truly think so.

She closed her eyes briefly, and when she opened them, the familiar hard edges began to re-form. "Just remember what I've said tonight. When you rule, you must put yourself above the people to lead, but you are accountable beside them."

I didn't think either of us had anything more to say on the brisk walk home. Some things my mother said...pain. It was pain I detected within her; the vulnerability clear. Whatever mistakes she'd made in the past, or whatever fears she still held, I knew there was more to my mother, and I was desperate to find out, desperate to have her see me as her equal.

As I lay in bed, warm under my covers, I knew of a way to prove I was ready and worthy to be queen: I had to find who was betraying us and helping the Dydairians.

NINE

BLOOD RUSHED IN MY ears. My heart pounded up into my throat. An iron fist twisted my stomach in knots, squeezing tight. Today was the first day of the trials. It was the first day I would see all the men risking their lives to compete, willing to sacrifice all the normal things a man should be able to do, in order to devote their entire being to me. My stomach rolled.

Responsibility sat heavy on my shoulders.

I stood behind my mother in the royal box, a raised platform set back in the crowds, high above the arena below. In a large circular shape around the arena, hundreds, if not thousands, from the city had shown up to watch; rows upon rows of people. Some of the people closest to us I could just make out, but the royal box sat high with a canopy above our heads—a welcome break from the high-noon sun. I dreaded to think what the contestants felt right now. The same as me? Nervous, sick? Dressed up in full protective armour, they must be sweltering. At least I was able to wear a thin strapped floor-length dress made from a light chiffon material. The lilac colour meshed well with the dark purple banding around my waist giving me more shape and holding the dress snug to my body. A good thing, considering my stomach quivered so much.

Yola had come into my room earlier, rudely awakening me from sleep, and then twisted my hair into an updo. I cursed her inwardly at the time, but now I stood grateful for the soft breeze whispering at my neck.

All around me, men, women, and children spoke animatedly, excited at the prospect of the next royal guard. My mother's chair sat to my left, her four personal guards surrounding her as they discussed something. I was too anxious to even listen in. Ha. What a surprise.

I wandered what the contestants would be feeling right now, but that made me think about Wren. Oh God. I'd tried not to think about him, determined to forget whatever it was about him that made my heart pound in a very different way to what it was doing currently. I didn't want to see him hurt even if the thought of watching him fight sent a tiny thrill shooting to my core.

Sheri and Yola sat behind us on small stools as assistants to my mother. A few notable families, some of whom had sons in the trials, sat behind them. I honestly didn't know how my mother made small talk with some of them.

I accidentally caught the eye of one of the big-headed nobles who nodded at me. His arrogant smirk clearly a sign that the pompous pride on his face had nothing to do with his son being in the contests, but the fact he'd made it to the royal box. He took a gulp of the expensive golden liquid served to him. Droplets clung to his thick beard as he stared at the serving girl's retreating behind. Yuck.

"You good?" Derril's light voice danced as he looked down from his position to my mother's right.

I released the fabric I twisted in my hands, smoothing down my dress.

"Umm, yeah, sure."

"Not nervous, are you?" he asked playfully, one hand resting on his sword. He gave me one of his lopsided grins.

"What...what were the trials like for you?" I couldn't believe I'd never asked him before. Of all my mother's personal guard, Derril was the one likely to have told me if I asked. His eyes clouded momentarily with a memory, but his smile stayed in place.

"Terrifying," he answered truthfully, and I sucked in a sharp breath. "But don't worry, little one. Only the bravest, sharpest, and truest can pass these trials. It's good to be terrified, gives you something to work towards."

Only Derril could say that and sound honest and not in the least big-headed. He quickly squeezed my shoulder when I smiled up at him.

"I guess I'm more nervous than I thought I would be."

"I'm not surprised. Four of these men will become your personal guard; they'll be with you twenty-four seven for the rest of your life."

"Thanks, Derril!" I squeaked, my breakfast making itself ready to come back up.

I also didn't want anyone to die for me in these trials.

Markin stepped forward and held his hand out for my mother,

who gracefully took it, coming to her feet in one fluid move. As soon as she stood, the crowd around the area quieted—no small feat considering the sheer amount of people—and they began settling into seats in anticipation of her welcome speech. For once, I felt the same way.

"Welcome!" my mother announced, spreading her arms wide, long thin sleeves on her deep purple dress swooping low. A wide smile filled her face, and the crowds latched on to her words. "Today marks the first of the guard trials, to find a group of strong, intelligent, loyal men for my daughter, Princess Rayleigh, heir to the Balmore throne. I want to thank you all for your hospitality within our city, welcoming those who wish to participate. Each applicant has been studied by some of our most senior and trusted advisors, who have then selected the top fifty contestants taking part today. This is by no means an easy achievement, and we should be proud of all who applied. As we welcome the fifty contestants to the guard trials, I urge you to remember that these can be bloody, dangerous, and ultimately, lives can be lost. If you have small children with you, please be cautious about what they may witness. Let the contestants in!"

With my mother's command, a hidden gate on the floor of the arena opposite us slid up and out walked men clad in armour and protective clothing of varying styles, shapes, and colours. Briefly, I allowed myself to wonder which one was Wren, but all had their heads covered in one way or another—impossible to tell. I pushed him to the back of my mind.

The men walked around the red-sand arena floor, waving and thrusting swords up at the wild crowd. The people of Balmore grew crazy. It was a big event; one the city had been preparing for nearly a year.

The contestants finished their lap and stood in five rows of ten, facing the royal box. I gulped. It would be impossible for Wren to make out the details of my face from where I stood, but butterflies still flapped anxiously in my middle, which was absolutely ridiculous. If he made it through the rounds, at some point he'd find out I wasn't some common townsfolk, but the princess and heir to the Balmore throne.

"Contestants," Mother's loud voice rang out, silencing the crowd once again. "You have all signed waivers acknowledging the risk taking part in these trials may have. However, there is no obligation to finish the trials. At any point, you may lay down your sword and thus forfeit your place. If anyone is seen attacking a contestant who has deliberately laid down their sword, you will be disqualified immediately. Around the arena are soldiers, each tasked with watching the contestants to observe their every move. It will not go unnoticed. The first trial is a general combat between you all at the same time. The last twenty-four of you standing victorious in your fights will progress to the next round. Do you all accept this trial and these terms?"

The contestants knelt their agreement and submission. I held my breath.

"Rise," the queen began, "and fight!"

Some were hesitant, others were quick to action, but the sound of clanging metal soon took over the arena. Cheers erupted as the fighters began their match.

I sat, gripping the arms of my chair. *Please don't let anyone die. Please don't let anyone die.*

"Psst." The sound barely registered as I noticed a fighter in dark blue and silver armour, taking on several opponents at once and winning. It was obvious, or at least to me, that he wasn't trying to seriously harm or kill anyone attacking him, but his actions left no room for doubt he would stop them permanently if they didn't stay down. "Psst." This time, I turned to the sound coming from to my right. Behind the royal guests, Fox's head peeped up over the edge of the platform.

He motioned his head, beckoning me to behind where the royal guests sat. I feigned the need for space, which particularly stung when the bearded man behind me smirked at my 'uncomfortableness'. I made an obscene gesture behind his back, which Derril and Loch witnessed. They turned a blind eye, Loch smiling and Derril hiding his laugh behind a cough.

"How's it going?" Fox whispered when we were as far away as we could manage from earshot. I could barely make out the fight standing here, but the sounds raged clearly in my ears. Loch glanced over at us, but instead of calling us out, he gave a tiny nod of approval. I smiled back at him, thankful he had my back.

"Um, it's going," I tilted my head. "What are you doing up here? Not that I'm not happy to see you."

Fox ruffled his messy mop of blonde hair, scrunched his nose up, and then, having decided he was going to tell me what he had come to say after all, said, "You can thank me later, but, I know what Wren is wearing." My eyes widened, and I motioned my hand in a turning motion to hurry him up. "He's wearing a tan leather chest protector with matching cuffs on his wrist. He's got an iron plate over his chest area and a helmet, but it doesn't extend anywhere else. That's about as technical as I can get...brave man, if you ask me."

"He's not got full armour?"

"Nope."

"Gods. Have you seen some of these men? Ruthless!"

Fox took my shoulder but quickly dropped his hands in case others turned and saw. "Calm down, Ray, I saw him practising in the yard earlier. Wanna know something that will make you feel better?"

I looked him dead in the eye. "What kind of question is that?"

"He can fight with both arms equally well. I'm not a fighter or a soldier or anything like that, but honestly, even I can tell the dude can fight and defend from both sides."

My heart sped up, and I knew it was with hope: stupid, stupid hormones.

"Thank you, Fox."

"What are best friends for?"

I smiled, but a thought quickly occurred to me. My eyes narrowed. "And why were you watching him?"

Fox scratched his head, and he looked everywhere but my eyes. "I just...he was...you were like 'oh Wren's amazing' with stars in your eyes, and I was just...I was just checking him out, okay? I wanted to see what he was like if he was competing to be in your personal guard, and you both had the hots for each other."

My jaw slackened, the action beginning to become a habit. "We do not have the hots for each other! And I didn't say he was amazing like that!" I socked him on the arm. Fox being the wimp he was, flinched and stepped back.

"You're forgetting that I know you, and it's written all over your face," he said and waved his hand in front of me. I angrily pulled my brows together.

A strangled cry echoed around us.

"Fox..." I trembled, registering the sound belonging to that of a dying man.

He gently took my elbow this time. "You have to go and see. You're their princess. This is your guard. You can do this. I know you can." He spoke slowly and in a low tone, a far cry from the sounds coming from the arena.

I nodded and numbly made my way back to the front, near where my mother stood leaning on the ledge, mirroring a similar stance to Markin.

What if the sound came from Wren? Please don't let it be Wren.

My mother turned when I eased closer. "Come, Rayleigh."

I stumbled nearer and then took my place next to her, my hands clasped in front of me. I took a deep breath and looked down. A man lay on the ground, crying out in heavy, heart-wrenching screams; three soldiers knelt around him.

I'd never seen a dying man, except the ones my mother had executed quickly, but I knew with a heaviness to my heart that he was close to death. His stomach lay open, blood spilling out and spreading around him like someone had dumped a bucket of red paint over him. It didn't look real, that amount of blood. No amount of medical attention could save him. Even I knew this. I glanced at Markin. His face confirmed what I feared. Those were the cries of a dying man. The ones my mother had killed had died so silently. Not this man. I imagined everyone in the arena could hear his gut-wrenching wail.

Some contestants hesitated and slowed their fights, watching. Others continued, using the distraction to gain an upper hand. I observed those men. Were they right to use the distraction to their advantage? Or were they wrong because this was a simulation, and these were good, honest men, not an enemy?

Markin scowled. A contestant attacked another as they stood with their fist resting across their chest in a sign of respect. I knew then what Markin believed. I followed his new line of sight and swallowed a gasp. Wren had been surprised by another contestant taking the distraction to their advantage.

He raised his arm and deflected the first blow, his leather covering and smaller chest plates offering more flexibility with movements than full metallic armour would have given. The other guy kept at him. I focused all my attention on him, my heart resting in my throat. The attacker moved more cumbersomely, thanks to immense armour, the thickness of it showing a ridiculous amount of wealth. I tried peering at the sigil branded on his chest but couldn't make it out from here. It didn't matter.

Wren ducked under his opponent's swinging arm, coming up behind him and using the butt of his sword on the man's shoulder blade. It sent him stumbling forward, but with how heavily protected he was, it did little else. I tensed; in my peripheral Markin leaned forward to watch closer, something about the grapple grabbing his attention. Wren didn't wait for the guy to catch his feet, and swung the flat of his blade against the guy's shins with so much force, the guy flipped into the air and landed on his back. His helmet rolled off with the impact, and Wren used the opening to reposition his hands on the hilt of sword and thrust it against the guy's neck.

My breath hitched. The guy held up his hands in surrender. The rules dictated Wren stand down, and he did. Even from up here, I could see his chest heaving as he stepped back.

A burning sensation filled my lungs, and I let out the long breath I'd been holding. Wren turned to watch the now deceased man get carried out. Sometime during his fight, the man had passed. As the body left the arena, ten warriors withdrew, and others continued to fight with renewed vigour. I guess knowing the trials were deadly was one thing, but actually experiencing it was a whole different ball game.

The crowd cheered, replacing the sombre mood: everyone knew this was part of the trials. While they cheered, I searched for Wren among those still fighting. I wanted to keep tabs on him, finally spotting him engaging with another warrior. I studied him and could only relax my stiff shoulders with the knowledge he was currently unharmed.

Fox was right. He was exceptional.

A commotion closer to arena walls drew my attention. One contestant pointed and shouted into the middle of the arena as he walked back into the fight. I followed his trajectory, and my heart jumped into my throat. It was the guy Wren had beaten. He grabbed his sword again instead of heading off the main arena grounds like he should have been. He'd yielded, but yet he stalked towards Wren whose back faced the defeated warrior while he fought another contestant.

The crowd booed and called out, but their voices became lost in the cacophony and chaos of the fight. I gripped the ledge before me, powerless. *Turn around, Wren!* I could do nothing as the man, an angry sneer spread across his face, raised his sword behind Wren's back.

TEN

HORROR CLUTCHED MY INSIDES, and I inhaled sharply through my teeth. The guy's sword swung high. Wren spun and fell back, thrusting his sword up at the last moment before the guy's weapon could impale him. I didn't care how he knew to turn, just that he did.

Blood spattered.

Wren's sword hit true and slid through the man's lower torso, a quick identification of the armour's weakness. I knew I visibly sagged but ignored my mother's frown pointed in my direction. Composure. She wanted me to keep composure no matter what happened.

I tried to mirror her poise for the remainder of the fight. Counting down the men who forfeited and those too injured to carry on, I continued following Wren's progress. Loch and Markin's heads bent together, discussing the fighters, and once or twice they pointed and studied Wren closer. I shouldn't be happy, for several reasons. But I was. When they announced the final twenty-four, and Wren's name was on the list, I couldn't help but smile.

Wren drew long broad strokes over the grey mare's side, his large hand following the brush to smooth down the fur just like he had when we'd spoken in the barn.

"You were magnificent," I whispered, the words from the trial finally escaping. I pulled on my bottom lip with my teeth because I knew exactly where I wanted those hands to be. Just like I'd envisioned the first time we'd been here.

He turned, closer to me than expected, and the horse behind him drifted into mist. Wren's green eyes shone with such intensity that I only remembered to take another breath as he stepped closer still.

"What do you want, Little Shadow?" His voice rumbled and I shivered in response.

"It...it would appear, you."

His eyes dipped to my mouth and fire sang through my veins.

"And *how* do you want me?"

I didn't answer with words.

Braver than my waking self, I reached up on my toes, planting my lips on his, and when his lips parted, his tongue deliciously teased mine. He grabbed my hips in firm hands, pulling me flush against his body, and my hands slid through his hair as we kissed.

Wren walked me backwards until my back hit the wall of the stable, and then he reached round and cupped my rear. I gasped for air, but it did nothing to cool me down. Wren's hand glided up, further up until it rested just underneath the swell of my breast and where it stayed as he continued to own my lips with his.

I broke away, my hands curling round the back of his neck, keeping him close.

"Don't stop moving that hand," I ordered. He smiled, and his hand smoothed across my body, until his thumb brushed against the fabric of my tunic, right over where my peaked nipple struggled against the materials restraining it.

My eyes rolled heavenward, and my head fell back on a moan. "More," I whispered.

Wren pressed his hips into me, pinning me against the wall, his arousal grinding against me. With his hips keeping me there, and one hand caressing my breast, his spare hand roamed higher until he was undoing the ties at my neck and pulling the tunic down. His mouth landed on my neck, kissing, sucking, licking his way down to my collarbone and then further as he tugged the tight seam of my under-top down, exposing the breast he had yet to pay any attention to. His teeth scraped across the delicate skin, getting closer and closer. I arched my back, desperate for his mouth to claim me. His tongue danced closer to where I most desired it.

"Please," I begged.

I felt his answering smile against my skin as he quickly moved lower and took the hardened peak into his mouth, lightly scraping his teeth over it and sending warmth pooling between my thighs.

He knew what I needed and drifted a hand lower until he

reached the hem of my shirt, lifting it before undoing a button on my waistband with one hand. He quickly left my trousers to free my other breast, his mouth immediately finding its target on that one. I cried out at the quick nip he gave me before soothing the pleasured sting by dragging his tongue over the area.

I ground my hips up against him, needing more of him. He moved his lips to my neck, settling there at the same time his hand reached under the waistband of my loosened trousers. Heat bloomed where his hand touched my skin and his fingers inched lower slowly, tortuously. I grabbed onto his shoulders, pulling him against me in a silent plea.

His fingers grazed the top of my...

"Princess Rayleigh!" Sheri shouted, banging on my door. I sat upright in bed, gasping for air.

I moaned, brushing my hands through my tangled hair, trying to steady my breathing and get rid of the tension rolling through my body.

"Princess Rayleigh!" Sheri shouted again, pounding three more times.

"Shit, shit, shit." I pushed the tangled covers off my bed and hastily grabbed a robe, tying it tight to hide the fact my heavily flushed chest was still showing signs of being aroused. My pointed nipples clearly stood to attention, and the room was hot as fuck. I couldn't have blamed it on the cold. My core heavy, I throbbed with need between my legs, a need that had not been met and rudely interrupted.

I yanked the door open.

"What?" I snapped, harsher than intended but not surprising given my lack of release.

Sheri's eyes widened in panic. "You're meant to be at a dress fitting!"

Now it was my turn for my eyes to widen. I ran back inside my room, no longer having to worry about any lingering arousal. I threw off my robe and dashed into the bathroom, nearly stumbling into the bathtub as I yanked off my nightdress.

"How mad is my mother?" I shouted through the door, grabbing a brush to yank through my tangles.

Sheri opened the door and dangled a plain dress from her arm, turning away to give me some semblance of privacy but didn't answer me. That was an answer in itself. I snatched it from her as I finished putting on my undergarments.

"Safe," I said, and she barged through to tie my hair in a quick loose tail at the nape of my neck, and I tied the dress at my front.

We ran from the bathroom heading for my bedroom door, and I swiped my father's bracelet on my way past the desk. Sheri stopped to throw some blue pumps at me.

"Shoes!" she squawked.

I hopped on one foot to put the shoe on as she shut my door behind me, and then I slipped my foot into the other and hurried down the hallway, Sheri close on my heels.

"Oh my God, Sheri, how late am I?"

"Be prepared, Princess," she said breathlessly.

Goddess be damned. She was going to send me to Lady Mila. I couldn't do that. I couldn't.

We reached my mother's rooms, and I paused, smoothing down my skirt and rolling my head as I mentally prepared myself. Just as I was about to open the door, Loch appeared from nowhere and stepped ahead of me to go inside first.

"Your Majesty," he said and bowed deeply before moving to stand next to my mother. "Apologies. I had Rayleigh doing extra training sets this morning and time ran away from us."

My mother's eyes darted to me and then back to Loch.

"I know how you get with training, Loch. Remember a clock next time."

Loch turned away from my mother and smiled at me. 'You owe me,' he mouthed, and I had to fight the urge to roll my eyes and give us both away. My mother always had much more patience for her guard than me, and on this occasion, I was incredibly grateful for it.

Fingers snapped in my face, and I furrowed my brows in annoyance at Yola.

"Out of that!" she snapped, and then helped the seamstress pull on the bones of a ballgown when I'd taken off the dress I wore. Amber material loosely fitted around my middle, and they helped me stand upon the small podium facing a large mirror. The seamstress started pulling in seams and pinning them, marking them.

"Markin mentioned he was getting Loch to go over some basics with you. How is it going?" my mother asked.

I stared blankly at her reflection in the mirror.

"Okay. Thanks?"

Her lips thinned in barely held annoyance. She took the cup of tea Sheri bought over and took a sip. "Can I not inquire after my daughter's activities?"

I caught Sheri's eye in the mirror who held just as puzzled a face as mine.

"Sure." And this is where I decided to push my luck. "How are things with the border patrols after the attack?"

My mother's mouth opened and then shut.

"Some things are best left for council discussions. Not dress fittings."

"All right, then. How about I meet you later for a 'council discussion'?"

"No."

I sagged and half turned to face her but stopped when Yola hissed at me to be still.

"Mother. This is getting ridiculous!"

"Rayleigh! You will not speak to me like that in front of guests!"

"You won't let me speak to you in any way that challenges you, or even at all!" I answered back, arms flying wide.

Her eyes widened, her back going rigid.

"That is because I am queen. *Your* queen."

"And don't you make that abundantly clear?"

My mother slammed her teacup down and stormed to the door, pausing in the entrance.

"You will do well to remember, daughter, that my word is final, and to speak against me to anyone, in front of anyone," she said, pointedly looking at the three women in the room, "can and will be considered an act of treason. Even you are not exempt from that," she spat, and waltzed out. Pain pulsed behind my eyes as I breathed in and out slowly.

I'd never heard such venom. Even Yola was quiet, her eyes not meeting mine as she got to work in silence with the seamstress. Sheri kept her head bowed, never once raising it to look at me, and so I stood, trying to control the shaking. It wasn't fear, but anger,

I tried to reign in.

It was later that night when I had one leg thrown over my window ledge, my body dipping to follow, when Markin pushed through my door and folded his arms.

"Do we not knock now?" I asked tentatively, and Markin's eyes fluttered close on a sigh. "Would you believe I was just sitting here to get some...air?"

"I don't know. The real question would be when did you think I was born?"

"Fair point," I muttered and climbed back in.

"Let's go, then," he said and made to move out of the room.

"Wait! I'm not dressed..." I mean, I *was* dressed, just not for proper company. I was in my woven trousers, an old cream tunic, and carried my battered cloak under my arms.

"That's the get-up I need you in. Come on. Let's move."

"Oh, um, okay."

I followed him to the hallway, but instead of turning right towards the main part of the palace, he took me left and then down a serving staircase. I blinked, realising that he wasn't wearing his usual fine clothing. He looked...common.

"Markin? Not that I don't trust you, but where are we going?"

"Put your cloak on, we're going out."

"Out?" I squeaked as he pushed open a back door that only servants typically used, and then ushered me across the back gardens.

"We're taking a visit to your tavern."

ELEVEN

I FOLLOWED MARKIN DOWN the familiar paths towards the tavern, trying to keep up as my mind whirled with what he'd just told me.

"My tavern?"

"Yes, like I said, I know more than you like to think."

"And you're taking me to conduct business? My mother okayed this?"

"Not precisely."

"I'm already in trouble with her, I can't afford to get into more."

Markin looked down pointedly at me. "You've never been worried about pissing your mother off before."

"True, but she might get angry with you."

Markin huffed on a half laugh.

"You know I can take her. Besides, you were going out anyway.

This way, *I* get to keep an eye on you."

"How very courteous of you—wait, I get to be with you when you're actually doing official crown stuff?"

"I wouldn't say official."

"Have you always been this cryptic with others?"

A small group of men passed us by, loudly cheering about the trials and the atmosphere of the arena yesterday. I shivered, pulling my cloak tighter, and Markin placed a steady hand on the small of my back to propel me forward.

"I'm meeting with someone off the books."

I frowned. "So it's not official?"

"He is one of my informants. He's been talking to people who wouldn't be so open with me if I asked."

"What's he been asking about?"

Markin gave me a sidelong glance. "I'm about to tell you this so you can be on alert as you insist on coming down here." I tried to contain my excitement, but the corners of his mouth slanted up quickly when he noticed anyway. "That traitor your mother mentioned? I'm actively investigating it, and I think it's someone who's been with us for years. I've ruled out all the new recruits." My mouth dropped open as we reached the doors to the tavern. It would make sense, wouldn't it? The Dydairians easily got onto the palace grounds, and who else would know the schedule and have the ability to help them? Markin clucked his tongue. "Stop gawking."

I followed him inside and through crowds of people—busy as usual.

"Evenin', Oliver, what can I get for yous?" one of the serving girls crooned affectionately, intimately. I tried not to wrinkle my nose. She ignored me and drifted closer to Markin, brushing her brunette hair over her shoulder.

"Just two of the usual, Mary, please."

Mary glanced at me, her eyes narrowing in recognition before she sauntered off. I hoped it was because she'd seen me here with Fox. Markin pointed me to a booth which someone had just left.

"She seems to know you well," I huffed.

"She's harmless."

"She likes you."

"Only when I'm here as Oliver."

I frowned. "What do you mean?"

"She enjoys the tips I leave as 'Oliver'."

"What is your purpose for coming here, then? Especially if you're investigating—"

Mary put two pints down in front of us. "There you go!" She winked at Markin and sashayed away again.

"You have more than one line of investigation going, don't you? That's why you need to be 'Oliver' tonight."

Markin raised a brow. "You learn quick."

"Want to tell my mother that?"

His face darkened, but before he could say anything, a man slid in opposite us and bobbed his head towards me. He was unremarkable. Hair to his nape, shaggy on top, a long cloak that he'd taken off and placed beside him. He wore clothes much like I did, and a faint scar ran along the side of his neck.

"Who's the girl?"

"No one."

The man studied me closely, and I watched him right back, trying to see who he was to Markin. "I've seen you before."

"No, you haven't," Markin answered for me, his tone leaving no room for argument.

The man's eyes darted back and forth between us before he nodded. "Noted."

Markin raised his hand to Mary and put his finger up. While we waited for her to bring the guy a beer, I watched the man engage in a friendlier conversation about anything but why they were there in the first place.

The man rubbed at his stubbled chin after Mary brought over another beer.

"Add it to my tab, please, Mary."

"Sure thing." She winked again and left.

"What do you need to know this time? I'm still looking into the last thing you gave me."

"I have some names I want you to ask your contacts to look into. Background information from before they came here. That sort of thing."

Markin slid over a piece of folded up parchment paper. The man took it, quickly scanned the contents, and then tucked it inside his front pocket.

"You could probably get this information a lot quicker without me, so what are the specifics? If I'm to use unofficial channels, it helps."

Markin leaned forward. "I want to verify their claimed hometowns. The people on that list haven't been 'home', nor had visitors here, for well over five years now."

The man bobbed his head. "Sending my *contacts* out will take time and money."

"Thought so." Markin unhooked a small black leather pouch

from his belt that I hadn't even noticed. "To start your investigations. More will be sent to you next week."

The man took the pouch, inspected it, and then concealed it on his belt without any visible reaction. "I'll be seeing you." He nodded to Markin and stood, casting me a quick glance before walking out.

"Who are you looking into?" I asked when we were alone again.

"I'm impressed you held your tongue for as long as you did."

"Markin," I whined. He finished his drink and turned to me.

"I'm sorry, little one, I can't share that just yet." I slumped back in the booth in defeat. "Come on, let's head back."

We slid out of the booth and made it to the front when two gentlemen stood between us and the door. Judging from the way they dressed, they weren't usual patrons from around here. I tried to hold back the frown that wanted to take root on my face.

"Alixus, Xander, what can I help you with?" Markin asked casually even though his back straightened: the only sign he was slightly weary.

"We need a word," the one on the right, Xander, said. "Privately," he added, looking at me.

Markin took a deep breath in and then turned to me.

"Stand by this door, I will be no longer than five minutes. Do not leave the tavern. Do not even move from your spot. That's an official order." He narrowed his eyes at me, and I knew how serious he was being, so I nodded and put my back to the wall, waving at him as the three of them left.

I reverted to people watching, a habit from making sure to spot anyone who could recognise me. I hadn't seen Fox yet but

I'd spotted Sadie serving customers. She looked okay, if a little pale. Some faces here looked vaguely familiar. They had probably been at the fair on opening night. A few tables away, a solitary figure sat—one of Markin's senior soldiers. Long hair tied into a half bun on the top of his head and no uniform. Dark trousers, dark jacket, no obvious weapons. Perhaps he was part of Markin's wider security. What was his name? Mahds?

"And who's this?" a male drawled, filling my view and blocking me from Mahds. His half open tunic revealed a lot of chest hair, and his bright eyes lit with excitement. The man brushed a hand over his short beard, his muscular bare forearms twitching. "You're a pretty little thing, aren't you?" he said, leaning in. He braced one arm on the wall behind me, his face close. The stench of beer filled the air between us.

"Not interested." I rolled my eyes and stepped to the left, still staying against the wall to wait for Markin. The man frowned and stepped closer, so close I put my hand out to halt him, but he moved until his chest pressed against it.

"A hand ain't going to stop someone like me," he whispered, dipping his head close to my ear.

"Ew. That's enough." I turned my head away from the fumes.

The man brought his other hand up and rested it on my hip. A shiver tore through me at the contact. Not a nice one.

"Back away," I snapped, trying to push his hand off me. The first kernel of panic sprung to life inside me. It was busy; no one paid us any attention. If I screamed or fought him, I'd bring the kind of unwanted attention that could betray who I was.

The man's hand started sliding round to my back and then lower.

"Want to take this outside?"

"Want to take your hands off me?"

"Look around, sweetheart, no one is paying us any bit of notice, and if you make a fuss, I'll say you're my disobedient wife who needs a good seeing to."

My heart leapt into my throat. "People won't believe that. I'm not a possession!"

"Law says differently darl'." He smirked, leaning into my neck.

I went still. My mind roared at me to use what I knew. I wasn't defenceless. But my body froze.

"I suggest you step away from the lady. Now," a deep voice commanded. I knew that voice.

The man at my neck glanced back, turning away from me enough so I could see who stood behind him.

Face dark with fury: Wren.

TWELVE

"**I**'LL REPEAT, GET AWAY from her," Wren said, his tone icy.

The man sneered and leaned away from me, looking over his shoulder. "And who do you think you are?"

Wren stepped even closer. "Someone you don't want to mess with." As he spoke, he held his hand out towards me. I didn't hesitate to reach for him, letting him tug me toward him when his large, warm hand encased mine. A muscle in the man's jaw ticked.

"You're welcome to the wench," he spat, stalking away from us.

Wren still held on, rough calluses from working with his hands for years brushing against my skin. It was then the memory of my dream flooded me, filling me with heat. With need. That hand had touched me in places that no one else had. There was something seriously wrong with me that I was thinking about that now: I needed to get a grip with reality.

He turned to me, and the intensity in his eyes hadn't wavered.

"Thank you," I said, not quite knowing what else to say.

He opened his mouth but then frowned, looking down. He focused on our hands, still joined. I pulled mine away and wrapped my arms around my middle to give them something to do and keep from reaching out to him again.

"Are you okay, Little Shadow?" he asked, gently tucking some hair behind my ear even though his jaw was still tensed.

I cleared my throat. "It appeared I just froze up, momentarily. I'm not sure why that happened." Why I felt the need to defend myself, I wasn't sure.

Wren's eyes hardened, anger seeping through even at his gentle touch. "I couldn't allow him to touch you like that."

His possessive voice caused a wild dance of butterflies across my middle.

"Thank you," I breathed. He captured my gaze, now curling the lock of hair he'd brushed back around his finger. My body heated, and I'm sure a flush worked its way up my chest and neck when his eyes dipped to my throat and then back up again, a small smirk playing at the corner of his mouth.

Shit. He had to go before Markin came back.

"I don't want to keep you waiting," I mumbled.

He dropped his hand, but the tension between us remained. He glanced down at the floor, but when he looked back, he quirked one side of his mouth up, showing off his dimple. My stomach clenched. Damn.

"See you around," he said, leaning in close to my ear, "Little Shadow."

I nodded, not entirely trusting my voice, and watched as he

turned and melted into the crowd, his broad back disappearing quickly.

I sagged against the wall, breathing deeply.

"You good to go?" Markin asked from beside me, appearing out of nowhere. I stood up straight, my eyes wide.

"Yes," I mumbled, and pushed past him to move outside, revelling in the cold air as it cooled my face's betrayal.

My sleep that night wasn't dreamless.

I stood in the woods bordering the palace grounds; darkness in the sky and the thickness of the trees thrust me in near pitch black. For once, the dark didn't comfort me. Outlines and silhouettes of wooden skeletons stretched out, trying to reach me with their branched fingers as I stumbled past.

The long skirts of my dress dragged across the frost-kissed leaves and moss. I could barely make out my feet as they crunched on the forest floor. Hiking up some of the material, I picked up my pace, scanning behind me, my heart hammering in my chest.

He was coming for me.

My long hair flew around me in wild tumbles, sticking to my sweat-soaked face as I ran. A deep male laugh echoed around me, booming through my ears: mechanical, emotionless, victorious.

"You can run, but you can't hide," the man's deep, lyrical voice teased. Fear spiked, coursing through my blood and drumming in my ears. I stumbled to a stop, twisting my head from side to side in sharp, jeering movements. My breath came out in uneven, jarring huffs, hanging in the air before me.

"Where are you?!" I screeched, no longer caring about my composure, my bones ice-cold, terror gripping them to stone.

A low chuckle grew louder behind me, every hair on my body standing to attention. I squeezed my eyes shut.

"Why here, of course." The man spoke from just behind me, gathering my tangled hair from over my shoulder and gently stroking down the length of it. A shiver tore through me, shattering any control I had left, and a soft sob escaped my pale lips. "Now, now. Don't be afraid. Turn around," the man commanded.

On shaking feet, I turned, keeping my eyes trained on the ground, scared to look up at his face. His icy fingers touched my chin and tilted it, bringing my eyes in line with his. Eyes identical to my own.

I screamed, falling backwards.

"Rayleigh!"

I ignored my name, continuing to release the fear through my scream.

"Rayleigh, wake up. You're safe." That voice. Calm, silken, distinctly male in a way that my toes curled in delicious anticipation.

"Wren?" I murmured, confusion firmly in place.

"Open your eyes, Little Shadow."

It was only then I realised my eyes were still shut, squeezed tight in fear of the face I just saw. My eyes.

Soft material wrapped around me, and a fire crackled not too far away. I blinked my eyes open and found Wren hovering above me—shirtless, I was quick to notice.

My eyebrows drew together as I surveyed the room, pushing up on my elbows to see my fireplace, the small table and chairs beside it, my bed. I ran a hand over the covers, not understanding how I got here.

"You just had a bad dream," Wren's voice caressed my mind as it always did. I stilled. What was Wren doing *in* my bed? I looked over at him. Yep. In my bed, not on it. Major distinction.

"What are you doing here?" I asked, my voice wavering. I wasn't altogether sure if it was because of the lingering dread of fear or because of the last time I dreamed of Wren. Of his hand sliding down my stomach...

He moved closer, one arm propping him up as he lay beside me. Heat emanated from him, drawing me closer. I no longer fought myself and leaned towards his comfort. The crackling fire flickered light across his features: full lips, straight nose, deep green eyes. I may have sighed. The corner of his mouth pulled up, showing that damn dimple, and he raised his hand to brush back hair away from my face, softly running the back of his hand over my cheek.

My eyelids fluttered close at his touch. I was pretty sure I still dreamed, but his touch was the same as it had been at the tavern when he'd taken my hand: electric, spine-tingling, warm.

I opened my eyes just as he dipped his head to capture my mouth in a delicate, comforting kiss. His lips lingered on mine, moving against them as if he'd kissed me a million times before. Perhaps we had, in another lifetime.

He pulled back all too soon and a soft moan escaped me. My eyes flashed to his, embarrassed, but heat pooled in his gorgeous greens. His hand once again found my face, softly cupping my cheek as he ran his calloused thumb over my skin, each stroke sending sparks of delight through my senses.

"I probably shouldn't be here," he said, his voice thick.

"Probably, but I don't want you to go."

"Let's just enjoy this, then. In the now. What we have…no one can take that from us." He took my hand, and I lay back; he kissed my knuckles before resting his head next to mine. "Sleep, Little Shadow."

I closed my eyes, reluctant to let go of the image, his face so close to my own, his body pressed against mine, his heat cocooning me.

My breathing deepened. I relaxed and slowly fell into sleep.

"Rayleigh!" a male voice commanded, a familiar one. I opened my eyes, and I was back in the forest, the sun just about to set. I turned in the voice's direction. Loch shouted at me to move to him, but my feet were glued to the ground. I wore my leather boots, riding trousers, a thin, metal, chain-link body protector, and had fabric wrapped around my body, cinching it all in. A sword rested in my hand. What was I doing? I followed the line of direction my feet pointed in and gasped. Wren, clad in protective armour like me. He faced someone hidden by the thick trunk of an aged tree and held his arms upright in surrender, speaking in low tones to whoever was hidden from my view.

"Rayleigh!" I recognised Derril's voice from behind me, but I continued to watch Wren, confused as to why he stood so far away and at the terror in Loch and Derril's voices.

Wren turned his head, his eyes pleading with mine, but I couldn't figure out what he was pleading for, couldn't figure out why two of my mother's guards were with me and Wren. A sword was plunged deep into the weakest parts of Wren's armour at his waist; the sharp, lethal tip protruding from his back.

A scream tore from my throat.

The attacker yanked his sword out and fled, his long, black hooded cloak concealing him as he ran away from his hidden spot. I sprinted forward and reached Wren just as he fell to his knees.

"I told you to go," Wren rasped.

I hovered my hand uselessly over his wound as my other wound around his back, but Wren's body was too heavy for me, and we slumped to the ground in a heap.

"Since when do I listen?" I teased, my sight blurring.

Wren laughed but blood spluttered from his mouth. His face pinched together as he tried to raise a hand to my face. I knew what he wanted: I placed my hand over his, cupping it to my cheek.

"I know we didn't have much, but to me, it was everything," he whispered, his face paling.

"I know," I choked, tears falling on his ashen skin.

"My heart...was always...yours."

"And you held mine from the moment I saw you."

The corners of his mouth tugged up in a smile so uniquely Wren, but his eyes fluttered shut, his hand now limp in my own. "Wren?" I whispered. "Wren!" I screamed.

Firm hands gripped my upper arms and dragged me upwards, away from Wren's body. He couldn't be alone. He couldn't.

"WREN!" I screamed, kicking away from whoever held me.

I bolted up in my bed, sheets falling away from me as I panted. The familiar fireplace simmered low in front of me, and I took in a few shaky breaths, pushing tangled, sweaty hair away from my face. I held my hands there, palms pressing against my cheeks as I desperately tried to calm my racing heart and throbbing stomach.

The dreams—nightmares—slowly faded from my trembling mind, but the gut-wrenching horror lingered. Even though I knew with stunning clarity that I was awake now, I couldn't stop the sense of dread, a sense of foreboding.

I got ready quickly, eager to leave the dreams behind me—or nightmare as it turned out. Markin and my mother would be discussing the next trials, and I wanted to be involved. It was the only thing my mother seemed to let me in on—I wasn't going to waste it.

Marching along the hallways, I moved past one of our maids' carts on the second floor outside one of the guest meeting rooms. The maid hummed to herself while she cleaned inside the room. I looked behind me at Markin's closed office door.

The idea formed with equal parts of my brain telling me it was both a brilliant idea, and quite possibly one of the worst. Refusing to be seen as a helpless princess, I had to uncover the traitor's identity and prove myself as a capable queen. No one approached as I casually stepped towards the cart and then opened the box holding an iron ring of keys. I knew which was Markin's. I licked my lips. It was a bad idea. But as I told myself that, I reached in and unhooked the key, hiding it down the bodice of my dress.

As I stepped away, the maid came out and quickly curtseyed when she saw me. I smiled tentatively back and almost ran down the stairs and into the soldier patrolling inside. I asked if he knew where my mother and Markin were this morning, and he directed me outside to the vast grounds surrounding the palace. They stood side by side, surveying the large expanse of grass, gazing into the forest that bordered the green. I gulped, gently rubbing at my right temple. The last event here had ended in beheadings. And it didn't take much to remember those nightmares based inside the forest either.

I shook my head, trying to disperse the negativity. Palace servers and soldiers worked together on putting together an extensive obstacle course along the green. By far the biggest I'd ever seen: logs formed high walls and hurdles, nets secured to the ground to crawl under, tight-looking tunnels made from large barrels. If I was being honest, it looked like it'd be fun, but I'd never be allowed near it—it wouldn't be considered very lady like.

Markin and my mother, engrossed in their conversation, failed to notice me as I walked closer to them. It wasn't until I was nearly upon them that they turned. It was eerie how similar their expressions were. Was I to become like that? A reflection of my guard? Or they a reflection on me?

"Rayleigh, nice of you to join us," Markin said. I stopped at his side, opposite my mother.

"What is the trial today?" I asked, nodding at the work being done on the lawns and studiously ignoring the key burning through my bodice. Or at least it felt like it was burning a hole.

"A trial of endurance," Markin answered, and my mother chuckled softly at some unspoken shared joke between them. "Each contestant will wear full armour, carry several days' worth of water and food, and any weapons of their choice. I will give them a map of the forest when they enter from the west side. Their task is to find their way through the forest, and once out, go through the obstacle course. Myself and the other guards will time the contestants and assess their performance."

"Performance?" Surely timing was the main focus for this task?

"Oh, Markin always has a sly trick up his sleeve," my mother commented, sipping at the tea she held. I frowned at him, waiting for his response.

"The maps are incorrect," he stated simply.

"But surely that's a bit, I don't know, unfair? Misleading?"

"Not at all. Your personal guard should use their intelligence and instinct even when some things say otherwise."

Again, I drew my brows together. These trials were going to give me wrinkle lines. "Shouldn't guards, all soldiers, follow orders as they are given, though?"

I jumped at my mother's bark of laughter. Markin smiled at me.

"Your guard should be able to think, reason, and act independently for both the good of the queen and the people. The queen relies on us to use our intelligence to know when things are wrong, when to question, when to do what we must—not what we should. There's a very subtle difference, and today is all about finding out which contestants have those skills."

"I never thought about it like that before." It made sense, but it annoyed me I hadn't reasoned that for myself before now.

I looked to the forest; Wren being stabbed clear in my mind again. I shuddered.

"I should get going to make sure things are in place. I'll meet you before the trials, Isla."

"Are you all prepared for later?" my mother asked me when he'd gone.

"I think so. Am I to expect Yola?"

"Absolutely. I'll be waiting in the sunroom for you shortly after lunch. The contestants will be due to come through during the afternoon."

"Only if they figured out the map is wrong."

My mother smiled and gazed into the distance. "Quite right. I shall see you later."

She walked off towards the palace, no doubt to make sure things were ready in anticipation of our guests. The trial wasn't open to the public, only to high-borns and influencers.

At least the event wouldn't be a total suck-fest because Fox was working as a server; I'd seen his name on the worker list. I smiled and turned direction for the kitchens, hoping he was already in. Talking to Fox and aiding in the kitchens brought me a sense of normalcy, even as a kingdom's heir.

By late afternoon, practically evening, I sauntered around groups of people on the lawns, attempting to appear calm and not at all nervous, while simultaneously avoiding eye contact. I didn't want to deal with some of these people and pretend to be interested when really all I wanted was to see Wren come out from that forest unharmed. It was purely irrational, my thinking. He was in the trials to become my guard. He would be constantly facing danger.

I scowled into the flute I held in my hand when a shadow approached.

"How you holding up?" Fox asked. The fake smile I had plastered on my face to prepare for whoever I faced turned genuine. He took my empty glass and tipped forward a tray of new ones for me to choose from. Impressed with the skill, I rose my brows at him—it didn't look easy.

"Thanks," I mumbled. Fox's knowing smile smirked back at me, and I fought the urge to roll my eyes at him; I didn't want anyone seeing and reporting him, thinking I wasn't happy with his service.

Fox twisted the tie at his neck with a free hand. He hated the black-and-white uniform freshly pressed by palace staff; he said it was 'too stiff' and 'itchy'.

"You nervous?" he asked while still pulling at his collar.

"I keep thinking I won't be, but then I am."

"The dreams you had last night probably don't help matters," he said, referring to what I'd whispered to him while helping in the kitchens earlier.

I huffed at his correct assumption. "You could say that again."

An elder gentleman and woman walked past, taking fresh drinks off Fox's tray. He bowed his head respectfully, and I took a sip of my drink, glancing away from the couple in the hopes they didn't stop to chat. I was in luck.

"Avoiding the chitter chatter of the elite, are we?" Fox mocked in his posh tone.

"Avoiding doing your job, are we?" I pushed back, trying to hide the smirk on my face. Fox pretended to look hurt.

"Well, I'll just leave you to all the important conversations you need to have with the more important people."

"I'm already having one with the most important person," I replied sweetly, pasting a huge smile on my face.

Fox turned his head at people gasping and squawking in wonder. The first contestant came out of the forest boundaries and approached the obstacles of the course. I struggled to see who it was at first, but the flash of silver and blue told me who.

"Looks like Mardy made it out first," Fox commented, using the name we'd recently dubbed for the silent one who always sat at the back of the tavern and refused to show his face. I didn't think I was someone who ever obsessed on looks, but I began to wonder why he never revealed himself.

"Do you think Wren's okay?" I asked quietly. Fox studied me for a second before answering in a gentle voice.

"I'm sure he is." Grateful for his approach, I sighed. Perhaps my dreams worried him just as much as they worried me.

In the distance behind Fox, Loch started scanning the crowds. If I had to take a guess, he was looking for me. I had a sixth sense with these things.

"I should go. They'll be wanting me near as more contestants come in."

"What are you going to do when Wren finally does come through?"

"He'll be too far away for most of the obstacle course, but I don't want to risk it just yet. I don't think I'm ready for that realisation. I'll think of an excuse to head inside as I also want to see if I can get into Markin's study while everyone is out here; I swiped the key from the maid's cart earlier."

"Mm-mm. I'm just going to not comment on that bad idea for now."

I grinned as he moved away, and I made my way over to Loch.

"The queen and Markin would like to discuss the contestants

with you as they come through. They think it would be beneficial for you to hear first thoughts."

"Of course, lead the way." I followed him to the front of the crowd. There was no royal box this time, but people kept their distance from the queen and Markin as they overlooked the obstacle course. It helped that Derril and Abe stood slightly back from them facing the crowds, hands on swords ready to strike if needed. They created a protective barrier that people wouldn't dare come near, let alone cross.

Loch and I walked past Derril and Abe, coming to stand just behind my mother.

"Queen Isla," Loch addressed, bowing as she turned around, and then she beckoned me to stand between herself and Markin. Loch stood back to form a line with the other two guard members.

"The first contestant has come through," Markin told me.

"I saw," I commented, and Markin frowned at me; I hadn't meant to sound so frosty. "What are your thoughts on his performance?" I asked in what I hoped was a gentler tone.

"Promising. He did well in the arena battles and has made good time through the forest."

"Even with an incorrect map?"

"Even with an incorrect map."

My mother leaned forward. "What do you think about him as one of your guards?"

"My thoughts?"

"Yes. He could be part of your guard. What are your instincts?"

I thought carefully for a moment, feeling like this was some kind of test from my mother and Markin. "I don't think I've seen him enough, but he seems competent. Although..." I trailed off, not knowing how to phrase my next thought.

"Although what?" Markin nudged gently.

I sighed. "I have no clue how he works with others, but I'd like to get an idea of that before I start making formal judgements."

Markin smiled, clasping his hands behind his back as he watched the next contestant come through. My mother also smiled but held her hands delicately in front of her. Did I pass this weird test of theirs?

My heart lurched into my throat when I recognised the next two people coming through from the darkness of the forest, one wearing the familiar protective leathers and tarnished silver chest plate of Wren's armour. He walked side by side with another contestant who moved with a limp. Neither were going fast, even when another contestant flew out from behind them and ran to overtake them as they approached the first obstacle. The man Wren walked with was one of the few contestants without a face covering, but he did have a thick collar around his neck, stretching up from the tough leather protective shield he wore around his chest and torso. It provided his neck with some protection at least. I could make out his dark shaggy hair, a sword strapped to his back rather than to a belt, and baggy trousers.

Wren and the unknown warrior made slow progress. Many contestants now arrived and surpassed them, but Wren never offered physical help to his comrade.

Markin and my mother moved closer together, their heads barely a whisper apart as they discussed something; a tingling sensation across my scalp told me it was about Wren and the contestant he walked beside. At one point, Markin even pointed to them. The pair were just about to navigate the tall wall of logs. Wren scaled the logs, sitting atop them, and shouted down at the other man making slow, painful progress. I couldn't hear what Wren shouted, but I knew he was helping even though his time was seriously going to suffer.

The two eventually made it to the finish line. I subtly tried to hide behind Derril's enormous form when they walked away, but Wren never turned toward us. He threw the other guy's arm around his shoulder and helped him to the medic tent. Now they had completed the trial, they wouldn't be penalised for his physical support.

"Markin?" I asked, unable to stop myself. "That contestant. What was his time? He could have made it much sooner." Markin studied me carefully before answering; I tried not to fidget under his scrutiny.

"There are still five others who haven't made it through. Probably still trying to figure out the map."

"So, what does that mean?"

"It means his time, albeit slow, is not the worst. But there is more than just time and numbers we look at."

I nodded, watching the other contestants complete the course when I realised this was the perfect opportunity to sneak into Markin's office. Everyone was focussed on the trial.

"I'm going to step inside for some ewater," I mumbled. Markin frowned at me.

"You all right?"

I was busy picking my dress up slightly, knowing exactly what excuse he wouldn't question. "Yes, but I think I'm getting a headache—I don't think I've had enough fluid today. I'll be back in a few minutes, if that's okay?"

Markin had already turned back to face the trial. "Fifteen-minute break, and then I'll be sending Derril after you."

Only slightly annoyed I had a time limit, I hurried inside.

THIRTEEN

I SWEPT DOWN THE halls, only coming across one serving girl in the whole time. Perfect. As I reached Markin's study door, I slowed down and looked around for any signs of someone else approaching. I pulled the key from my bodice and unlocked the door, quickly shutting and locking it behind me.

Ok. Part one complete.

I breathed deeply and moved to the desk to flick through papers left in folders, not even sure what I was really looking for. Maybe a report on what happened at Cilla would be a good start. Markin hadn't told me the whole thing—I knew it. Fox's name flashed at me, and I realised I was looking at the list of approved serving help for the trial being held currently. I put the file down and opened the desk drawer on the left. Nothing but pens and bric-a-brac. I tried the drawer on the right and pulled out a parchment pad of names. It wasn't an official document. Markin's handwriting lazily scrawled over the page, but something about the names was familiar.

I sat in the large office chair, tapping my fingers on the desk, and then left the pad of paper on top as I grabbed for a file I'd already flicked through. I opened it again and flipped through the pages scanning for anything that stood out. *Cilla*. The name froze my hand.

My stomach tightened as I scanned the report. It was basic, but the attack had been brutal, coupled with a handful of druids actually aiding the humans in crossing the wall near Cilla. My heartbeat sped up: the druids were attacking the border and helping the Dydairians? Markin's handwriting littered the margins with notes.

Who had been to the wall? Who was new to the village? What soldiers had visited Cilla before the attack?

A few names stood out, so I grabbed the pad of paper, comparing them. Many of the names on the list were soldiers who had fallen in the attack. Some had been relocated, the details of which I found on the next page of the report. But one name stuck at the bottom with a question mark next to it: Mahds. He was a senior rank—trusted, or so I thought. Was his name here because he was under suspicion?

Scratching whispered at the door, a key in a lock. I shoved the pad back in the drawer and closed the file up, hoping that I put it back exactly where I'd found it. Panicking now, I stood back up. I did not have a back-up plan, and it would take too long to open and climb out a window. As the door slowly pushed open, I ducked down and climbed under the desk, pulling my skirts in after me.

"I don't know why you had to come with me. I told you I'd get it." My jaw dropped open. Mahds.

"And I already told you I'd come to cover your back," another man replied, someone I didn't recognise. Another soldier?

Mahds huffed and walked across the room to the desk, thankfully staying on the other side. Paper rustled when Mahds moved through the files I had just rifled through.

"This is the one."

"The report from Cilla?"

"Everything so far—the official lines, anyway. I've already checked, Lucien, your name is not in there."

So the other guy was Lucien. The name still wasn't ringing a bell. Lucien scoffed.

"I think he'll still want to see this in any regard. Is Markin going to miss the file?"

"No, he's finished on that for now. Moved onto something else, so you have a bit of time before I'll need to put it back."

I sagged in slight relief at the sound of feet moving towards the door.

"Don't forget tonight at Madame El's. And don't be late again."

Mahds took a deep breath. "You know why I was late last time. I'd been pulled for duty. I'll be there when I can get there," he snapped and shut the door, key going back into the lock.

I sighed, thankful they had left, but now my head whirled. Mahds was working with someone behind Markin's back? And who the fuck was Lucien? I climbed out from under the desk and quickly unlocked the door to leave, knowing my fifteen minutes must be coming to an end.

As I made my way back outside, I knew I'd have to sneak out to Madame El's tonight to find Mahds and Lucien. If I could figure out what they were planning, my mother would have to take me more seriously. This was how I could prove myself. I smiled as I walked outside and greeted the others, determination swarming my core.

Later that night, after everyone had left from the trials—from which six had been eliminated—I took off my father's bracelet, putting it safely on my desk, and then grabbed my boots. I laced them up and wrapped my cloak around my shoulders, leaving the hood down for now. By my estimation, most of the palace would be asleep.

I paused by my window before listening to my gut and then turned to take the door. It wasn't my usual route, but I headed down through the serving stairs and kitchens. When I opened the back doors of the kitchen, rounding the corner towards where I would have dropped down from my window, a guard stood on duty. He would have been hidden until it was too late had I left via my usual escape. I snatched myself back from the corner just in time.

Shaking my head and keeping my feet light, I tiptoed the opposite way and round the gardens we'd been in earlier. Things had been cleared away from where spectators had stood, but the obstacle course had been left. Wren slid into my mind again and I smiled to myself.

Enough of that, Ray.

I got to the gated wall where Markin and I had gone through and double checked behind me that there were no guards walking this way. With the path clear, I started climbing the wall, using the gate to help me shimmy up when I came across smoother patches of stone that offered no holds. I startled at a noise behind me just as I reached the top; one guard was coming over this way. In my panic, I rushed and slipped, scrambling down the other side in a less than controlled manner. My hands and knee grated against stone as I slid, and then I landed on my butt. Hard. Fuck.

I stifled the moan and lay still, waiting for the guard to pass before I even dared move. Getting caught now would mean that I wouldn't find out anything.

The guard passed by the gate, his noise receding the further he got, and then I sat up, wiping my hands on my knees. Great. I had a hole in my trousers. Pinked flesh peeked through; I'd definitely lost a layer or two of skin, but at least I hadn't broken it and bled through. The same for my hands. Perhaps luck was on my side tonight.

I darted away from the wall. Even though I was no longer inside the palace, I was still within visible range. I picked up the main path and burst out next to the first building leading toward the city centre. Smiling, my feet moving quicker now, I turned my head to scan behind me, mightily pleased I'd escaped, and then collided with a male chest, bouncing backwards. He reached out, gripping my upper arms in warm, steady hands. Déjà vu slammed through me, and I squealed, my feet sliding out from under me; the man pulled me closer to counter it. My hands came up and rested on his chest, his scent wrapping around me and finally registering: hay, sweat, woods, that deep male musky scent that sent heat to my middle. Wren.

"Little Shadow?" he asked, a small faint smile ghosting his lips as I still clutched onto his front. "Are you okay?"

"Er...yep. What are you doing out here?"

He tilted his head. "No 'thanks for saving me from falling'?" Amusement lilted his voice.

I rolled my eyes. "Thank you, Wren, for saving me from falling...after you walked straight into me without looking...again." I couldn't help it after the humour I'd heard in his voice. Wren's answering smile helped spread one on my own face.

"Fair point." He smirked. "Do you still need to cling onto me? Or is that because you can't get enough of me?"

Heat rose into my cheeks at his brashness, and I stepped back, immediately missing his warmth.

"Yes, well, I needed a moment to re-stabilise." I frowned. Was that even a word? "What are you doing out here?"

"What are *you* doing out this way?" he countered. I crossed my arms and stayed silent. "Ignoring my question?"

"Ignoring mine?"

"You're quite the stubborn one, aren't you?"

I beamed. "I've been told once or twice."

Wren's smile dropped slightly. "It really isn't a safe time to be out and about. Especially here."

I frowned. "Outside the palace?"

"In general. What are you doing out here, alone?" he narrowed his eyes behind me, clenching and unclenching his hands as if he was mad. He wasn't angry at me, surely?

I considered what to say, putting my hands on my hips. If I told him what I was really doing, he would probably try to talk me out of following the lead I had. But then again, I *could* try to persuade him to come with me. The extra muscle wouldn't be a hindrance given I had no back-up. I was taking a risk going tonight, but I wasn't entirely stupid.

Although maybe that could be debated.

I nodded to myself having made a choice. "I'm following a lead. I overheard two people who may or may not be working with the Dydairians. They're meeting with someone at Madame El's."

Wren's brows rose. He opened his mouth but then shut it again and finally settled on crossing his arms over his chest. Damn. Those muscles bunched again. My body tingled, remembering the dream where he held me in those arms, pulling my body closer to his.

"What?" he finally answered, and I shook my head to quash that particular trail of thoughts.

"Weren't expecting that were you?"

"Can't say I was. Where the hell did you hear something like that?"

I shrugged, ignoring the question. "So…?"

"What are you asking me?" he asked, his eyes narrowing on me this time.

"You're not going to try to stop me?"

"Would there be any point?"

I beamed again. "You catch on quick."

He shook his head, trying to hide the small smile I saw creeping up at the corners of his lips.

"And you?"

He looked down to face me, frowning. "And me?"

"What are *you* doing *here*?"

Wren glanced around, even though there was no one about, and raised a hand to grip the back of his neck.

"Patrolling," he said eventually.

"Patrolling? You know you don't get extra points outside of the trials, right?"

Wren rubbed a hand over his mouth before crossing his arms again. "I do, yes. It doesn't hurt to try, though."

"But—"

"You have your thing. I have mine."

I pursed my lips. "Touché, but fine. Okay, bye."

I gave him a wave and turned on my heel to speed off down the path again, heading towards the closest buildings, smiling to myself when his steps sounded behind me.

"Hey, wait! You can't just go by yourself!" He grabbed my elbow, turning me back to face him, and damn it if I didn't step closer to him on purpose.

"Why not?"

He paused, searching my face. "Because you just said you were going to investigate a potential mole. It could be dangerous. A trap. Anything. Is this from a reliable source?"

"Yes."

He scanned my eyes, darting his tongue out to wet his lips. "That still doesn't mean you can do the palace guard's job, or the personal guard's jobs."

"Why not?"

"For the reasons I mentioned above: dangerous, trap, you name it. I really don't think this idea is a wise one."

"Wren, you're not going to stop me going unless you physically restrain me." He looked at me like he might be actually considering it. After a moment, he dropped his hand from my arm.

"I'm coming with you. I feel like someone has to keep you out of trouble." I smiled at him and started walking again.

My stomach danced in a strange, delightful twist. His arm brushed mine as we made our way down the path, and I wondered if I had more trouble at my side than where I was going. Just being near Wren did things to my body, my mind, that I'd never experienced before. Things that were forbidden.

FOURTEEN

"So," Wren said, pushing hands into his pockets. "Do I want to know what Madame El's is?"

"Probably not."

"It sounds like an establishment for more...dubious behaviour. And I'm not talking about the dubious behaviour you're about to participate in."

"Want me to just tell you so you stop rambling?"

"I wasn't rambling. You ramble. I—"

"Was rambling. It's a place people go to drink, gamble...and find entertainment of a sexual kind."

"I thought so. Won't you stick out? Aren't girls normally *the* entertainment?"

I frowned at him. "What backwards village are you from? No, men *and* women work there."

"Women go there as patrons? To view men? Men work there

like the ladies do?"

"Yeah. And sometimes women go there to watch other women or men go to watch other men." I raised a brow at him when he signalled to me that he got it. "From what I hear, anyway."

"You've never been?"

I snorted. "Gods no. There's one thing me being at the tavern, another thing entirely if I got caught at Madame El's."

"Caught?"

Crap. I shouldn't have said that.

"I just mean that if my family were to find out, there would be more than hell to pay."

He nodded, understanding enough.

"Why do you sneak out, then? I've seen you at the tavern twice now without an escort. I assume your family doesn't know about that either?"

"You could say that. I like the freedom that comes with deciding things for myself."

"Is that why you're following this lead?"

"Partly. I want to prove that I can do something useful."

"Why do you need to do that? You shouldn't have to prove yourself to anyone."

"Says the guy partaking in the guard trials—to prove himself worthy of being in the personal guard."

His lips thinned. "Point taken. What's this intel?"

"One of the senior soldiers has perhaps been consulting with someone on the outside."

"A senior soldier? We're following a senior soldier? This is bad. You should take your concerns to the—"

"Palace? Yeah, because number one: why would they listen

to me? And number two: I don't want my thoughts getting to the wrong someone. Who knows who else is working with the Dydairians?"

"I can see why you might think that, but I still don't think *you* should be investigating this."

I scoffed. "Thanks for the vote of confidence."

"I didn't mean that, and you know it."

"Do I? I barely know you." And wasn't that a sobering thought? I'd have to let my lady parts know. They weren't at all fussed they were lusting after someone who was barely above a stranger.

He side-eyed me as we passed some late-night wanderers. "I'd say we know enough to be doing this together," he said after a moment's thought. "Although I'm questioning my choices that led me to being dragged to this place, to go spy on a senior soldier of all people."

I nudged his arm with my elbow. "Shut up." I still smiled.

We stopped outside a building where a large sign written in fancy swirling letters read: Madame El's. People who lived here knew what it was. Otherwise, you'd have to step in before it became apparent. However, it was so out of the way of the main drag that it wasn't usually an accident that people came by here.

"Ready?" he asked, a hand on the door. Now I was here, I didn't think I was if I was being honest with myself, but I nodded anyway, and he pushed open the door, going through first. I followed behind his big frame, entering the lowly lit establishment. He stopped to take in the environment, and I moved to stand next to him. A bar sat to the right of the room and next to that, a platform. On the platform, three scantily dressed ladies and one man moved in a sultry tango of a dance to the low timbre of music playing from somewhere. A cloud of smoke hung in the air atop a group of gentlemen seated in the middle of the room. Tables and booths scattered across the floor, some with topless ladies and men sat on laps and...yep, that was some grinding going on next to us. A few ladies stalked around the room, again, barely dressed. One walked past us, her hand entangled in the front of a guy's shirt as he followed her beyond a sheer curtain on the opposite side of the room. I didn't want to guess what was going on the other side of that.

"Are you okay with this?" Wren asked, looking down at me, and I realised I'd been clutching the clasp of my cloak together to keep it shut. Talk about a metaphorical string of pearls.

I cleared my throat. "Yes. Why wouldn't I be?"

"Because this is a very explicit place for a young lady to be exposed to," he said, gesturing to the room in front of us.

I stormed over to the woman working a small cubicle to our right, a rack of cloaks hung up behind her. I passed mine over. She ran her eyes up and down my body, noting the hole in my trousers and my scruffy tunic. Her appraising look of Wren was met with a pair of bright eyes and smug smile as she leaned over the counter.

"Here for something specific?" she drawled.

"No," he huffed and then took my hand, leading me over to a small couch. I wouldn't have considered it spacious enough to be called a two-person couch, but there we were, squished right next to each other.

A server came over, a short skirt barely covering her behind and a scrap of material over her bust.

"Hey, what can I get you?" She winked, putting her hands

behind her back so her chest thrust up.

"Two waters thank you," I said icily. She eyed me, her nose crinkling.

"Two beers," Wren corrected, and the woman left to get our order, her hips swinging. "Ordering water in a place like this will make you stand out more than what you're wearing," Wren said.

I looked down at myself, annoyed he had a point. "Some of the guys here are dressed way worse than me."

"None of them have your face, though."

I froze. Did he really just say that? I dared a glance at him. He sat forward, arms resting on his knees and his brows drawn together.

The busty server brought our drinks over and placed them on the small table in front of us. Wren hiked his hip up to pull out some coins from his back pocket and gave them to her. The movement meant he pressed into my side. I reached for my beer and drank deep, needing to calm the turbulent feeling it left inside me.

"I take it you know what this guy looks like?"

I scanned the room, seeing too many backs to know if he was in here with us.

"Yeah. Although not the guy he was talking to—nor the person they're meeting."

Wren put his beer down, wiping his top lip of foam as he scanned the room, too, and then looked to me. "What's your plan for when you see them?"

"I hadn't quite got that part down in my head yet."

"Thought so."

"What's that supposed to mean?"

"I obviously don't know you very well," he started dryly, referencing what I'd said earlier on, "but I'd say you're someone who acts first, thinks later?"

"You make that sound like a bad thing."

"Not always."

"But in this case…"

"There are so many unknowns to this 'plan' of yours that I'm itchy."

I pulled a face at him, silently laughing. "I think you're weird."

"Says you who sneaks out of her house to come to a brothel of all places, to spy on a senior soldier."

I shook my head, taking another drink of my beer, and then spat a bit out. Shit. Mahds. He stood with a brooding dark-haired male behind him, his equally dark eyes darting about the place.

"He's here," I whispered, repeatedly tapping Wren's arm. "What if he sees me?"

"You're only *now* worrying about that?"

"Wren!" I hissed, my heart pounding. This was a bad idea. A really bad idea. He was going to see me in this place. He was going to kill me. Or worse, everyone was going to know the princess of Balmore frequented Madame El's. My mother would go nuts. And oh shit, he was moving closer this way, just behind the other man.

I turned my head into Wren's arm muttering about being caught. Wren huffed and reached over, dragging my furthest leg up and over his so that I straddled him. I yelped when his strong hands ended up on my hips to pull me closer.

"There, stay close and it'll look like we're making out."

"Making out?" I squeaked.

"To fit in."

"But I'm not...naked."

"You don't have to be," he said, clearing his throat. "Plenty of others are doing it." I looked around us. He was right. Several patrons were indeed getting close with others who weren't necessarily working. "You might want to look a little more like you're not under duress, though."

"Right. Yes. Um, what shall I do?"

Wren studied me a moment before running his hands up my sides and then down my arms, raising them and placing my hands on his shoulders.

"Don't be afraid of touch for a start."

"Mm-hmm..." I murmured, close to him. Wren's hooded eyes scanned my face. His hands roamed back down my sides to settle on my hips again, heat flaring at his touch.

"Who am I looking out for?" he asked, and it took me a moment for the words to settle in my brain. I blinked.

"Tall guy, velvet jacket, blue. Light hair bound back, light beard. In his forties. That's Mahds. The other guy, I think he was wearing a dark tunic, no jacket."

Wren nodded and placed a hand on the back of my head to bring my head closer still. His nose pressed against my ear.

"Found them," he whispered against my skin, the action sending an excited shiver across my neck. "They look like they're arguing."

"About what?"

"I haven't got super hearing."

"Right. Yes. Of course." I struggled to think with his scent so close, his light stubble scratching at my chin in the most spine tingling of ways. This was definitely not a great plan. I couldn't think straight. I said as much out loud. Out fucking loud. Wren frowned at me.

"Have you done this before?"

"Huh?" Words weren't even coming out of my mouth now.

"This. Sit like this. Be close to someone."

I didn't answer, my heart rate speeding up so much so, it'd be a miracle if he didn't hear it. Wren's brows suddenly rose on his face from the frown he'd been giving me, but now a small smile tugged on his full lips.

"You haven't, have you? That's why you're nervous," he said.

"I'm not...nervous," I breathed.

Wren's small smile turned into a smirk, but before I could even think about doing something—like shove off him—he yanked me closer, pulling my hips down on him so my chest rubbed up against his. I shuddered, gasping as I ground over him, and Goddess help me, he didn't do all the work for that to happen. I finished rocking my hips over him, closing my eyes at the pressure building between my legs.

"Tell that to your body," he murmured close to my mouth. His hand dragged up my side, over my shoulder and up the side of my neck, gripping some of my hair. His breath fanned over my cheek as he placed a soft kiss there.

"That's not nerves," I managed to get out in a breathy whisper. He pulled back slightly and met my eyes, something indescribable in them. His eyes flashed behind me quickly.

"They're coming this way," he said and used the hand in my hair to pull my head close. I stilled as he brushed his lips over mine, slow and lazy. I opened mine beneath his and he pressed harder, catching my top lip between his. His tongue ran across it in a feather-light touch. Moaning, my arms tightened around his neck, and my own hand now dragged into his hair. He pressed a hand into my back, arching it, and I pressed my chest further against his, desperately wanting to feel his hands under my tunic. I'd been kissed before, but not like this. Heat sparked between my legs, an ache forming that only lessened when I rocked against him.

He pulled his head back only marginally, and I hated how much I wanted his lips back on mine. His arms clenched tighter around me, and his throat bobbed as his eyes found mine. Hooded. Dark. I just made out with him in a public place.

"I shouldn't have done that. I'm sorry," he whispered.

"It was to keep our cover. I should be the one apologising for putting you in that position."

"No. Don't apologise," he said darkly, frowning.

"But..." I finished weakly, embarrassment sure to be clear on my face. He gently swiped his thumb across my cheek.

"They went behind the curtain."

I frowned and looked behind me. I couldn't see them. Turning back to Wren, I leaned back and then scrambled off him, his arm keeping me steady when I nearly slipped off onto the floor. I grabbed my drink and downed a few more gulps, wishing I could drink more before I stood and marched over to the curtain. Wren made a sound, but I deliberately ignored his presence to focus on following Mahds.

When I got to the curtain, I went straight through. Wren cursed and then his heat pushed against my back.

"You can't just go storming into places like that!" he hissed.

I ignored him as I faced several nondescript doors down a

corridor. Moans and screams filled the air.

"What's going on?" I asked.

Wren gave me a pointed look. "I'd say more than making out is going on in some of these rooms."

"Why are there some people screaming?"

"I really didn't realise you were *this* innocent," he muttered, his lips thinning.

"Sorry," I said automatically, and he turned his frown on me. Again.

"Why are you apologising?"

"I don't know." I didn't get any further when a door opened up ahead of us. Wren acted fast, pushing me against the wall and shielding me from sight. His arm rested on the wall by my head, blocking me from view as his body slid closer. Standing under him like this, I only reached his broad shoulders. He dipped his head close to mine again and rubbed his nose against the side of my neck, the flesh tingling where he touched me. He grabbed one of my hands and ran it up his chest.

"You really need to get better at blending in." He smiled against my neck, and I shivered again.

Mahds walked past with the same man I saw earlier, the man who must be Lucien. Lucien turned and scowled at us, luckily not able to make out my face under the cover of Wren's arm, before they both pushed past through the curtain.

"Who's...Who's in that room?"

"And I'm not a mind reader. We should go."

I ducked under his arm and Wren cursed again.

"I came all this way," I muttered to him.

"And who knows who's in that room. It could still very well

be a trap."

"Practise for you, then."

"Practise? No, stop!" he hissed, but I was already pushing through the door.

A woman in long skirts stood in the middle of a room, a bed pushed up to one wall and a couch behind her. Her head shot up, an angry scowl creased deep between her brows.

"What are you doing in here?" she accused, her eyes narrowing on us.

"What were those men after?" I asked and her face blanked.

"Nothing that concerns you, girl. If I were you, I'd walk out and forget everything you saw here. My boss don't take too kindly to strangers getting in his business."

"Is that a threat?"

"Just stating a fact, miss."

Wren put his hands up. "Sorry to have disturbed you." He tried taking my elbow in his hands again, but I stepped away from him.

"No, I need to know what was going on in here. They were barely in here and even I know...it doesn't matter. What can I give you? Money?" I asked, stepping closer to the woman who folded her arms on a huff. She eyed me up and down.

"What do you have that I can't get for myself? Money isn't always the currency of choice, if you get me." She winked.

"W-what is it that you would consider as payment?" Damn it. My voice wavered. What a way to look confident. The woman's sly smile crept higher on her face. Her face tilted to one side, contemplating.

"No." Wren snarled, yanking me closer to him this time. "Nothing like that."

"Fine," she huffed. "What's under your shirt, girl?"

I looked down, momentarily confused, and then pulled out the thin gold chain holding a small blue gemstone. I'd forgotten to take it off before I left.

"You want this?" I asked, and she nodded. I hesitated for only a moment before I reached around to unclasp it and hand it over. It wasn't particularly special, so I hoped no one would notice its absence.

"I've always liked pretty trinkets," she murmured, turning over the gemstone in her hand.

"Now, tell me what I wanted to know."

She pocketed the necklace. "They took some information that my boss was passing over to them. A date and a coded message."

"What was the message?"

"It was coded," she replied, rolling her eyes.

"And the date?"

"Two weeks from now."

"What's two weeks from now?" I asked. She shrugged, but Wren stiffened next to me. "What's two weeks from now?" I asked him again.

"Nothing. It's probably nothing."

"What is it?" I demanded, turning to face him.

"The finalists' ball at the palace." I froze, and the woman moved to go around us. Wren shot out a hand to stop her. "It goes both ways. You didn't see us here."

"I'm not stupid. I've only stayed alive as long as I have by not telling on everybody's business." She left the room, but Wren frowned after her.

"What?" I asked.

"She shared that information with us quickly considering her parting remark about not telling on 'everyone's business'."

"She got the necklace, though. We can trust her because of that, right?" I tried hiding the quiver of uncertainty in my voice.

"You really are innocent, aren't you?" He wasn't teasing this time, rather, watching me intently. I looked away from his scrutiny and opened the door to leave.

FIFTEEN

I FINISHED UP THE stupid, pointless essay for the history professor on the role of art in architecture over a hundred years ago. Why the heck I'd need that knowledge was beyond me, but I completed the task to avoid my mother's continual threats about spending a day with Lady Mila. I shivered. That woman was deplorable.

"Princess," Sheri curtseyed from the doorway of the sunroom where I'd been writing, "your mother wanted me to remind you that you're expecting a dinner with Lord Allen, his wife, and their son, George."

"Oh joy," I muttered, having completely forgotten about it.

"She wanted me to tell you to be in your rooms to be suitably dressed and arranged by Yola and that this was an important dinner you won't be late for," Sheri finished, looking down as she did so, and I sighed.

"It's okay. I know she made you say those exact words to me."

"Thank you, Princess," she breathed a sigh of relief. "Would you like me to send your work to the professor?"

"That would be great, thank you. I guess I'll go up and get ready for the torture to begin." I passed her by, spying the small smirk she was trying to hide at my comment.

Once upstairs, I gritted my teeth against Yola's stern words, even sterner hands, and let her put me in the pink frilly dress and tie my hair up. I was going to get a headache with all my hair piled up like that, but I didn't complain. Mostly because I wanted this dinner to go so smoothly, my mother wouldn't be able to say anything against me, and then I could sneak out to see Wren quicker. We'd agreed to meet at the tavern and discuss what we'd seen at Madame El's.

I glided down the stairs like the elegant, high-born lady my mother trained me to be, and swerved into the entrance hall where my mother was already welcoming the lord and his family. I rolled my shoulders back and plastered on my best 'you don't really disgust me face'.

"Lord Allen, how wonderful to see you again so soon," I sang, and he bowed deeply. I caught my mother's glare. Perhaps I was coming on too strong, although she must know I wouldn't be here voluntarily.

Lord Allen's wife stepped forward, offered a quick curtsey, and then took my arm, a light glinting in her eyes. "It's a pleasure to see you, Princess. The debacle at the meet and greet must have been such a shock! You poor thing, why don't you tell me about it?"

I let her lead me, following the butler's steps into the dining room. The long table set with the queen's finery; five places already set up.

"I'm sure there's been enough gossip about that now. Oh, you must be so proud that George made it through to the second trials before he was eliminated!" I twisted it, making it seem it was a good thing. Her face faltered for a second before putting her smile back on.

"Oh yes, we are very proud of him."

Lord Allen and George followed behind us, my mother in between them.

"He did extraordinarily well. The calibre is just so high—but there are indeed other positions that would need skilled people such as yourself, George," my mother said, gesturing for them to take seats at the table.

George took a seat to my left, his parents opposite us and my mother at the head of the table. Silently, coming from the shadows, servers moved in to fill our glasses with pale golden bubbly liquid. They placed a bowl of soup in front of me, and I waited until my mother took a sip first before etiquette dictated the rest of us could start.

"That is what I wanted to discuss with you, Your Majesty," Lord Allen began, smacking his stupid, thick lips together. My mother would have to tread carefully in meeting his requests; he may be a despicable human being, but he held a lot of land and provided us with many men for our armies on the wall. He was also generous in financial contributions. I'd figured this all out by overhearing conversations at events. Sometimes it paid to be seen and not heard.

"And what is it, exactly, that you wish to discuss with me?" my mother asked, folding her hands on her lap.

"You are aware of the presence I have among your people and the money that we so willingly donate to the kingdom and the upkeep of the wall. We are also happy to keep supplying men to the armies responsible for guarding the wall."

My mother smiled, her lips staying pressed together before she spoke. "Of course, you are a significant support of this kingdom and my crown."

"So perhaps we could arrange an agreement between your daughter and my son to continue such a good rapport between us?"

My mother carefully placed the spoon down she'd just picked up and folded her hands across her lap. Her head tilted to one side, and she pursed her lips. "I'm afraid that wouldn't appear as a good match to the kingdom. Your son fought in the trials, which meant he was willing to give up his entire life and take the oath. The oath binding him to my daughter's safety and reign, forgoing all relationships in order to fully serve the crown. He would not have been allowed to enter a marriage. Which means him entering into one with her now would belittle the oath he would have taken had he been successful. It would put into question his loyalty."

"His loyalty?!" Lord Allen scoffed.

"To be so willing to disregard that oath and that life."

"But that is nothing of the sort!" he argued, his face growing a shade red.

"I'm afraid Princess Rayleigh will enter into a marriage con-tract to help further the success of our kingdom, not question the very foundations it stands on."

"But George is a courageous and upstanding civilian!"

"That he is, and I'm sure he will find an exquisite lady who can help secure his lordship within the kingdom. But Princess Rayleigh will marry into royalty when the time is right. I'm sure you understand."

I had to hide my frown. I didn't want to marry at all, let alone into another royal family. Uck. At least I could escape George and Lord Allen. I hid the smug grin I knew was desperate to be seen.

"Are you sure you want to risk my generosity towards this kingdom?"

My mother stilled before drifting her gaze to focus on Lord Allen. He had the good sense to swallow thickly.

"Are you sure you want to sound like you're threatening the queen, Lord Allen?"

He sputtered, his face reddening even further. "No, no, Your Majesty, that isn't my intention at all."

"Good. Then I shall expect the same amount of contributions you have so gracefully given this kingdom up to now, and I shall look forward to the match you secure for your son. I'm sure he will be very successful in finding lands he can acquire of his own—as long as that generosity continues. Of course, should that slip, so may my good graces and my ability to look the other way at certain...discrepancies." She narrowed her eyes at him. I had no clue what she was referencing, but Lord Allen certainly did. He nodded and hastily shoved food into his mouth. Silence followed my mother's words.

It was much later than normal when I marched down the city's winding alleys towards the tavern. My mother insisted on upping patrols, so it had taken ages to find a suitable gap to leave without being seen. I just hoped Wren was still at the tavern.

As I hastily re-wrapped my cloak around my shoulders to ward against the extra chilly night, I slammed shoulders with a stranger I hadn't seen approach.

"I'm sorry!" I gasped, the force of the collision spinning me around to face him. A man in his thirties stood close, his long, greasy hair hanging limp around his face and a scar running over his right cheek. I tried not to hurl at the decaying stench that came off him in waves. He sneered, his too-thin nose pinching, and my head pounded in warning. He stepped closer, and I scanned my surroundings as discreetly as possible, cursing myself for not paying more attention. We were alone.

I looked back at him, realising he'd followed my search and noticed the same thing about a lack of witnesses.

"Well, hello there," he hissed, his voice low and gravelly with a touch of an accent. His hand shot out, grabbing my shoulder, and he dug his thick, meaty fingers into my flesh. He slammed me close to him, bringing his other hand up to my mouth to cover it before I could even think of shouting. The foul smell of rot and earth filled my nostrils as I fought for calm.

His dark eyes lit up with excitement. I slammed my foot down onto his, drawing a yelp, and managed to push his arms off me. I didn't count on the flash of silver gleaming in his hand when he made to approach me again, though. He grabbed my upper arm in a tight grip, pinching the skin through my cloak. I sucked in a sharp breath when his other hand stopped at my neck—the one holding a knife.

I was better than this. I was trained better than this.

His eyes roamed my face, recognition lighting them up. I was determined not to show my fear even while it soared through my trembling body.

"I cannot believe I just happened to come across you. Tyton will be pleased."

I frowned. Who was Tyton? I didn't want to find out. I had no clue what this guy had in store for me, but I knew this: I had to get away. He tried shoving me, but I set my feet apart to stay immoveable, refusing to co-operate.

"Move, little wrench!" he hissed, showing his stained and crooked teeth. My hands fisted in his jacket, trying to push him away. Pain pulsed through my head, settling at my temples as dark spots appeared in my vision.

Not now, not now, not now.

My hand found the skin at his neck, and I hit and scratched at him in the little wiggle room I had. He sucked in a jarring breath, clutching at his neck. I hadn't hurt him enough to cause the reaction and I panicked. His wide eyes darkened, the whites almost completely disappearing.

We both jumped at a clattering sound down the alleyway; I used it to my advantage, my brain kicking into action. No way was I letting him take me anywhere. I brought my knee up into his gut, and when he doubled over clenching his midsection, I fisted my hand—remembering to un-tuck my thumb at the last moment—and punched, hitting his jawline. He cried out and fell to the ground.

A sharp pain speared my knuckles, but I didn't wait. I ran

towards the nearest alley to get to the other street in the hopes someone was around. If not, I'd have to leg it back to the palace. *Please let there be more people, please.*

I stumbled through the alleyway, looking behind me when I heard the guy follow, cursing me as he did. Without looking forward, I ran into a solid body. I yelped; a familiar scent wrapped around me and strong hands gripped my shoulders, preventing me from ploughing into the ground.

Recognition hit me and I sagged in his arms.

"Little Shadow?" Wren asked, eyebrows drawn tight together, searching my face. I shamelessly gripped onto his arms.

"Guy behind me, knife," I panted. Wren's face changed: concern leading to hardened warrior. He tucked me behind him, peering into the alley. He made to move forward, a hand on the hilt of his sword as it rested against his hip, but he had no protective gear on. I gripped his hand. "Wait!"

His eyes, full of concern, looked down on me, but under that concern was a trace of...anger? "I'll be fine. You'll be okay here for a moment. I won't be gone long. I'll just take a look."

I nodded, unable to shake the fear and worry. He squeezed my hand and entered the darkness. Pacing, I nibbled on a nail. I should have gone back to the palace, got help. Wren was on his own down there. Then again, Wren was a fighter, a damn good one.

Before my feet decided what direction to go in next, Wren appeared, a grim look on his face. I threw my arms around his neck, relieved. When his arm circled my back, I realised too late what I'd done. His calming scent claimed me; his arm a powerful band of safety behind me.

"He got away, I'm sorry." His gentle voice caressed my ear, his head curved close to my neck.

I shook my head, laying it on his shoulder. I'd give myself this moment to indulge. Just this one moment while my heart calmed its erratic beating.

"When you didn't come to the tavern, I grew concerned and came looking," he offered without me even asking. My heart skipped a beat knowing he'd come searching for me.

"Thank you. You didn't have to go after him, but you did," I mumbled into his chest.

"Part of the job I'm signing up for," he replied, and we both stiffened at the mention of the trials.

My heavy heart thumped painfully when I stepped back and cleared my throat.

"I should go."

"I need to walk you back. The streets aren't safe right now."

"It was just one guy–"

"Dydairian," he interrupted. I froze. He brought up his hand holding the knife the guy must have dropped. "Dydairian metal," he explained.

"They're in the city?"

"I need to report this, but I need...I want to escort you to wherever you are going. I can't leave you here, alone. I can't." The hardness in his eyes told me there would be no arguing with him this time. But if Wren reported another Dydairian attack in the city, my mother wouldn't hesitate to stick more guards on me day and night. This would be my last chance to see Fox.

"The tavern," I replied.

"Are you sure?"

"There are plenty of contestants there, right? Plus Fox."

Wren nodded, his face a mask of emotion I couldn't decipher. We walked side by side in silence as we made our way down the main streets, people now everywhere. Where had they been a moment ago? Wren constantly checked behind us for signs of being followed, but we made it to the tavern without a problem.

I stood awkwardly at the door, not wanting to leave the safety I felt with Wren, despite the capable warriors who waited inside. He made no move to speak, his face giving away nothing, so I hesitantly started pushing open the door.

Wren reached out and gently took my elbow, pulling me close enough to him that the slim slither of light from inside the tavern illuminated those bright emerald-green orbs of his. I blinked at what I saw there. Desire danced in his eyes, his pupils large. His tongue darted out to wet his lips.

"He escorts you back. Understood?"

"Okay."

"Be careful, Little Shadow, please," he begged, his voice thick as he brushed the back of his hand across my cheek.

I nodded, not quite trusting my voice. His brows drew together, his eyes distant, and then he turned away, walking off into the night to report the attack. The countdown began. I'd say a quick goodbye to Fox and Sadie, before making it back to the palace before the queen sent someone to check on me—which she'd no doubt do when she heard of the attack.

My hands trembled as I manoeuvred the busy tables at the tavern. The contestants may be down to the final sixteen, but many stayed to see out who made it to the guard. Fox was clearing the bar as I approached. I ducked under a group of tall men who bashed their drinks together in some celebration.

"Fox!" I called, rushing into his side to hug him tight. Fox stumbled under my sudden appearance, but his arms wound round me and squeezed back all the same.

"What did I do to deserve this?" he asked, bemused. I stepped back and pushed away the tendrils of loose hair that brushed at my face; they must have come loose with the attack. "Are you okay?" Fox dipped his head, eyes serious.

"No. Listen. We don't have much time. This is probably the last time I'll be down here. I wanted to say goodbye properly."

His eyes widened, and he pushed at his messy blonde mop in frustration. "Hang on a minute, Ray. Goodbye? What's going on?"

"There was an incident earlier, one that might mean I can't sneak out again. Look, Fox," I said, grabbing his hands in mine, taking in his wide eyes, "I know this is rushed and not what we planned, and I'm sorry. I'm really going to miss coming here, but I'll still see you at palace events, right?"

Fox opened and shut his mouth before frowning. "When I get the jobs," he mumbled.

"I'll make sure you do. I'll pass on Sadie's medicine to you there."

"Ray, I don't want to say goodbye. You're my best friend. Who else am I going to chat utter crap with and discuss all the hot gossip?" His eyes became full and his chin wobbled, but I launched myself at him again, squeezing him tight.

"I'll come and find you on event days. I'll help you in the kitchens or whatever. Hey, it'll look good to support the staff and all that," I tried to sound nonchalant as I lightly punched him on the shoulder. "I need to say goodbye to Sadie," I added, my smile falling. I knew this one really would be a goodbye if I could never leave the palace alone again.

Leaving Fox, I scanned the tavern and found Sadie talking with some popular patrons. She waved when she saw me, leaving the table of customers she'd been chatting to.

"Ray! It's good to see you. The trials are doing wonders for my business." Her old eyes crinkled around the edges, her familiar raspy voice one I'd never forget. My face remained serious, though, and her eyes immediately dimmed. "What's wrong?"

"This is the last time I'll be able to get here as Ray, and I just want to thank you for everything you've done for me and for Fox over the past few years."

"Oh child," she rasped, wafting a hand in front of her face to dismiss the comment. "It has been nothing but a pleasure. Well, except for Fox, he's a pain in my aging derriere."

I laughed. "But I know you love him like family."

"Right you are, dear. The same as you." She placed a wrinkled hand on my face, the skin smooth despite its appearance. "You look after yourself, young one."

"And back at you. You need to make sure you get rest for that hip; I'll send medicine when I can via Fox."

Her cackled laughter filled the air. "I can rest in me grave! Oh Rayleigh, I hope I'll be honoured to see you ascend the throne one day."

"Me too. I want to see your face at my coronation celebrations!"

We both laughed, and I hugged her thinning frame tight. I asked Fox to walk back with me, more out of wanting to spend even just that bit more time with him than Wren's order.

By the time I got back into the palace, the hum of its nervous energy reached out to me, growing louder with every second. I rushed to get inside before my mother sent for me. After feeding the fire with haste, I changed from my city clothes into a plain grey dress with long sleeves. I took my hair out of its messy plait before I rushed towards Markin's office, finger combing through my long locks on the way over.

There were answers I deserved to have.

SIXTEEN

WHEN I ARRIVED AT Markin's study on the second floor, it became clear I wasn't the only one who wished to speak with him. Markin only really used the fairly small room when he had loads of paperwork to be getting on with. The dark stained wooden walls had always created a pleasant warming feel whenever I spent time in here, but this visit, after sneaking in here, all I felt was judgement. Could walls judge? The lights on his desk didn't illuminate much, but I knew it was because he both preferred it that way and it was late. Loch sat opposite Markin's desk and turned his head as I approached. Another officer stood by the door, but I couldn't see his face from the direction I was coming from, his body hidden in shadows.

"We really should shut this door more often," Loch dead-panned. Ouch.

"Gee, thanks, Loch," I said, eye-rolling. Loch gave me a tired half smile and stood.

"I'll leave you to it."

"Thank you both." Markin dismissed the two men. The grim look on Loch's face made it evident Wren had already been. I stood back to let them exit and stifled a gasp. Mahds exited behind Loch. He drew his brows together at me as I stepped back from him. I hadn't been expecting him. Mahds of all people. Of course, he was a senior soldier, but I hadn't expected to see the guy I suspected to be helping the Dydairians here. Now. At this very moment.

"You all right, little one?" Loch asked, stepping back by my side.

"Yeah," I squeaked. I was *so* not a subtle person. Loch made a point of shutting the door for me; at least I wouldn't have to worry about Mahds listening to me with just me and Markin in the room.

"Mahds came to find me when you arrived back at the palace," Markin said, distracting me from my thoughts. Wait.

"He was waiting for me?"

Markin nodded. "On my orders. You had another ten minutes before I alerted your mother. As it is, I need to discuss this with her urgently."

From his tone, I knew that meant I had a short amount of time to talk with him.

"You heard, then."

"Yes. This isn't good. I'm afraid our next recourse is to ensure you don't leave this palace alone."

I opened my mouth in protest, even though I knew it was futile, I still had to fight it. "You can't do that to me, Markin!"

"Oh, I can, Rayleigh. Let's not pretend that your mother

wouldn't order it anyway. And no, you won't be able to sneak out anymore—I can see the idea forming in your eyes. I, and a few others, permit you to leave, and I have someone watching your tavern to make sure you arrive."

Now I really did let my jaw fall slack. "You mean, I never truly leave without being detected?"

"I told you I know more about what goes on here than you realise. If giving you that small freedom allows you any sort of enjoyment, you know I'd do everything in my power to make it happen. And it gives you the opportunity to practise what you've learned from us. You really think I would have a gap in our defences enough to let the princess escape all the time?" His tone wasn't rough, but it made me question all the times I thought I had snuck out, and my heart started thumping faster. Did he know I'd snuck into his office? He couldn't have. He definitely would have confronted me about it already. I tried to calm the racing beast so it wouldn't give me away.

"But what about the attacks on the palace we've had? Why let me go at all before now?"

Markin's face fell as he sighed, leaning his arms on the oak desk in front of him. "Yes, well, I'm working on that. And don't forget that I send someone to the tavern to make sure you get there."

"Someone like Mahds?" I asked, my voice smaller than I had intended. He nodded. "Markin, Mahds—"

He held up a hand. "Think carefully about what you're going to say next, Rayleigh."

I sat in the chair Loch had left. "I don't trust him."

I had to tread carefully; he couldn't know I'd spied on Mahds by breaking into his office. I'd lose his trust, and Markin's belief in me was the only thing holding me together when it came to my mother. I couldn't lose that.

"I do." That was it. That was all he said.

"But what if someone was working from here, from high up on the inside to help the Dydairians coordinate the attacks, getting through the wall, through the city, into the palace!" Markin sat still, barely blinking. A thought struck me. "You already think this."

"I've already told you that things are in hand," his tired voice responded, but he didn't make eye contact.

"Should I be worried?"

"We will have the situation under control—"

"No, Markin. I don't want the spiel my mother would give. You said yourself that the personal guard should be able to think independently of the queen. So, what are your personal thoughts on my safety?" I questioned, feeling strong and confident enough to speak like this for the first time. Markin looked up and met my eyes, his shining with a worry I hadn't seen before now.

"You should be worried about your safety, always, but this will be under control soon. Myself and the personal guards are working around the clock to figure out who could be helping the Dydairians. It is only speculation at this point, and we need to tread carefully. It is imperative that we find you a loyal guard and that guard is heavily vetted by us to ensure your safety. That is your main priority right now. Worry about the Dydairians later. And trust me when I say I only send people out to watch you whom I personally trust."

"But Markin, I overheard–"

I stopped abruptly when he held up his hand again. "And

that is why you cannot leave without an escort, not anymore. You shouldn't have overheard anything. When you overhear parts of a whole, you can never fully rely on what you hear. Understand me?"

"What if people are lying to you?"

"They are, and that is why I trust only a few with you—Mahds is one of them. Not everything is as it seems, Rayleigh."

"I want to help, I need to help," I whispered, fiddling with an imaginary thread on my skirts.

Markin sighed. "I know, I know you do. But this is far more...complicated than you realise."

"So why can't I help? This will be my role in a few years. As soon as my mother steps down, I'll be in charge, and I can't help the people of this kingdom if I don't know what's going on."

He was quiet for a long moment before he spoke softly. "Please don't make me force this upon you. I would much rather you agree and just stay inside the palace."

"But my mother will force it."

"Let me worry about your mother."

I paused, speculating. One good thing could come out of my compliance. "One condition." Markin's eyes narrowed in my direction. "Approve my friend Fox for permanent work at the palace."

"Fox? He's worked for us before, hasn't he?" I nodded. "I'll move him to the permanent acceptance list once we clear him."

"Then deal," I responded, smiling somewhat triumphantly.

Markin sighed and began clearing his desk, ready to go and speak with my mother. I turned to leave him to it, wanting to be nowhere near my mother when she found out about the latest attack.

"Markin?"

"Mmm?"

"The trials tomorrow? I don't want anyone else to die in them."

"I know," he answered, the harsh lines on his face softening. "But they are a part of the trials. Some will fall and fall permanently, however, they always have the opportunity to stand down, forfeit their place in the trials and keep their lives."

"Would you?"

"Would I what?"

"Would you lay down your sword to keep your life?"

Markin's silence told me all I needed to know. "No, no, I wouldn't. I'd compete until I won or lost my life, just like I would in real life."

His response is exactly what I was afraid of for Wren.

"Oh! For goodness sake, child!" A voice chided, and one I immediately recognised: Yola.

"Yola?" I mumbled as my arm was yanked away from my face. Yola's harsh face surrounded by daylight stared down on me. "Don't you knock?" The last thing I remembered was taking my headache tonic and lying on my bed, worrying about Wren and the trials and how much my body yearned for him, even though it shouldn't. I'd never reacted this strongly to someone before.

Never.

"You're going to be late. Come on. Bathe, now! What were you doing last night?" Yola asked, scrunching her nose before yanking my arm again to encourage me out of bed. "Hurry, child! Your mother is not in the best of moods, and I refuse to let her see you this unpresentable before the trials. Now go!" She shooed me towards the washroom where I focused on the tasks ahead. I'd see Wren soon enough in the trial.

"Please protect him," I sent a whispered plea to whatever gods might listen.

SEVENTEEN

T RIAL THREE. A TRIAL of one-to-one combat where skills and abilities of each contestant were tested to the max. I made my way to the royal box of the arena, following my mother, but nerves trampled my stomach like a herd of rambunctious elephants.

I kept smoothing down my dress even though there was no need given the thick, sturdy material. It was paler than my mother's rose-coloured ensemble, but we still matched—never a coincidence. She and Yola always had meetings to discuss outfits. Apparently, what we wore reflected our opinions and positions, so 'we must always project a sense of unity and togetherness'. Whatever. I just wore what I was told to do at these things.

I fiddled with the thick, corded twists of the same blush pink colour that spun round my waist and over my shoulders. Glancing down at my fussing hands, they once again smoothed the material. My uncovered arms were a slight blessing; nerves heated my blood plenty hot enough. The neckline cut straight across my neck where a small gold pendant lay. I'd had to feign ignorance when Yola tutted and stormed about my rooms trying to find the 'lost' necklace. Why did it have to be 'that' necklace of all necklaces that she wanted?

I stepped onto the royal box, Yola tutting again and rushing forward to smooth some hair that had come loose in the breeze. She'd twisted the front section back in the same style as the corded material on my dress and then secured the entire mass of hair in a long braid, the intricate twists spinning down my back. I tried not to flinch when she poked me with another hair pin. Again.

Derril's warm face greeted me, a welcoming difference to my mother's lady-in-waiting. He held my hand up and bowed. He performed the same customary greeting with my mother while Loch and Abe stood behind our chairs; a barrier between us and the high-born joining us. I wasn't oblivious to the way Markin's eyes darted over them and came to rest on Loch's, some unspoken communication being held between the two men. Was he worried about the leak in our systems being from one of the high-born? I hadn't thought about that, thinking it was someone who worked for us. Not that I was completely over the idea it wasn't Mahds. Markin hadn't told me the whole story, but something didn't feel right. Although, I knew my mother and Markin could very well be hiding even more from me. In fact, I almost expected them to be doing so.

I stood in front of my chair, hands clasped, as my mother opened her arms to signal she was ready to begin.

"People of Balmore," she bellowed, allowing the crowds' high excitement to dull enough to be heard properly. "Welcome to trial three where we will test each contestant's capacity to think, their skills in battle, and their endurance through a trial of combat. We have divided the last sixteen contestants into groups of four and they will fight each member of their group back-to-back. They may be afforded a brief break, but this is at the mercy of the pair before them as the break will be as long as that fight lasts—up to a total of twenty minutes. My guard and senior officials within the palace army will watch closely and make decisions about whom to put forward for the final eight." A roaring cheer interrupted my mother. She let the crowd indulge for a few seconds before raising her arms again; the crowd's excitement died to a temporary whisper. "The winners of each match are not guaranteed a spot in the final. All performance to date will be considered, however, winning is of course beneficial. Remember that the trials can be bloody and deadly; if you have small children, proceed with caution."

The gates down in the arena opened and the sixteen remaining contestants walked out. Noise in the crowd soared with tangible anticipation. Each contestant stopped before the queen in the royal box and dropped to one knee. I kept as far back as I could—not that Wren would recognise me dressed the way I was. I hoped.

My mother addressed the men. "As before, if at any point you decide to lay down your sword, you will keep your life guaranteed, but you forfeit your place in the trials." She paused for dramatic effect, not that she needed any in this atmosphere. "Let the trials begin!" she commanded, and the crowd howled with excitement.

All but four contestants stayed in the middle. One of the palace soldiers signalled to the two who would fight first, and I was slightly relieved to see Wren wasn't in the first group.

The heavy clang of metal rang through the arena, but I paced behind the tall-backed chairs my mother and I were supposed to be sitting at, unable to focus.

"Rayleigh, please," my mother chastised. She'd been standing to one side with Markin, discussing the two fighters. Loch and Derril studied the fight, too, but Abe kept shooting me glances. When he caught me glancing back at him, he lowered his head and raised one brow. I translated easily: *you okay*? I nodded and gave a tense smile, sitting heavily on the chair as the second fight began.

It may have been round two or something when a flash of red hair caught my attention. The guy with long auburn hair fought well. His movements were strong. And while they seemed chaotic at first, I soon recognised a pattern. His movements reminded me of Abe and how he fought. Maybe this guy was originally from the same area as him. Abe leaned over the barrier, watching the fight intently. He recognised the moves, too.

I also recognised the guy Wren had helped in the second trial, surprised to find myself pleased he at least looked like he was doing well. If Wren thought he was worthy of helping, I wanted to see how he fought. I overheard Loch telling my mother his name was Essiah. The first group's battle flew by so quickly that I wasn't sure if that helped my nerves or not.

When Wren's group finally entered the arena, my already tangled body of nerves twisted into an unrecognisable mass within my churning stomach.

Wren was up first, but I shouldn't have been so worried. He was confident and attacked and defended with precision. I knew for a fact Markin was taking a special interest in him after the second trial. A small tug pulled at the corner of Markin's mouth when Wren struck his opponent with such force, the guy dropped his sword and stumbled forward. Quick to action, Wren changed the angle of his thrust to hit the guy's head with the heel of his sword, thus knocking him out. They declared Wren a winner, and I breathed a sigh of relief.

My sigh of relief turned into a sharp intake of air. Wren's name was called to fight again in his group. He'd have no rest period.

I gripped the arms of my chair when he walked back into the centre of the arena, his chest rising and falling heavily, adjusting the front of his body plate. All four of my mother's guards leaned forward with heightened anticipation. The short horn sounded. The fight began.

Wren's beastly opponent roared, raising his sword as he swaggered into the arena. He stood much taller than Wren, and his impressive dark armour was clearly more expensive—and newer. The man twisted his sword around in his wrist, the sharp blade glinting dangerously in the late morning sun. He lunged first. Wren went on the defensive, dodging strikes and blocking hits.

The guy teased Wren, making him work harder to stay in the fight. If anything, it looked like he knew Wren had no break and used that to his advantage, hoping to tire him down. He never gave Wren a window of opportunity to fight back.

My dress was now balled in my fists as I stayed glued to my seat. *Come on, Wren.* The man raised his sword and slashed in an upward direction; Wren barely had time to stop the blade from hitting him in the chest as he yanked his sword up and across his body defensively. His arm muscles bunched as he struggled to push him away. The other fighter used the distraction and punched into Wren's protective helmet with his sword-free fist. Wren's head snapped back, and he staggered away. The man came at him again, hitting him in the side. Wren's brief cry of surprise mirrored in my gasp; I stood up, leaning on the edge of the platform.

Wren landed on his back, his helmet flying off. His body sagged momentarily before he attempted to get up. He failed, pressing a hand to his side. A suffocating gasp stuck in my throat. Was he hurt? His opponent moved swiftly forward, sensing victory. I had no idea if this guy allowed his opponents to live or not. He was within his rights of the trials to kill Wren.

My heart lurched forward when Wren inched on his side towards his sword, painfully obvious he wasn't going to get to it in time. A dull ache behind my eyes made me grind my teeth. Sweat beaded at my neck as I counted down the seconds the guy would be upon Wren: four, three, two, one. I pinched my eyes shut, expecting to hear horrified gasps of the crowd, but instead, the sharp clash of metal pierced my ears, quickly muffled by loud cheering. The crowd rooted for Wren.

I kept clenching and unclenching the material of my dress in my hands, forcing myself to open my eyes. Wren had somehow reached his sword, but he was still on his back, putting him at a grave disadvantage. He held his sword up, an end in each hand, blocking his opponent's attempt to cut down right in front of him. His grip on the hilt shook, and the flat of the blade pressed heavily into his arm cuff as he protected his head. Even far away, I could make out the visible pressure his arms took from the downward force.

On a loud cry from Wren, he kicked his foot up into the guy's crotch. When the man doubled over, Wren swiped his feet from under him and yanked off his helmet before he even fell to the floor. He straddled him, quickly delivering three quick blows to his opponent's face with his fist. I couldn't see the guy move anymore. Wren climbed off, kneeling on all fours as a horn blared.

Wren won. He bloody won. A smile stretched tight on my tense face but faded quickly. Wren limped off the arena in obvious pain. He still had one more fight left. Could he beat a third opponent while clearly injured? Would that person seek out Wren's injuries and use them against him?

Wren's name reached my ears and I stilled, aching to overhear a message being carried by a soldier to Loch in the royal box. Loch nodded and thanked him before moving over to discuss whatever it was with Markin. I swore I heard 'medic tent'. How seriously injured was he?

As the next two fighters came on, I moved over to my mother and Markin.

"Mother, may I be excused for this next fight? I'm feeling a little under the weather. A quick lie down away from the crowds will be most appreciated." I even curtseyed, which may have been a step too far. However, she seemed only half interested as she nodded at me.

I hastened down the steps and out towards the serving tent where I knew Fox was working to deliver drinks to the crowds. His dirty blonde mop and trademark scowl served a rather rowdy group. I pushed my way through the crowd but many parted when they recognised me.

"Fox!" I hissed. He looked over, confusion etched deep in his face. He hurried to where I stood.

"Princess Rayleigh?" he mumbled, trailing off when I yanked his arm and dragged him outside, round to the back of the unmarked tent my mother and I used just before the trial. The entire arena was well-guarded overall, but I still took a moment to ensure the tent was safe for us to enter.

"I need a favour," I hissed quickly, already untying the thick twisted cord belt from around my waist.

"Whoa, there! What are you doing!?" Fox shrieked, but then lowered his voice when I glared at him.

"I need to swap clothes so I can sneak into the medic tent and make sure Wren is okay."

Fox held a hand to his head. "There is so much wrong with what you just said, and judging by the urgent tone in your voice, I don't feel like I have time to address any of it."

"I need your clothes, Fox!" I snapped.

"Alright, missy! Calm down. You can't see Wren. If he's injured, he needs time to heal. You'll probably make things worse."

"But I need to see if he's okay. What if he needs help? I can't offer that as Princess Rayleigh. He needs Ray."

"Again, there's a whole lot of wrong there. You are the same person except one wears pretty dresses. They both boss me around," he mumbled at the end.

"Are you going to help me or not?"

"Fine. But you so owe me!" Fox turned his back so I could take off my dress. He threw his tunic over his head, and it landed at my feet. I pulled it over my head, rolling up the long sleeves and took the rest of my dress off. Fox's trousers needed pinching together, which I did with the pin I found on the small wooden folding table holding spare hair and makeup things. Fox stood in just his undergarments before he stepped into my dress and slid it up his body, shimmering his shoulders through the straps.

"Do I look pretty in pink?" he jested. I grabbed his discarded jacket and rifled through the pockets for a hat to cover at least half of my icy-blonde sophisticated hair style.

"That you do," I replied, winked, and ducked out. Fox's chuckle followed me out from the tent, and I prayed no one would enter trying to look for me. It wouldn't end well for Fox to be found wearing my clothes and me nowhere to be seen.

I wound my way through the busy crowds and past the temporary tavern tent—I wasn't sorry to see the creepo boy looking flustered as he tried to manage with a man down. This time, I was bumped into and pushed numerous times, which meant no one recognised me. People really were so unobservant.

The medic tent loomed up ahead; I ducked inside just before a large group of people moved past the entrance. Quietness washed over me; I'd have to be even quieter inside so I wouldn't stick out. A couple of contestants lay on the beds, one half asleep and another sporting a bandage to his face. A few nurses milled about but most were through the connecting tent corridor and in the main medical room. It sounded like a surgery was going on. I peered inside, but the rushing around of bodies and harshly barked instructions from doctors told me they were too busy and distracted to come into this area.

Holding my head high, I tried channelling the energy of my mother: I belonged here. I wasn't out of place.

I scanned the array of beds. Wren sat on the edge of a small bed near the back, hunched over his side. He'd taken his gear off and his tunic, both of which lay discarded in a pile on the floor. I moved closer, wincing when he grunted; his head bent near a bloody bowl of water resting on the short stand beside the bedframe. His hand held a rag pressed to his side.

"Need a hand?" I asked softly, coming to a stop just in front of him. He looked up, and I expected to see confusion, but instead, fatigue faced me and...I swallowed hard. Failure shone in his eyes.

"I'm fine," he huffed, stiffly moving the rag back to the bowl to rinse. I rolled my eyes at the stereotypical blasé male reaction and took his hands in mine, trying to pry the cloth away. He stared pointedly at me, and I narrowed my eyes at him. Two could play at this game. He seemed to sense I wouldn't relent and let go of the rag. He sat back up stiffly.

I twisted excess water out of the now stained rag and placed it over his side as I sat down beside him. His wound could definitely be worse, but a nasty gash stretched round his ribs with a mottled blue and purple cloud already surrounding it. Gods, that bruising must hurt.

"Why aren't the nurses helping?" I grumbled, frustrated at seeing him in pain.

"They aren't allowed to help in the middle of a trial. I would forfeit if I allowed it. They're too busy anyways, so I have no choice but to do this myself."

"Not anymore," I whispered. "Did his armour do this?" I asked quietly, knowing the gash wasn't a sword wound. He frowned to himself, pinching his eyes shut when I pressed a little too hard. "Sorry."

"You were watching?"

"Err, yeah. Then I saw you come into the medic tent." He must have been dealing with the pain as he didn't detect the hesitant lie out of my mouth.

Wren nodded. "He wore armoured gloves with razors on the knuckles, so when he punched me..." I inhaled sharply. "That was precisely my reaction," Wren mumbled.

"How that's fair is beyond me," I said tightly. I needed to have a word with Markin.

"You'd think so, but battles are seldom fair, are they? Got to make do with what you've got. Unfortunately, my time in the trials has just ended," his voice lowered and pain not from his physical injuries clouded his eyes.

"Hey, look at me," I commanded and waited until those troubled green eyes met mine. I kept the rag pressed to his side and gripped the arm which rested on his thigh with my other hand. "You're better than this, Wren. Do you think the guard would accept someone who so easily gives up? Even if you lose the next fight, it doesn't mean you haven't made it through. Fight with honour, Wren, and I'm confident you'll pass."

He studied me for a long minute, and I struggled to look away. How could he hold so much intensity without saying a single word? I forced myself to focus on cleaning the wound best I could, being careful not to wipe too hard. He'd have to clean it again when he was less tender, but it would do for now.

"Ray," he began, his voice both soft and pained.

"Let's get you bandaged up," I said quickly, hoping to distract whatever negative thing he looked like he was about to say. They had left the bandages on the side behind the bowl, so I grabbed them and unwound the start of one roll.

"Why are you doing this?"

I made sure the long rectangular gauze was clean before carefully pressing it over the wound, making a note to grab some ointment from the palace later.

"Are you just going to ignore me now?" he asked again.

"Yes."

"Why?" he asked, exasperated, and I slowly began winding the bandage over the gauze and around his torso. I leaned closer to wrap it around his back, passing the bandage roll to my other hand. I even took a second to praise myself for not acting a fool around his half naked, very defined, body.

"Because I don't want to hear it, okay? I probably shouldn't be here, you're right, but is it stopping me? No."

"If you know that, then I need to make a better effort to stop seeing you."

I stilled briefly before wrapping my arm around his back to pass the bandage to my other hand again. I cleared my throat. "Wren," I sighed.

He covered my hand with his as the bandage came to a stop on his stomach.

"We both know this is bad. I'm not immune to you even though I should be, because that's precisely what I'm willing to sign up for. In another life, another time, maybe I would be free to get to know you better, but for now...this is making it harder." He looked down at our connected hands.

I grabbed the tape to secure the bandage.

"Wrendor?" a male voice announced from the front of the tent. I turned to see an official-looking man studying a document in his hands. "Looks like you're on in a few minutes. Get ready," the man stated and promptly left again, not even fussed by the sight of me. Fox's clothes worked to conceal me at least.

Sighing, I looked up at him, taking in every inch of his face with my eyes knowing this could be the last time I saw him as Ray.

"I know what I just said, but thank you for helping me. I needed reminding what I'm here for." I sat back as he redressed, struggling to put his top on and hissing as he moved. Ignoring his protests, I helped secure the chest plates over his shoulders. He leaned forward, softly grasping my head in his hands, and kissed me tenderly on the forehead. His lips lingered there, and my stomach tightened with desire and comfort at the same time.

He stood and I followed suit while he tightened his sword belt around his waist. His face may have been pale, but his eyes lit with a new strength and a determination I knew wouldn't let him down.

There was nothing else to do but walk out of the medic tent and start his next fight, but he remained still, a nervous, torn energy filling the space between us.

Reaching out with one hand, he tucked some loose hair behind my ear. "Bye, Little Shadow."

He left and I shamelessly watched his broad shoulders disappear out of the tent. I couldn't let myself wallow. I had to get back to Fox, swap clothes, and get back to the arena before my absence started arousing suspicion.

A single tear tracked down my cheek. I swiped it away and pushed my shoulders back. I followed Wren's footsteps out of the medical tent, forcing my tensed fist to open before I split the skin with my nails when I walked in the opposite direction he had gone.

EIGHTEEN

B UTTERFLIES DANCED IN MY stomach, and my heart
squeezed on and off in nervous anticipation.

"Hold still," someone said. The voice came from one of the
team of women my mother had hired to make us dresses for the
finalists' ball tonight. She tutted at me as I fiddled with the burnt
umber coloured material. I glanced down at where the dressmaker
knelt, holding pins as she tried to do something on the seam of my
dress; I smiled apologetically.

Wren would be at the ball tonight, a tradition when contestants were down to the final eight. Held in their honour, it would
enable me to get to know the candidates better. I shivered, trying
not to clench the silken material. I wasn't ready to show Wren who
I really was. My nerves were so fried that even meeting the other
contestants wasn't worrying me in the slightest.

Sheri and Yola conversed with my mother while they tended

to her dress, getting it on and fastened. We both stood on circular podiums to enable the dresses to be worked on from all angles. As usual, our dresses were similar in colour but differed in style. My long-sleeved, off-the-shoulder dress hugged my waist, showing off my curves before flowing out wide around me. The seamstress huffed again when I shuffled from foot to foot, trying her best to attach the individual sparkling golden leaves that tumbled down one side of my torso and onto the skirt of the dress. I didn't want to admit it was spectacular, even though it could be considered a piece of art.

"Stay still, Rayleigh," my mother chastised. Yola finished tying the intricate laces at the back of the queen's bolder, golden-hued ballgown. When my mother turned, a fine sheer layer over the top of her dress caught the light. Adorned with elaborate crystal designs that snaked around her waist and up over her shoulders to her collar, my mother radiated power.

"Sorry," I muttered.

"There is nothing to be nervous about. This is a relaxed party."

I raised my brows at her as she moved some of her hair away from the high collar of her dress.

"We're literally in ballgowns, mother."

She clucked her tongue, stepping down from the podium—Yola walked over with the queen's crown, golden and bright like her dress, to rest on her head. She quickly styled some remaining pieces of hair over the sides. Yola worked her magic, weaving the crown onto her hair in a delicate embrace.

"Are you okay?" my mother asked, glancing over at me for the hundredth time.

"Yes," I squirmed. "Just nervous." At least that wasn't exactly a lie.

"You'll have fun. It's a time you get to meet with the final contestants. Four of these men will be in your personal guard. Don't forget."

I rolled my eyes. How could I possibly forget?

My frayed stomach knotted further.

Maybe I should have told Wren. Maybe Fox was right. Maybe I should have just come clean before the ball, so he had time to adjust. I'd always known he was part of the trials, but he hadn't known I was the princess he was competing to protect. I groaned inwardly. If the roles were reversed, I know I'd be upset, angry, maybe even feel betrayed.

The seamstress began packing away, so Yola got to work on my hair, twisting it half up and half down; the elaborate twists tumbled from a small bun near the top of my head, and the rest fell in waves down my back. She secured a golden leaf broach just under the bun to tie in with my outfit.

This time, I wasn't getting away with no makeup and had to endure her torture. But when she finally finished with me, I managed to persuade my mother I needed a few minutes alone and was—miraculously—granted it.

"Do not mess up your dress or hair. Do not make trouble!" she ordered.

I dipped my head at her as I left. "Yes, ma'am."

I glided through the hallways trying to muster all the elegance and formal training I had as I approached the kitchens looking for Fox.

He turned when I entered, and like most of the staff in the kitchens, continued to pour drinks into glasses and finish last-minute touches on canapes spread over wide silver trays. However, as he worked his mouth slackened. It was good to see someone else have the same reaction I often did at Yola's transformations.

I gave him a twirl. "You like?" I asked.

Fox studied my dress, a gleam of appreciation in his eyes.

"Like? I love it. You look stunning; it suits you," he said, inspecting the material and the hand stitched leaves closer.

"I'm glad you approve because I'm nervous as hell." I placed a hand over my quivering stomach. His eyes softened from admiring the dress, to understanding.

"I know. Do you have any idea how you're going to approach this?"

"No. I just...what if he hates me?"

"He couldn't hate you." Fox continued to pour drinks and pass them to one of two serving girls preparing the trays, lowering his voice so they wouldn't hear. "He'd be lucky, privileged even, to work alongside you. You both know you wouldn't have been able to have any sort of," Fox lowered his voice even further, "relationship. He wants to be in the personal guard; no outside relationships allowed. You'll eventually have to marry for strategic strength, some stuffy noble high-borne, no doubt." We both crinkled our noses. "Either way, you being the princess doesn't affect the outcome." One girl took away the tray of drinks Fox finished setting up and the other went to fetch more glasses. Fox started on another tray while he waited, taking a cheeky sip out of one without anyone seeing. His eyes widened. "Ooo, that's nice. Your mother has good taste."

I rolled my eyes but smiled. "You could be right about Wren. I don't think the nerves have got the memo yet."

Fox stepped closer and laid a hand on the side of my arm.

"You got this, Rayleigh. And you look spectacular; you're not going to make this easy on him."

My cheeks heated just thinking about Wren seeing me in the dress and getting the chance to dance with him. My mother already informed me I'd be dancing with all the contestants during the evening. Those dancing lessons she'd dragged me through would be paying off tonight.

Fox's eyes drifted somewhere over my head, so I turned to see what caught his attention. Markin. He manoeuvred his way round servers and kitchen staff with seamless grace. Fox quickly got back to work.

"Ah, Rayleigh, I was looking for you," Markin began, surveying the working area. Many averted their eyes and hurried their movements at his study. While I suspected he often gave everything a once-over, I knew he had to have been highly suspicious of nearly everyone right now.

I smiled at him. "Is everything okay?"

"Yes, shall we?" he responded curtly, swinging an arm out to indicate I should proceed ahead of him. I snuck a quick glance at Fox who smirked at me and then I sauntered out. I really had no desire to head to the ball, but Markin's tight tone intrigued me. "Guests are arriving. No problems so far," Markin said when we exited the room and began walking down the long corridor towards my mother's throne room. I was at least a little relieved to hear that.

"Are you sure?"

"Of course."

"What about Mahds?"

Markin cocked his head to one side. "What's this about? I already told you I trust him."

My stomach churned. I should tell him. If everything was fine so far, it might mean it won't be later. Shit. Consequences be dammed. "Markin, I know that Mahds has been meeting with others, and someone sent him a coded message with today's date." I couldn't even look at him. He stopped and spun me round to face him, his hands clutching my shoulders.

"Again, I think I need to repeat that you shouldn't be listening to half conversations and spying on people. That is not your job and will get you into more trouble than you could imagine."

"But Markin," I pleaded.

"Listen to me, I know what Mahds is doing, okay? I need you to trust me."

My lips trembled as I reached up to hold his hands to my shoulders, my eyes slowly filling.

"I do trust you, I do. But that date, today's date, wouldn't this be a good time to be attacked?"

His eyes closed on a sigh, and when he opened them, he cupped my face in large hands. "Yes, hence why we have tripled our normal security for something like this. I told you, I already know about Mahds. There is too much at play for me to explain it all, too much risk for you, but you are drawing the wrong conclusions. Please, don't do anything rash and just have faith."

I sniffled, rubbing the back of my hand against my nose and then dabbed under my eyes so the ink Yola had painstakingly applied to my lashes wouldn't run.

"I just want to help. I'm so in the dark and everyone has left me alone. I feel so alone, Markin." My voice trembled, and Markin pulled me to his chest, gently stroking a hand down my back.

"I know," he whispered. "I know. Please forgive me for that."

There was nothing I could do but nod in response. I trusted him, I did, but I was losing faith. The weight on me was becoming unbearable, and I didn't know how much longer I could stand it.

He pulled back and held his arm out once again, forcing a smile onto his face. I took his outstretched arm, and we carried on down the corridor.

"Your mother wanted to meet with you in her throne room before going to the ball, to meet the final eight." That had me stopping in my tracks, forgetting the last five minutes entirely. A single room with just the eight? There'd be nothing to hide behind, no façade. Nothing. Wren would see me clear as day. I'd been hoping for the cover of lots of people to show myself.

"Oh?" I squeaked. Markin squeezed my fingers as they rested on his arm, taking my tone for general nerves—thank the gods. I didn't know where I'd begin trying to explain Wren to him.

"I know it can be an unnerving thing, meeting these young men, but we're not bad, are we?" he joked, and I smiled at his attempt to calm me. In truth, I adored my mother's personal guard. Whether it was because they became pseudo father figures after my father's passing, or because they genuinely cared for me, I didn't know, but they were fine men.

I blinked.

"What if I don't like them like I like you guys? What if they're not...?" I asked, horrified at the intrusive thought. A pang of guilt twinged, melting and mixing corrosively with the nerves. Would gaining my own guard mean I lost my mother's?

"Rayleigh," Markin began, a serious edge to his tone. "We will always be happy to be a part of your life and will be until we pass. You don't have to worry about that. Besides, you've known us for nineteen years. Give these potential new guards at least a dance before you make any harsh assumptions, okay?" He winked at me.

I cast my eyes heavenward for dramatic effect. "I'll try."

"Now, before we get to your mother, I came to find you about something specific."

I raised one brow. More? How could there be more? "What's that?"

"One of the contestants wrote to me saying they are unwell and cannot attend tonight. They assure me they are fine to continue in the trials, but as the ball is not one of the trials, they have stated their desire to continue without attending tonight."

"Oh," I muttered, not sure what else to say. Markin tried to describe who it was to me. I'm pretty sure he was describing 'Mardy'—or at least that's what Fox and I dubbed him as.

"But it is entirely up to you."

"What do you mean?"

"Do you wish for him to continue in the trials even though he is not present tonight?"

"Well, it's not a trial, so I don't think we can hold this against him. How is he performing thus far?"

"Exceptional in some areas. Probably leading the trials."

Tilting my head to one side, I pondered. I thought back on his performance: he'd fought well in all trials and was even first through the forest and over the obstacle course. 'Extraordinary timing' Abe had commented at the time.

"And it's down to me to decide?" My mind bounced between a

few different thoughts before I settled on 'pleased'. Giddy pleasure washed over me. My opinion mattered. It didn't happen often. "Then I see no problem," I finished as confidently as I could. Markin smiled as we turned the corner and approached the throne room door.

During the short walk there, I'd forgotten about the pressure, forgotten the nerves that trampled my defenceless body, forgotten that through those doors Wren would see right through me and the deception I'd offered up to him before now.

I tried to reconcile that it wasn't really deception: I stayed true to my morals and personality—mostly. Perhaps grinding over someone's lap, moaning when they kissed me, and having sex dreams about them wasn't my normal behaviour. But on the whole, I was 'me'. I hadn't really lied. *I* wasn't a lie.

I repeated that in my head trying to fool my nerves into quitting already.

Markin reached for the door and time slowed down. I unnecessarily smoothed my dress down, a habit I had to stop, and let out a long and steady breath to attempt expelling what negativity I could.

Hold your head high, Rayleigh. You can do this. This is *your* guard.

The sturdy oak doors swung inwards, and Markin led me into the room.

"Your Majesty," he announced to my mother and bowed, stepping aside to leave me out in the open.

A row of seven finely dressed finalists stood to one side, each immediately bending a knee before me.

And there he was. Magnificent in his suit, dark hair swept

back. A strong jaw clenched tight with nerves—I'd come to recognise—as his head dipped respectfully. His green eyes dashed sideways to catch a glimpse of the princess he was competing in the trials to protect.

My heart stopped as a bolt of electric heat flashed wildly between us.

NINETEEN

M Y EYES HAD NEVER darted away so fast before. I focused on my mother, standing regal as ever in front of her throne, and concentrated with every fibre of my being on not falling to my knees under Wren's scrutiny.

The short walk to my mother went on forever, all the while trying to still my shaking hands. In the corner of my eye, the contestants continued to kneel, their heads bowed in respect as I made my way towards the queen. A smile on her face and a twinkle of pride pulsed off her. It helped ease some of the tension that all were invisible to, all except Wren and me.

"My daughter, Princess Rayleigh, heir to Balmore kingdom," she announced, releasing the finalists from their positions. They stood as one, like a well-oiled machine founded from strict discipline.

My brain worked overtime to keep my eyes from glancing at

Wren. Do. Not. Do. It.

My mother addressed the men. It wasn't easy to feel anything other than dread, but I found myself pleased to see Essiah again. I'd heard he twisted an ankle early in the forest during the second trial but had been determined to finish. Loch and Abe had been discussing both Essiah and Wren often; I wasn't ashamed to admit I paid close attention—not spying, just listening in. They were discussing my potential guard after all.

Next to Essiah, a tall, slender man with dark shaggy hair, stood with his hands clasped behind his back and stance shoulder width apart. His impassive, blank face revealed nothing. An inked guy with tattoos snaking up under the collar of his pressed white shirt stood next to him. I moved my eyes onto the shortest of the lineup, then to a man with a huge scar running the length of his face, then one with long fiery hair tied back into a double looped tail and then, of course, Wren. I'd run out of finalists to study.

Damn you, Mardy, for not being another face to look at!

Wren stared ahead, hands clasped behind his back in a stereotypical soldier stance. It did nothing but encourage my pathetic hormones to rage to the surface. I both did and didn't want him to look at me; torn between wanting to know what he truly felt seeing me and fearing what his eyes might tell me.

Taking a quick breath, my eyes flickered towards his direction. A wealth of hurt shone brightly, tugging on my delicate heartstrings. A deeper pain I couldn't decipher flashed before he looked away, the memory of his eyes already haunting me. I knew he was trying to piece it together, who I really was and how it had been me all along. But the hurt I'd seen on his face sank its claws into me, piercing straight through me like a physical punch to my gut.

I homed in on my mother's words of welcome, trying to drown out the sinking grief already tearing at me.

"Rayleigh?" my mother's voice echoed.

"Sorry?" I mumbled, my brain rapidly catching up.

"A few words to your finalists?" she prompted, her smile turning slightly icy as she realised I hadn't been fully listening.

"Um," I began nervously, all pairs of eyes turning to watch me. I studiously refrained from locking eyes with Wren again. My mother's confident aura and my formal training gave me the strength to continue. "I want to say thank you, to all of you, for your bravery, your skills, and your dedication shown thus far. It has been an honour to host you and my pleasure to speak to you all tonight. Our kingdom is truly blessed to have such fine warriors seeking to defend and uphold its honour, and I feel privileged to know that four of you will become my personal guard and continue to serve this kingdom as I one day take the throne. I can't wait to have you by my side and succeed together."

The men nodded their heads gracefully. I even noted Essiah trying to hide a grin of pleasure as he attempted to maintain his stoic composure. I smiled at him. Markin instructed the finalists to follow my mother and me into the ballroom.

My mother held her arm out. I took her hand gently, walking beside her as we made our way down the steps and towards the double doors to leave the throne room.

Standing outside the hall doors, two soldiers bobbed their heads at us when we neared. They hauled the heavy doors open, the doors swinging outward into a sea of people dressed in fine suits and exquisite silks.

I took a deep breath, feeling Wren's eyes on my back like a

beacon: both nerve-wracking and strangely satisfying at the same time.

Let the party commence.

I'd successfully been able to avoid dancing with Wren so far, but I knew my time of procrastination was coming up. It was expected I dance with *all* the finalists here. Obviously, the one who wasn't in attendance, I wouldn't be dancing with, and I briefly wondered what he might look like again. Fox was right; it only added to the air of mystery around him.

The man with a scar down his face stepped all over my toes when we danced and didn't say a word throughout the whole time. I can't say I got to know him very well. Tattoo man was so focused on the dance routine—which was basic at best for this purpose—that he barely said two words to me either.

Essiah was an interesting guy, at least I knew his name. The previous two hadn't even introduced themselves to me. Essiah was quiet but talked more than the previous men had, which was a welcoming break from the silence. He was very polite and well-spoken, indicating he came from a certain level of wealth in order to receive the education. I hadn't seen him at the meet and greet, but he must have been there. He mostly discussed politics and the way the kingdom ran with me. The joke was on him because he probably knew more than me with my mother's constant keeping me out of things, but I didn't mind the topic. It meant I got to know what he thought. We actually seemed to share many a view, which I was incredibly pleased about. But while he was formal and stoic, I still noticed small beads of sweat near his hairline. I smiled warmly at him, trying to ease his nerves as we danced.

Dancing with the fiery-haired warrior next, Bo, was the most fun. The most talkative of all of them, he spoke a word a second I was pretty sure. Even though he looked the complete opposite to Derril, his personality was comfortingly similar. I laughed with Bo—like deep, belly-shaking laughter. I didn't think my grin could have been any wider. He talked about his family and how proud they were of his desire to do something with his life and work for a kingdom he truly admired.

We laughed and joked about some of the more formal men in the room, Bo's relaxed accent and attitude letting me know he grew up anything but a high-born. I liked him.

The music changed and Markin stepped in, dancing with me next. He respectfully took my hand in his and placed his arm around my upper back. Formal as always.

"You looked like you enjoyed yourself then," he commented, a twinkle in his eye. I smiled back at him, finally relaxed.

"He was funny, reminded me of Derril, actually. Does that count? Can that count in the trials?"

Markin's smile grew a serious lilt to it. "It could. Your opinion matters the most."

"Really?"

"Absolutely. This is your guard." I'd never really thought I had much influence. His words churned in my head. "You just have one more to dance with. It's a shame about the eighth finalist—whilst this isn't a trial, it's a very important event for you."

Markin's voice drowned out as I zeroed in on his words: 'you just have one more to dance with'. Wren. I'm not sure Markin noticed my sudden quietness, but I continued to smile and nod all while panicking.

Being up close with Wren. I couldn't help but think about when he'd pulled me over his lap at Madame El's. My thighs clenched at the thought.

"Ah, I'll let you step in," Markin said out of nowhere, looking above my head. I gulped and gave a tight smile to Markin as he placed my hand in a large, warm one, the contact making my skin tingle.

Wren's face swam into view. I took in the powerful line of his unshaven jaw, the pinched expression around his mouth, and worst of all, dull, blank eyes staring back at me. Nothing like the heat we'd shared when he kissed me the other night.

Wren slid his other arm around my waist, not as high as Markin had left his, but careful not to drop below my lower back and become inappropriate. Of course, my mind screamed at him to lower his arm and pull me closer. His scent wrapped around me, and I clenched my thighs again to ease the building pressure between my legs. Instead of voicing any of this, I stayed quiet, afraid to shatter the fragile tension we already held between us. Unlike the other contestants, his arm was the only touch that sent trembles up and down my spine. I tried really hard to suppress the shiver that ached to escape.

We started moving in time to the slow steady beat of the music. Wren cleared his throat.

"You look lovely tonight, princess." I winced. His tight voice rigid like his body.

"Thank you," I whispered back. "You, too." What a lame reply.

One corner of Wren's mouth jerked up quickly, so quick I almost missed it.

"Great music," he commented.

"Quite."

"Great food."

"The best."

"Great–"

"Are we going to ignore this?" I asked, not able to stop myself interrupting him.

He sighed, looking everywhere but my eyes. "Is there any point? Will it actually change anything?" His accusatory tone thankfully sent a much-needed spike of anger through me, chasing away some of the guilt I'd been harbouring since I walked into that throne room.

"No. Nothing about our situation would have changed even if I wasn't who I am. But I never changed who I was on the inside. You met me earlier than all the other contestants. That's all," I finished, keeping my voice down so others couldn't hear, but the harsh tone remained firmly in place.

"That's all?" Guilt, for some reason, marred his features. "You know exactly what you did."

"And what was that exactly?"

"Lead me on, pretended to be..." he trailed off.

"Lead you on? With what exactly did I lead you on with? You came along with me to...that place. *You* pulled me onto *your* lap!" I hissed, hastily looking around me to make sure no one listened to us. Heat rose in my cheeks. I needed some space from him. Space to think as I struggled to do it near him, his scent filling and surrounding me so intimately. "If you'll excuse me." I didn't await a response and dragged my hand out of his, turning to the doors.

I stalked out without making a fuss, giving a nod and a smile to Loch. He smiled back quizzically but nodded to say he was okay with me leaving.

I was so in my own head that I missed the steps behind me until a large hand grabbed my elbow and yanked me sideways into a dark room. I gasped as a hand slammed over my mouth.

TWENTY

WREN SHOVED ME INTO the small closet storage space, shutting the door behind us and pushed me against it, his hand still over my mouth. A low light from a lantern hung on the wall beside my head, swathing the room in a delicate glow. Shelves of cleaning supplies stacked around the small room, and to our right there was a short ledge with a sink, a mop, and a bucket. A cleaning closet?

Wren yanked his hand away from my mouth but didn't move from where he pressed in close to me.

"Why didn't you tell me?" he pleaded, a desperation clung to his voice that I didn't understand.

"It wouldn't have changed anything. And I liked just being me. I didn't have to pretend to be anybody else." I looked away, expelling air as I tried to keep tears at bay. Why did he affect me so much?

"Why won't you look at me?"

"Because I can't bear seeing it."

"Seeing what?"

I closed my eyes, my head still turned away from his. "Your disappointment in me," I whispered.

Wren's fingers took my chin and moved my head to face him. He leaned down close to my face.

"Little Shadow, I'm not disappointed in you. Frustrated: yes. Angry: yes. But never disappointed."

I frowned. "You shouldn't be saying those things to me. You shouldn't even be in here with me."

He huffed, his jaw clenching. "Yes, well. There are a lot of things I shouldn't be doing. But you keep drawing me in. I'm drawn to you, and to be frank, it's pissing me off."

I placed my hands on his chest to push him back, but he only relented a small step, his head cocking to one side. Danger, my inner voice said. My stomach somersaulted, heat sparking lower. I wanted the danger.

"I don't know whether to hit you or kiss you for saying that," I muttered, my hands fisting into my dress to stop me from doing either.

His eyes flashed. "Kissing me would get you in trouble. Get me in trouble. If I'm successful in the trials, I'll be taking the oath. No relationships. And you're the princess. You're expected to marry someone of importance. Kissing guards isn't a part of that."

"So, we definitely shouldn't kiss."

"No. We shouldn't."

"I don't like following the rules."

"Me neither."

We clashed in a frenzy of lips and hands. He pressed his body firmly into me, backing me up against the door. One hand curled around my hip, gripping me tight, while his other snaked to the side of my head. His fingers reached round to the back of my neck, holding me in place, while his lips claimed mine. I parted my lips below his when his tongue stroked against them, welcoming him. I roamed my hands over his dress shirt, reaching the collar and using my grip there to rise onto my toes to get closer to him still.

He moved his hand to cup my chin, fingers biting into the skin, and positioned my head so he hovered over me. Regret flashed through his eyes.

"You're too pure for this," he whispered onto my lips, and I shivered. My grip on him tightened as I released a soft whimper.

"I decide what I can do." I kissed him. He tightened his hold on me, pressing his hips into mine against the door, the bulge in his trousers rubbed against too many layers of this damn dress to provide any sort of release.

"Not when you're the princess of the fucking kingdom," he growled, shoving off me. He ran a hand through his hair while I mourned the loss of his heat, his contact. "I can't do this." He rubbed a hand over his face, breathing heavily.

Something cracked inside my chest. I stared at the ground, blood rushing into my ears. Foolish. I was foolish. What we were doing was treason. At best, he'd be exiled, worst, executed. He was risking his life to be here. With me.

"I shouldn't have compromised you like this; you won't have to worry about me speaking of this to anyone. I'm sorry." I turned and grabbed the handle, but his hand closed around mine.

"That's not what I'm worried about," he whispered into my

hair. I closed my eyes as his arm wound round my waist, his warm hand settling over my middle.

"Then what are you worried about?" I breathed, leaning my head back against him.

"You're young. And beautifully innocent. I'd be taking that away from you."

"Why do you keep saying that like it's something you can just take from me? I'm not as innocent as you think. And I can decide what I want for myself. Ultimately, I have to follow rules, but why can't I choose what to do until then?"

"You shouldn't be choosing me, princess."

"Tell me you don't want me, then I'll leave and forget about everything." His silence met my back, his thumb brushing against my middle as he pulled me closer still. My free hand rested on his arm. I turned just my head to look up at him, and he rested his forehead against my shoulder. He met my eyes when I spoke again. "Tell me you don't want this."

"I...can't," he strained out.

"Wren? Please just kiss me."

His lips hungrily brushed over mine.

I reached my arm back, winding it around his neck to hold him, but I didn't need to fear him leaning away from me. His hand moved down my torso and then around to my hip before he stroked up against my side and rested it under my breast. My dream flashed through my mind where he'd done the same. But I had too many layers on.

Growling, I spun in his arms and pressed my body tight against his, trying to get some relief from the pressure building between my thighs, from the heaviness of my breasts. He walked us backwards until my lower back hit the ledge. Wren gripped both my hips and lifted me onto it. I yelped, my arms flailing out in response.

Wren looked at my hands and shook his head with a playful smirk. I reached out, gripping his jacket to yank him towards me at the same time as I opened my legs. With no uncertainty that I wanted him, he stepped into me, standing between my thighs. He cupped my face in his large palms and kissed me, angling my face to deepen it. He kissed across my cheek, to my neck, placing a soft kiss beneath my ear.

"Princess, I—" he groaned.

"No, don't do that. I want this, you hear me? You're not taking anything away I'm not willing to give."

He rested his forehead against mine, breathing heavily. "But you—"

"Have no control over my life, Wren. This should be mine to control. I should be free to do this."

"You want freedom?" he asked, his eyes piercing mine.

I nodded. "Craving freedom was how you met me in the first place."

"Freedom," he repeated quietly. "I'm going to hell for this." He slammed his lips against mine again.

I pulled back just enough to speak, moving my hands up his torso to grip around the back of his muscular neck.

"If you're going for this, then so will I."

"You won't, you're too...perfect," he whispered, frowning to himself. I laughed and squeezed my thighs around him; his eyes closed. "You want freedom?" he asked, opening his eyes again. I nodded, pulling my bottom lip between my teeth. "There are different ways to feel free other than sneaking out at night."

He quirked one side of his lips, his eyes lighting up as he pressed in close to me, his arousal rubbed against my many, many layers. I huffed in frustration, and he kissed me again; he smiled against my lips and ran one hand down my side and over my thigh. He squeezed gently before gathering material in his hand and moving it up to gather around my waist.

Wren looked down at my legs, stroking my bare flesh, running his hand closer to the tops of my thighs. He then looked up into my eyes and leaned in to brush his lips over mine, deepening the kiss as he gripped my bare thighs closer to him. I leaned in, too, groaning into his mouth when he rocked against me and without as many layers to dull the sensation...I tipped my head back, eyes closed, and he trailed kisses down my throat.

"So innocent," he murmured against my skin, but I could feel his smile as he teased me.

"Shut up," I whispered, no heat behind the words.

"What if I were to do this?" He stroked his right hand up and brushed his knuckles against my underwear. I gasped, opening my eyes to look directly at him. "And this?" He stroked his thumb over the most sensitive part of me, gently applying pressure as he moved his thumb round in small circles. I grabbed onto his shoulders, my mouth opening on a silent pant, my eyes closing. Wren chuckled. "You like that?"

I nodded, not sure if I could even articulate words at this point.

He continued to rub in small circles through my underwear. He used his other hand at the base of my neck to tilt my head back. Pressure built and built, my core tightening. He must have seen it on my face because his hand came around to cup the side of my face. He kissed me softly. I gripped onto him tighter, panting now.

"That's it, my Little Shadow, hold on to me."

"Oh Gods!" I cried, tensing my body as the pleasure built to an almost intolerable amount, and then it crested. Light exploded, my arms trembled, and I clutched onto Wren, my legs shaking. I panted, my head resting against his shoulder as the waves of pleasure washed through me. He moved his hand to my thigh, still holding me to him as I came down from the incredible high.

He dragged my head back to kiss me again, his tongue stroking against my lips. "Never forget," he breathed against me, "that it was me who gave you your first orgasm."

I frowned through my hazy state. "How did you know I hadn't?"

"Your face gave you away," he whispered, rubbing his nose against mine.

"I thought I'd had them before, but never...like that. They were never like that, no matter how hard I tried."

He smiled. "I like thinking of you with your hands on yourself." My face heated, and he stroked the blush with his thumb across my cheek.

"I—"

Wren gripped my chin to stop me from turning my head away. "Don't. Don't use that brain just yet. You wanted freedom. Just feel that for one more moment. Let me give you one more moment."

He kissed me again, deep, his fingers curling around my head, holding me possessively, and then he stood back and helped me down from the ledge. I smoothed my skirts down as Wren swiped a thumb over his lips, wiping some of the wetness away. He then stepped forward and did the same to my lips.

"Thank you," I said, unsure what I should say after what he did. Wren's lips tipped up, his dimple making its appearance, and feeling bold, I reached up to touch it. "Sorry," I whispered automatically.

Wren gently took my hand, kissing my knuckles. "Stop apologising."

He looked behind him at the door and his shoulders fell.

"What happens now?" I whispered.

Wren swallowed, his lips thinning. "Now we pretend nothing happened here." I nodded, but my face fell; I studied the floor until Wren put a finger under my chin and lifted until I faced him again. "You know it can't be any different," he said, pressing his forehead to mine again. "Thank you for trusting me to give you a few minutes of freedom."

I smiled. "What about you?"

"It wasn't about me."

"Did you not want...to do...anything?" I asked, my stomach churning at the thought of his rejection.

"I will not take that from you in a closet. You deserve so much more than that." He took my hand and tugged me towards the door. "We should go before you're missed. I'll go first in case there're any issues. Follow in thirty seconds."

After Wren returned to the hall, I waited for that thirty seconds before leaving to avoid entering the hall simultaneously. I didn't want to risk anyone becoming suspicious. I wasn't supposed to want Wren. I wasn't allowed Wren. But my heart beat painfully as I followed him out, pushing my shoulders back and holding my head high, trying to forget the incredible moment I'd just had.

TWENTY-ONE

MY HEELS CLICKED ACROSS the smooth marble floors as I made my way down the hallway. I smoothed out my dress, taking my bottom lip between my teeth as I thought about what Wren had just done to me. No one had ever touched me like that before—not even *I* had touched me like that before. Or at least, I hadn't had that same response.

"Rayleigh. Your mother is after you," Abe said, shocking me from my thoughts when he appeared from out of nowhere.

"Huh?" I was sure the heat on my cheeks would be obvious, but he didn't comment, or didn't accurately guess what the blush was for.

"This way, come on." He sighed, placing an arm around my lower back to propel me forward. "How has your night been?"

I blushed again. "Good, yeah. Not what I expected."

"I remember this night when I was competing for your mother's guard. Did you know I spilt my drink down your mother's dress?"

I spluttered out a snort. "No! How did I not know this? You're the most graceful of the four of you!"

"Nerves. I was so nervous. Turns out, your mother didn't mind it, and it gave us something to talk about. It's all she's been reminding me of since your guard trials started." He smiled.

We turned the corner towards the hall, and I stopped. All seven of the contestants stood around my mother, the rest of her guard behind her. She addressed them seriously. Her face tight and pinched. Her eyes met mine and her lips thinned.

"How good of you to join us for *your* ball," she spoke steadily, but her eyes narrowed on me. How had I pissed her off this time?

"I wasn't aware I had to be present at all times," I shot back as I stood in between Wren and Bo. Abe went to join my mother, and I swallowed nervously. Her hand flexed by her side. I wanted to step behind Wren, behind safety, but I held my ground. I didn't want any of my potential guard seeing me act so pathetic, let alone my mother.

"Well, now you've graced us with your presence, perhaps we can get on with the matter at hand?"

"What matter?" I asked before I could stop myself. She closed her eyes, but when she opened them, she looked at my guard potentials one by one.

"I hope you're all prepared for what you're signing up for. Rayleigh will need copious amounts of guidance before she even takes the throne, as you can see."

I opened my mouth, but nothing came out. Did she really just say that? In front of her guard? The contestants? A dull ache made itself known at the base of my head. This was the worst timing. I couldn't afford for it to get worse. I couldn't afford to black out. I took deep breaths, trying to control my anger, knowing it only made my head worse.

She finished her spiel about what the contestants had to do tomorrow and what was expected of them. They had to pack a bag, and my mother was delivering the task herself—something about a message to a neighbouring town. I couldn't listen. My blood boiled with anger at her audacity to embarrass me like that. As she finished, I tried to stop shaking and rolled my shoulders to release tension, but a sharp, stabbing pain throbbed at my temples.

"I assume I'm no longer needed—I shall take a short break to think about my inadequacies." Before she could reply, I turned and walked away, probably just earning myself a day at Lady Mila's, but I couldn't care any less at this point. I was mad. If I stayed, I was going to say or do something that would probably earn me house arrest *with* Lady Mila, or I'd pass out from this headache. Storming away was the best I could do.

Nobody followed, for which I was thankful. I pushed through the sunroom doors and to the outside courtyard, resting my hands on the stone railing. Closing my eyes, I inhaled the refreshing night air and rubbed at the ache at my temples, trying to put pressure where it hurt the most. The doors shut quietly behind me, muffling sounds of laughter and drink. I planned to go back to the party and face my mother shortly, but for now, I let the cool air dance lightly on my skin and inhaled the floral scents from the garden wafting through the air. I couldn't see much ahead of me, just what the lights behind illuminated, but the nearly full moon dusted everything ahead of me with a light, silvery glow.

When the doors opened behind me, letting out a short snippet of noise, I didn't need to turn around to know who was behind me; his scent forever imprinted on my brain.

"I apologise, my lady," Wren said behind me, both of us now overlooking the moonlit gardens.

The pulsing slowed and I smiled, remembering how he first called me a lady when I bumped into him. "Don't be. What have you got to apologise for?" I asked, the roles reversing on apologies for once.

"I followed you as soon as I could."

"Why?"

Wren sighed. "Honestly? I don't know. I know why you crave that freedom you speak about, though. Is she always like that?"

"Yep."

"I shouldn't have said it like that. I didn't mean—"

"It's not like I'm going to go running to her and tell her what you said. She's an ass."

"I thought you'd be spoiled, you know? But now I see that you've not had much in life in the way of choice. I guess I already knew that—you being the princess and all—but it's different. Seeing it with my own eyes." He trailed off, speaking into the dark night. I took a deep breath, exhaling as the pain continued to ebb further away within his presence. I turned to look at him.

"You thought I'd be spoiled?"

"That's what you picked up on?"

"Well, yeah."

"I'm sorry. I had opinions. They were wrong. I was wrong." He sighed, his brows drawing together.

"What are you saying?"

"You're here by force. A choice you don't have. I thought I didn't have a choice either. But I'm beginning to question everything. Because of you."

His cryptic talk annoyed me, and I frowned, too.

"I think I preferred it when you were mad at me."

"I was never mad. Especially not now."

"You mean after what we did in that closet?"

He nodded but rubbed a hand around the back of his neck, huffing out a big breath.

"This isn't what I thought it would be."

"Where does that leave us now?" I asked, finally plucking up the courage to look at him again. As he surveyed the grounds, I studied his profile as the light from behind cast his face in shadows.

"I use my choices to forfeit the trials. There's got to be other ways to accomplish what I need to do," he whispered to himself, into the night.

"What?!" I sputtered. I don't know what I'd been expecting, but that wasn't it. He'd wanted to serve his kingdom, seemed so passionate about it. "But why?!"

"You don't need to be seeing me every day. It'll be hard on us both—"

"So I don't get a choice again? You're just going to take off because my life is too much to handle for you? Just go." I turned away, a part of me worried this wasn't affecting him the same way it was affecting me. Silence followed for several moments, but he didn't move.

"What would you have me do? Please, tell me," he pleaded. I finally turned to look at him. I stepped forward so we were nearly chest to chest. A desire burned in his eyes, and my body responded, growing almost feverish with need.

"You can't forfeit the trials. You're an honourable man, one who would be a great asset to this kingdom, to me."

"I'm not that man. Look at what I did earlier—an honourable man wouldn't have touched you. And all I want to do is rip that dress off you and touch you in all the places I couldn't earlier. Would an honourable man do that?" he snapped.

"Are you trying to get me to push you away?"

I wasn't sure how long we stood facing each other, close, but not close enough, our eyes locked in a battle of struggles neither of us knew how to approach.

"You've changed everything for me," Wren breathed out, his voice sending quivers to my nervous stomach and heat to my cheeks.

A short cry from the dark gardens shocked us out of our trance. I frowned. Wren's hand gently took my elbow and pulled me to his side. Not that I wanted to complain at the gesture, being tucked close to Wren was all I could think about, all I wanted, but I didn't want to be treated like a small child. I tried stepping forward off the patio.

"Rayleigh!" Wren whispered, pulling me back towards him, his grip even tighter.

"Wren! That is the cry of a small child."

"Go inside, then, and I'll check it out."

"I think not! I'm the heir to this kingdom, and I will not leave a small, frightened child to cry."

His eyes hardened against the fight I was willing to give to go myself.

"As a member of your potential guard, I assure you I am equipped to handle a small child. Now go inside where it is safe," Wren commanded.

"Guards take orders from the throne. That's me. Someone is in distress. I will go and see that they are okay, and you may accompany me." I was stern and I was strong. I didn't let my flare of confidence disappear.

Wren ground his jaw before muttering something under his breath. "Fine, but you stay behind me." I nodded, smiling as I did what he asked and followed him off the patio and across the grass. The wet blades brushed against the hem of my dress; if Yola could see me now, she'd give me a good talking to for dirtying this dress.

We approached the noise, the light growing dimmer by the second as we left the glowing halo of the sunroom. A small bundle huddled on the floor in front of us.

"Are you all right?" I asked, moving around Wren to kneel next to the body. A child jumped up, perhaps a boy around five or six, and sprinted away into the darkness. My skin prickled with unease.

Wren took my hand again and pulled me back to him; the moon illuminated his watchful eyes and tense jaw.

"See anything?" I whispered.

"Let's go back," he replied, equally as quiet.

"But the boy?"

"We'll tell the soldiers, and they can send out a group. That note we got from the woman at Madame El's specified today's date. What if...?" Wren muttered, scanning the darkness before us. Unease scratched at his voice.

"I talked to Markin. He said he'd tripled security..."

Wren tilted his head, and I wondered if he felt the same as me: a screaming voice inside our heads telling us not to turn our backs to the darkness. My hand tightened its grip on Wren's. He squeezed back, his thumb gently stroking across the back of my hand. His comforting presence eased some of the tension I carried across my shoulders.

"Rayleigh, look out!" Wren yelled and pushed me aside as a long blade, brilliantly catching the moonlight, sliced down where I had just been standing. I stumbled a few paces backwards, away from Wren, when thick arms banded around my middle, pinning my arms down.

"Wren!" I screamed.

TWENTY-TWO

WREN TOOK THE BRUNT force of an attack as he faced his assailant head on, who was dressed head to toe in the same black armour the Dydairians had worn when they attacked before the trials. But I didn't have time to see if he was okay: I had my own problems to deal with.

The guy pinning me to his front wrestled me backwards; I threw my head back, a sharp pain radiating from my head as I connected with his face. A deep 'oof' vibrated through my back. I used the opportunity to spin and face him, noticing he was also in the same black armour.

How the hell had they gotten through Markin's security?

I quickly jabbed with my fist, hitting him in his stomach and then face. He fell to his knees, and I responded with one of Markin's many lessons. Quickly stepping behind him, I now used my height advantage to wrap my arm around his neck. Using the crook of my elbow as a force against his throat, I pulled on my wrist as hard as I could. The guy stopped moaning, immediately and wildly flinging his arms, thrashing and slapping at mine, but I stood firm, one leg keeping his apart so he couldn't stand back up. Markin always said a man gasping for air was dangerous, but they'd quickly lose consciousness if pressure was continuously applied. I did that now, pushing past the screeching pain in my muscles, unused to the action they were using. After a few moments, the man slumped forward, the weight of his body dragging me down, but I counted in my head to make sure he wasn't playing me.

Eight, nine, ten.

The guy fell into an unmoving heap on the ground when I released him. Whether he was alive or dead didn't matter to me; he trespassed, broke laws, and attacked my home. I snapped my head up to look for Wren. He knelt over the guy who had attacked him first. Wren delivered a final blow to the man's head which snapped back, and he stilled on the ground in a heap.

Wren wasted no time, grabbing for the man's fallen sword and jumped up, spinning towards my direction.

"Rayleigh!" he shouted, body tense, but when his eyes landed on me, travelled down to the body at my feet, and back up to my face, I couldn't help but smile at the mix of surprise and pride on his face.

"Yes, Wren?" I said as innocently as I could muster, even placing my hands on my hips.

Wren's chest moved up and down in deep movements, but when I found hooded heat in his eyes, I knew it wasn't all from physical exertion.

"We should get going," he mumbled, reaching out a hand for me.

I took it, smiling. "Not what you expected, huh?"

"I'm beginning to think I've only just scratched the surface where you're concerned."

"Not so fast," a male voice snarled from the darkness, and a group of at least six men emerged from the shadows. All dressed in the black armour. I pressed my back against Wren's as they circled us like sharks. "Think you're so special, fighting off my men one on one? I'd like to see how you do against us." My stomach churned at the guy's violent tone, threatening to spill everything I'd eaten tonight. Wren's hand tightened around mine, his shoulders tense.

"Can you use a sword?" Wren whispered.

"Yes."

"We're too far away to run. Ready to fight?"

"Unfortunately."

"Stay close to me if you can."

I nodded. "Always."

And then they came for us.

Wren passed me the sword he'd taken only moments ago and sprang forward without a weapon. I spun the foreign metal in my hand and raised it high to stop the downward trajectory of another coming at me. Fear for Wren without a sword twisted its ugly limbs inside, but I pushed it out to concentrate. I would not freeze up again.

Although I had only been going through exercises with Loch, I was able to pull forth all the lessons Markin taught me, thanking him for making me start up a fitness regime again even if I was tiring quickly now.

I ducked under a swinging blade, slid under an arm, and sprang up behind one of them. A quick knee thrust to his back was all it took for him to crash to the ground. Sensing movement, I stepped back just narrowly escaping a sword to my side. As my attacker's sword carried forward, not stopped by my flesh, I used the surprise to swing wide and cut into his side. The man cried out, fell to the ground, and clutched his wound. He wouldn't be a threat for at least a few moments.

A guy to my left lunged forward, but I spun at the last second, slicing down my sword to fend off his attack. As he slipped forward, I kicked him in the head to silence and still him: not my finest or graceful of moments, but it was effective. I yanked my torn dress back, cursing at its hindrance.

With a short blade in each hand, Wren could now fight off two guys at the same time. I barely had time to ponder how he had gained two weapons when a battle cry to my right startled me. Another Dydairian raced toward me, sword high and an angry sneer across his face. I had just scarcely lifted my arm to stop his sword finding its target in my body, but he'd come at me with such force, my arms shook with exertion to keep his sword away from my face. I gripped the hilt with both hands and clenched my jaw as I fought to hold the stance for as long as I could, refusing to go down when suddenly the pressure was gone.

Wren swung in front of me, taking the force off me as he replaced it with his own weapon and then pushed back the attacker with some unknown strength. I put my back to him and together, we defended and attacked against the last two standing Dydairians.

With the men down, my chest heaved in time with Wren's. I scanned his body looking for a sign of injury. His appraising eyes met mine at the same time, sparking heat between us in the cool night air.

"You know how to fight?" he asked, a ghost of a smile on his lips.

"Told you I'm not what you would expect."

Wren nodded in agreement, swiping his thumb over his bottom lip. "So it would seem."

Commotion across the grounds near to the sunroom spilled over into my senses, interrupting the moment. A handful of soldiers, my mother's personal guard, and my mother herself marched towards us. My mother pointed and gave the soldiers a sharp order; they ran over to us to check on the Dydairian bodies by our feet. They secured a couple still alive by binding their hands.

"Rayleigh!" my mother shouted when she closed in. It wasn't an angry tone, nor was it relieved. In fact, she sounded just like I expected the queen to sound when met with an attack on her lands.

I glanced down at my dirty, streaked dress; a rip ran down the length of it and my hair spilled out of its design, tumbling over my shoulders. My mother's gaze landed upon the sword I held. I gripped it tighter.

"Yes, mother?" I tried to reply, equally calculating as she had sounded. While her face held the stony expression of a hardened ruler, pride beamed from her eyes. I blinked, not expecting it. She gave me a curt nod. My stomach fluttered nervously. It was approval from my mother.

"I see you came across some unwanted guests," she stated, not asked. "Dydairians?" she directed her question to where Abe knelt near one of the dead bodies.

"It appears so," he answered.

She turned to face Wren, who immediately straightened under her scrutiny. "And you're responsible for getting rid of the threat?"

"Yes, Your Majesty. With a lot of help from Rayleigh." My mother raised a brow at him. "From Princess Rayleigh, Your Majesty," he quickly corrected. I'm not sure why my mother looked so pointedly at him; if Wren were to become part of my personal guard, he'd use my name informally a lot. Her personal guard didn't call her 'Your Majesty' or 'Queen Isla' all the time. I shot her a small frown, but she ignored me while she sent out more orders.

"Abe, you are to coordinate the guests getting home tonight. I don't want anyone leaving by themselves without an escort. Loch, I want you to take soldiers and do a thorough sweep of these grounds to ensure there are no more Dydairians, and I want to know where they entered my property. Derril, use this as an opportunity for our finalists. Pair two to each of you; this one here will stay with Markin." Her personal guards nodded their heads and got to work. I knew how my mother worked, and it took little to work out that Markin, Wren, and I would be accompanying her for a thorough breakdown of events.

I groaned.

My mother turned on her heel and stalked back towards the sunroom. Markin gently took my sword off me, handed it to Abe, and then followed my mother, gesturing for Wren and me to do the same. I started forward.

"Where are we going?" Wren asked quietly.

"You're about to get a small audience with my mother."

TWENTY-THREE

WE FOLLOWED MY MOTHER and Markin into the throne room; Markin immediately shut the door, and my mother turned to face us, clasping her hands in front of her.

"First, I am impressed that you both held off an attack such as this." I smiled at her, unable to hide that I was happy she showed some degree of warmth toward me. "However," she began, and just like that, I winced, readying for her disappointment. "What I want to know is why you two were so far away from the palace? Why were you able to be ambushed?" She tilted her head slightly to one side, meaning she already expected she wasn't going to like what I said.

Okay, here went nothing. I opened my mouth to speak, but Wren jumped in before I could utter a word.

"It's my fault, Your Majesty. I heard a small boy crying and went to investigate. I should have brought Princess Rayleigh inside first and found help.”

“Your name is Wrendor Netero, isn’t it?”

“Yes, Your Majesty, people call me Wren.”

“Well, Wren, thank you for telling me—”

“Mother, wait!” I snapped, and Wren faced me with a puzzled look. “It wasn’t Wren’s fault, honestly. I heard the boy cry, and Wren actually tried to make me go inside, but I ordered him not to.” My face heated. My mother narrowed her eyes on me. I knew then that she always knew I was at the heart of this story, and she hadn’t believed Wren in the first place. Was this going to affect his place in the trials?

“Why didn’t you listen to the warrior? He is clearly skilled enough to protect you, and then you wouldn’t have been in harm’s way. That is precisely why we have personal guards.” She spoke quietly, filling me with more dread about the punishment she was sure to give than if she had shouted.

I wanted to cower under her impressive glare. She may have been proud of how I defended myself, but not of how I got in the position.

Holding my head high and squaring my shoulders, I answered her. “I couldn’t allow Wren to go on his own. Neither could I allow what appeared to be a small boy, a small boy from *my* kingdom, continue to be in distress. I have a duty to these people, and what sort of potential leader would I be if I let one of my people stay in distress just so I could watch safely from the palace?”

My mother took a step closer to me, lowering her voice even further and speaking as if it were just me and her in the room. “While I admire your resolve, Rayleigh, and I admire your dedication to do well by these people, that is not the way to do it.

Sometimes I wish I could work with my guard, they are there to protect me after all, but I have to think about what could happen to me and the ripple effect that would have. If I got injured or killed, who would take over?"

"Me," I answered, looking down and away from her steady gaze, not liking where she was going with this.

"You are not ready for that responsibility yet."

"But—"

"What if you get injured or killed?" she said, and I opened my mouth to speak, but I couldn't say anything. "This kingdom would lose its heir. They'd lose hope, and with everything going on right now, with the Dydairians—"

"What about the Dydairians?"

"Nothing. You have to understand that while you may want to fight and step into danger without a second thought because it might make you a good leader, it goes beyond that. Big picture. There is always a bigger picture." I brushed away at the stubborn dirt on my dress, refusing to look at anyone. I wasn't ready to be a ruler because I had considered none of what she was saying, but more than that, I was being left out of something important. Again.

"What about the Dydairians?" I asked for a second time, trying to sound as firm and unnerved as I could. "Why are they in our kingdom? *How* are they getting across the wall so much at the moment?"

My mother walked away a few paces before exchanging a quick glance with Markin. I couldn't read his face, but clearly my mother could. She turned away in a silent huff and closed her eyes.

"Not now, Rayleigh."

"But as you said, if something happens to you, I lead. How can I lead if I am not taught how? I should be involved with this to learn how to deal with it so that if it happens again when I am on the throne I know what to do!" My veins were alight with fire as I took a step forward. She whirled around and marched right up to my face.

"I said, not now, Rayleigh!" Her words were ice and her eyes vacant. I gulped, fearing her for the first time. I slowly stepped back until I was closer to Wren, his presence immediately offering a sense of calm and stability to my frayed emotions. "You are dismissed," she commanded me. "Markin? See to it the soldiers outside this room accompany her and assure she stays in her room." Her eyes narrowed on mine, and I swallowed a lump in my throat.

I faced Markin who closed his expression off to me, the face he reserved for soldiers and others. Not me.

"Markin?" I pleaded, hoping for…I wasn't sure what. Something akin to guilt and unease flashed across his features, but it was gone before I could truly identify it. I knew he would follow my mother's orders even if he didn't agree with how she was treating me. "Markin, please. You know this attack isn't my fault."

"I know, but this is bigger than one attack," he said softly.

I turned to my side, facing Wren. He watched me, confusion and conflict warring in his eyes. I ached to hug him, ached to make sure he wasn't injured after the fight.

"What about Wren?" I asked my mother but kept my eyes on him.

"Wrendor will stay here, assigned with Markin, to help clean this mess up and ensure our people's safety."

I faced her then and didn't hide the slowly growing contempt uncurling in my body. "So he gets to learn, but I don't? Why not make him heir to the throne?" I slammed down the guilt: my anger was aimed at her, not Wren. Markin opened the doors and motioned for two soldiers stationed outside to come forth. I stalked towards the doors; I'd damn well walk out on my own and not be manhandled out of here.

Markin relayed instructions to the soldiers and they stepped forward, but paused when I narrowed my eyes.

"Don't even think of touching me." Hiking up the bottom of my ruined, muddied dress, I marched ahead of them until I was alone in my room. I passed the floor-length mirror and froze. There, I studied my reflection: my ruined dress, flushed face, my tumbling hair. I was heir to this kingdom. I'd just fought against Dydairians who wished to hurt me—and I did so well. Why was I still being treated like this?

Wren's confused and conflicted eyes flashed in my mind. While he might become my guard, the power of command truly lay with the queen until I ascended the throne. Would he see to her commands before mine? I rubbed at an ache in my chest at the thought of him placing her before me, but I pushed it aside. He was more than that. Our connection, whatever it was, had to mean something. My choice had to mean something.

I swiped at the tears I couldn't keep back.

TWENTY-FOUR

W HETHER IT'S BECAUSE I sulked like a teenager, or because I tried to teach my mother a point, but I refused to come out of my room the day following the ball. Thinking about it, I was pretty sure that made me look like a moody teenager, but I just couldn't deal with my mother for fear of saying something I may later regret. I honestly had a hard time trying to reconcile with her words and actions toward me.

Not to mention that I'd had to take an extra tonic yesterday as my head wouldn't stop pounding. I may have to apologise for scaring Sheri when I'd passed out after she'd bought me food. My anger really didn't help matters. In fact, I was sure it made my headaches worse.

But today was a new day. My head was back to its usual background ache, barely even noticeable, and I decided to try and approach the day differently, and less sulkily. I was done being treated like a child, and that meant I had to act like an adult. I'd see my mother and calmly explain my side of things, try to get her to see how valuable it could be to let me learn alongside her. Something spooked her about the Dydairians, and I intended to find out what.

I flounced down the stairs trying to muster the biggest smile and air of indifference I could manage. My outfit consisted of a pale pink dress with long sleeves, a square neckline, and my hair pulled back into a low ponytail. I felt I was presentable, demure, and above all else, appealing to the queen.

My mother and Markin ate breakfast together in the breakfast room near the serving quarters. They huddled close like they often did, deep in conversation. My mother was first to notice me and sat straight.

"Rayleigh, it's nice of you to join us."

I pressed my lips together and waltzed over to the spare seat, helping myself to fruit and toast, pouring juice as they both stared at me.

"Yes?" I asked, proud I'd said that and not snapped 'what' which came to mind first.

"It's good to see you up. We can discuss the finalists and the last trial," Markin responded for my mother, ever the professional.

"Yes, I think that would be fruitful." Both pairs of eyes lingered on me as I buttered some toast.

Ha! Take that you two. I could be a 'lady' and speak properly.

Markin cleared his throat. "I was saying to your mother that each finalist has been paired with a senior soldier in the palace army and sent to a nearby town for their last trial." I schooled my face before looking at him. This was Wren's last trial, the one my mother had told the finalists at the ball to pack a bag for...before everything went awry. "They are to deliver a message to a specific person and then receive a message back, which they are to bring back to the queen. They do not know the contents of either message and have been instructed not to look."

"Would you look?"

Markin smiled. "Of course."

"Can I ask why?" I queried, biting into my toast.

"To make sure it was nothing I should deal with straight away. To ensure that in the event the message was damaged or lost, I could still relay the contents to the queen. It's important for me to verify that there is no potential harm to the queen without my awareness. It also might mean I need to change my plans to detour for more information, act on whatever the message may be, or travel back as fast as I can rather than take my time."

I frowned. "You're not one to take your time anyway."

"No, but I would need to stop for food and rest. If the message was time urgent, I would ride for as long as the horse could manage, stopping to only secure a new horse."

"You make good points. I wonder who will read the message?"

"It's not quite as clear cut as that. I have ensured there will be obstacles the finalists have to overcome."

"Obstacles?"

"They will lose their horse and their provisions. Then there will be an injured person asking for help on route—staged, of course."

"I see. You want to assess how they deal when things go wrong, but the injured person? I don't get that."

"An injured person from Balmore, a kingdom they are swearing to protect. Yes, the queen is our primary focus but beyond that, the kingdom and its people are an extension of her."

I think I was understanding the layers to this task. "And have you given them a time in which they have to make it there and back?"

"Yes."

"So, helping this injured person would seriously delay their trip?"

"Yes again."

"What are you expecting?"

"I would have already read the message and would be able to assess its urgency effectively. If it was an urgent matter that affected more people within the kingdom, then I would deliver my message with the promise of coming back for them. I would leave some food and water. If it wasn't, I would take them with me and ensure they received help."

"Ahh, there is so much to this trial."

"Oh yes," Markin replied, a smile on his face. At least he looked less burdened than he did the other night in the throne room. "Once they are back, my senior soldiers will discuss with us what they saw and then we'll run over the entire trial process with you."

I finished my toast, thinking of how to approach wanting to talk with my mother about my training when she signalled for breakfast to be cleared away and then turned her attention on me.

"Rayleigh, I will be busy for the day, but I want you to speak to all of our staff and ensure they are doing okay after the night of the ball. This is a time for you to get to know their worries and try to help them feel comfortable and safe. Reassure them."

"But...what?" I spluttered, completely surprised with this

task.

"But what? This is part of being a ruler. Isn't this what you wanted?"

"I wanted to stay with you, learn from you!"

My mother's coy smile spread across her face. "And this is what I, the queen, am ordering you to do." She stood up and said goodbye to Markin, walking out of the breakfast room and leaving me stunned for words.

I was now being side-lined with a useless job to do. Throwing my napkin down, I stood and then breezed out, trying not to alert people to my boiling anger as I did.

I spent the whole day speaking to nearly everyone who worked at the palace and was left eating a rather large portion of humble pie. It had been a sleepless night, tossing and turning, recalling all the people I'd spoken to. My people. People who worked in this castle.

This morning, as I brushed my hair and tied back two front bits with ribbon, I remembered how mortified I'd felt—and a little ashamed—the more people I'd spoken to.

Everyone was so pleased, grateful even, that I took the time to enquire about them and ask how they were. I listened to worries, gave reassurances, and became a general ear to unburden on. I thought I knew the staff well, but this was the first time I ever felt I truly acted as their princess, the heir to the throne. It was the first time I ever felt an emotional bond with these people. They seemed to enjoy my company, too, and I theirs. Maybe my mother had been right after all. I pulled a face at the thought.

Eager to continue speaking to the staff, I stepped into my comfiest pumps and slipped on my bracelet. I planned to find Markin after I finished speaking to everyone. I hoped that on his own, he might share more about the night of the attack and share what Mahds had been doing. He told me I'd gotten it all wrong—but had I? Maybe if I was included in on things, I wouldn't have to 'jump to conclusions' as he'd put it.

I passed the mirror, ignoring the slight blush staining my cheeks, putting it down to excitement and not at wishing to see Wren again. The trial would come to an end at some point this morning, and I'd be meeting with the contestants who'd become my guard. My steps faltered. When had I become excited about the guard?

A little voice inside told me the reason quickly enough: Wren.

By lunchtime, I'd finished my mother's task, and I practically skipped to Markin's personal rooms. Situated pretty much next to my mother's, I knew she wouldn't be far away—I just hoped he was on his own right now. I headed straight to his sitting room and found him and my mother, deep in hushed conversation. Again.

"Mother," I announced and marched in. They both looked up at me expectantly, but I sensed the tinge of unease reflected on both their faces. "What's wrong? The finalists?" My heart hammered in my chest. What if something happened to him...to the finalists?

"Something unforeseen came up," Markin began. "The finalists were all attacked."

"Attacked? By the Dydairians?" My mother's face paled, her hand covering her mouth as she faced away. Something deeply bothered her to show it outwardly that much.

"Yes," Markin continued.

"What did they want?"

"By all accounts, to sabotage the trials."

"The contestants?" I breathed, not sure I wanted to hear if anyone was seriously hurt or killed.

"Our contestants are made of finer stuff than the Dydairians." Markin sneered at the word. "Along with the senior soldier they were each paired with, they successfully fought off and stopped the attack."

I breathed a sigh of relief, but then paused. "Why do you not look so relieved?"

"Because attacking eight separate pairings on different routes takes coordination and..." Markin trailed off, but I knew what he wanted to say.

"Knowledge."

Markin nodded. "We have a breach in our security. High. Perhaps multiple leaks. More than I originally suspected."

"What are we doing? What about Mahds?" I asked, trying to stay strong even though my world turned on its axis. People we trusted worked with or for the Dydairians. On top of that, I didn't even know what the Dydairians wanted because my mother refused to bring me in on it. To just come into Balmore and attack? Why? Why now?

Markin snapped his head toward me. "Drop it, Rayleigh. Mahds is clean."

My mother frowned at me but in annoyance, not confusion. Clearly Markin had already told her my suspicions about Mahds. She moved closer to Markin before speaking to me.

"We have another problem to deal with first. The attack revealed something about one of the finalists," she said.

I took a deep breath before I answered her. "What's that?"

Both Markin and my mother shared quick glances again before focusing on me.

"It's best you see for yourself," Markin finally said. I dutifully followed both of them to the throne room, my heart hammering at a hundred miles an hour, thoughts whirling round my head. Did they somehow find out about me and Wren?

My thoughts tumbled haphazardly until we reached the throne room and all thoughts died, my mind going numbingly blank.

I followed my mother to the front where the eight finalists stood in a row. The soldiers they had been paired with stood slightly behind them and then my mother's personal guard stood near her throne chair. It was an unnervingly full room.

My mother shot a glance at Loch, who then shut the doors. My eyes immediately found Wren's, my relief instant when I saw him mostly unharmed, just tired and looking like he needed a hot soak in a bath. I scanned the line of men, and my eyes popped out of my head.

At the end of the line stood Mardy, or who Fox and I had nick-named as such. Mardy's face was finally uncovered, and instead of seeing, well, I'm not sure what I expected to see, but it definitely wasn't a girl. Her jet-black hair fell out of its plait, I assumed styled so she could secure it under her helmet.

I scanned her face. There was absolutely no denying her feminine features now that she faced me.

My mother spoke. "During the attack, the finalist stepped in to protect our soldier. In doing so, her helmet came off, and her identity was revealed." Mardy lowered her head for a second before raising it high, her eyes focussing straight ahead. "She is what we call an imposter, and impersonating a warrior is a high crime indeed. Do you deny this?" she questioned Mardy.

"No. I do not," she answered firmly.

"Imposters in this kingdom are at worst, sentenced to death, and at best, exiled. Do you understand the consequences of your actions?"

"Yes, I do, Your Majesty."

"Then why did you do so?"

"To prove that women are just as capable as men, Your Majesty."

I smiled inwardly. I liked her already.

"Is she an imposter?" I suddenly asked, surprised by my own outburst. All eyes, including my mother's, landed on me. "What I mean is, she wasn't impersonating a warrior as by all accounts, she is one. Markin?" I hoped he'd back me up here. "What has her performance been during the trials?"

Markin turned to my mother, sharing that silent look they often communicated by. She nodded.

"Exemplary. She is one of the best of the finalists I would argue."

My mother now faced me. "Well, Rayleigh. What should happen now?"

"What?" I squeaked.

"It should be you to decide the fate of this contestant competing to be in your guard. You have the facts. Decide."

My mind struggled to keep up with my thoughts. I was making the decision? It was down to me?

"What is your name?" I asked her.

"Shar, Your Highness."

"Nice to meet you, Shar. I cannot argue with your performance. Your place in the trials is secure."

She gave me one small smile before returning to her hard appearance. Someone ushered out the finalists, and only myself, my mother, and her personal guard remained.

Derril placed a comforting hand on my shoulder, winking at me. "You did well there, kiddo," he whispered.

"The guard and I will run through the trials and our findings with you, and then your final choices can be made," Markin announced.

"Wait, choices? I thought there would be a top four?"

My mother chuckled, and I nearly recoiled at the foreign sound. When had she last laughed?

"The final choice on your guard was always down to you, Rayleigh. Just as I chose mine." She smiled affectionately at her guard as she spoke, the connections she had with them clear as day.

"Me?"

"Yes, you. Take all what you can from my guard, Rayleigh. They've been watching closely. They will give facts as well as personal opinions. I want you to trust them, trust them like I trusted my father's guard, and choose your own protectors."

TWENTY-FIVE

CHOOSING MY OWN GUARD put me in a predicament. What should I do about Wren? Speaking to Fox would have been the best thing for me right now, but I wasn't sure I'd ever be able to sneak out of the palace in time. Not with all the extra security focussed on keeping me in.

I paced my room, waiting for the moment I'd have to go to the arena and make my speech. A speech! As if I didn't have enough to worry about right now.

If I chose Wren, would we have this 'thing' hanging over us? Would I be choosing him because I wanted there to be more between us? But if I didn't choose him, just so we wouldn't constantly be in that position, did that make me selfish? Markin said he was one of the top contestants—an exceptional thinker were his exact words. I needed a thinker, right?

I gripped the material of my dress in frustration before remembering the delicate fabric and gently smoothed it down. Yola had really gone all out on ensuring my dress was perfect. The deep blue contrasted against my icy-blonde hair which Yola had left down, soft waves balancing out the harsh lines of the dress and matching the delicate silver circlet of the crown on my head.

Beautiful stars, each encrusted with silver gemstones, nestled on my dress, reflecting the light when I moved. I put on the bangle that had been left for me, moving it up to encircle my bare arm, before adding my father's bracelet around my wrist. I ran my fingers over the twisted metal, aching for what never was. Would he be here now, offering me words of wisdom as I paced my room?

I stood in front of the mirror. Sheri had said I looked regal, and now that I really studied myself, I was reluctantly in agreement. My appearance may have been different to my mother's, but we certainly carried the same air around us. I didn't think I was ready for this responsibility. I had chased freedom and choice for so long, and now I was being given this monumental task...and I was lost.

A knock sounded at my door. The thud, thud, thud thrummed in time to my heart. Markin beat me to the door as he opened it and walked straight through.

"Rayleigh, you ready?"

I flashed him a tight smile. "Sure. Why not?"

"Remember your speech?"

"Oh, my mother made sure I had that down and made me practise all night. I'm exhausted."

"That sounds like your mother," Markin chuckled. "Are you happy with your choices?"

I quieted for a moment. No one yet knew of my decision on who my guard would be since I would announce it at the ceremony. While practising my speech, the finalists plagued my mind, not letting me have a moment's peace. I kept wondering if it was ethical or moral to choose Wren. Would choosing Wren cause us both more heartache? Right now, we could part ways and mourn what never was. If he was constantly in my life, watching me fulfil my duties to someone else, how would that turn out?

Then there was the issue of the others. There were some I definitely preferred; but was it about preference, or those who could do the job effectively?

"Could I have your counsel, Markin?"

He smiled warmly at me. "Of course, I was expecting no less."

We moved over to my small table, sitting down in the comfortable armchairs.

"How am I meant to decide? Do I base this on each person's needs? Their abilities? What about how much I like them? Can I even choose them based on who I like?" I rambled like an idiot until Markin leaned over and placed a comforting hand over mine.

"You liking your guard is perhaps the most important factor. Getting on and being compatible is at the heart of this partnership. You will get to know each other incredibly well because you will be together nearly all the time—at least one guard most of the time. Of course, liking them has got to be a top priority. Don't forget that each of the finalists are capable fighters and warriors, so that shouldn't be concerning you, or I'd at least try to not let it concern you too much anyway."

I think I knew all that deep down, but hearing it from Markin reassured my frayed nerves.

"Thank you. I guess I'm panicking. It feels like such a big decision with a long reaching impact."

"That's why we didn't say it would be you making the final choice until the last moment, so your thoughts throughout the trials wouldn't be swayed either way and colour your perception of a contestant."

Little did he know I had a very swayed perception of a certain someone. I cleared my throat to hide the uncomfortableness of the whole situation lest he detect something I most definitely didn't want him to learn of. Ever.

"Wise."

"Look, Rayleigh, on something as big as this you must follow your gut instinct. Who do you think you would feel safest around? Who would you feel comfortable sharing your deepest and darkest secrets and moments with? Who would you trust to act both in your place and for you in the way you would want?"

My stomach somersaulted several times. The answer to every single one of those questions screamed in my head. I smiled at Markin.

"You're the best."

He winked. "Always have been."

"You okay, my lady?" Sheri asked, watching me pace before the gates leading to the arena. We waited inside the foyer, a stone walled room; one door led further into the structure where there were rooms and such for warriors. And then there were the gates which led to the arena. In the arena, the finalists waited for me.

The arena would be full of spectators by now; my mother and her guard arriving from the other side, greeting the finalists. And Wren.

I moaned into my hands. When I looked up, I found Sheri watching me intently.

"Sorry, Sheri, I'm just…feeling stressed." I took a deep breath in and released it slowly, trying to regain a sense of calm. My stomach flipped. Yeah. That wasn't happening.

"It's understandable."

"Ugh! Why do I have to do a stupid speech?" I cried, looking up to the ceiling as if that would suddenly solve all my problems. I gave her a pointed look when a short giggle escaped her.

"You'll have to get used to it when you're queen."

"Oh, please don't remind me about public speaking. I'm nervous enough as it is."

"Have you actually decided who your guard will be yet?"

I huffed. "How did you know?"

"That you haven't fully decided? I've watched you grow up. No way you've been able to make a decision this big yet. Plus, you always leave things to the last moment."

"I do not!" I huffed indignantly. She narrowed her eyes. "Okay, well, yes, I do."

"Is now the time to tell you that you have about five to ten minutes to decide on your guard?"

"Is now the time to tell you that you have five to ten minutes before I run away screaming?" We held the stare for only a moment before we both laughed. "Oh Gods, I needed that, thank you."

I breathed deeply, dispersing the last of the giggles.

"You're very welcome. Any time. But...you do have to choose and choose quickly."

"I know." I sighed. I had a good idea of who I would pick, but I kept swinging back and forth on the matter. "I'm hoping when I get in front of them that my choice becomes clear." I pointed my hand in a straight down motion to emphasise the point. It was a good plan. I'm sure of it.

"Well, the gates are opening, so you haven't got long to see if your plan works."

My eyes widened as the gates opened and bright sunlight streamed through in the room. I walked out, entering the arena with the crowd roaring and cheering. I raised my hand and waved, smiling, trying to make it seem genuine when really, I was a bag full of quaking nerves inside. Some queen I'd make.

The final eight contestants all lined up in front of my mother, but they parted in the middle for me to get to her. Of course, Wren would find himself right in the centre. I brushed past him, deliberately making a whisper of contact. His woodland scent hovered over me, and a sense of calm took over.

I made my decision. I think I'd known from the moment I was told the decision was mine. I just hadn't trusted myself enough.

Turning around to face the finalists, I raised my arms either side of me like I'd seen my mother do many times before, signalling to the cheering crowds that I was ready to speak. They quieted to a murmur, eager to listen to the first public speech of Princess Rayleigh.

I looked around at the sea of faces, my head spinning; then I focussed on the line of fine warriors before me, finishing my study with a pair of stunning green eyes greeting me with warmth and respect.

"People of Balmore, welcome to the unveiling of the final royal guard," I began my speech, speaking loudly as instructed. "Four of these fine warriors will become my personal guard and see me from now to when I am queen, and beyond. It has been an honour to welcome all the contestants into our kingdom and see such a display of skills. We are down to the final eight. Each of these contestants has shown exceptional fighting skills, precise thinking, a natural instinct, and an aptitude for protection. I cannot thank them enough for their service. I want to introduce now, the final four." I focussed on the finalists standing before me and stepped before Bo, the one who made me laugh at the ball with his quick humour. He wore no helmet now, his fiery hair pulled back into a low tail.

"Bo, I choose you to become one of my guard members. Do you accept?" He beamed at me when I spoke the words I memorised, and his eyes danced with excitement. He knelt, bowing his head before me.

"I do."

I moved to the next contestant. His skin was darker, his clothes loose and baggy rather than tight and defined, but his fierce determination echoed loudly.

"Essiah, I choose you to become one of my guard members. Do you accept?" He, too, knelt before me.

"I do."

My next choice was easy.

"Take your face covering off," I whispered to Shar. The crowd closest to us collectively gasped. I rose my voice for all to hear. "For the first time in history, I am asking a female to become one of my guards. Shar, I choose you to become one of my guard members. Do you accept?"

The corners of her mouth tipped up slightly before she knelt. "I do!" she shouted triumphantly.

Now for the hardest decision I was ever going to make. I moved to the middle of the line and stood before Wren. His eyes were a mass of rolling emotion, never staying on one feeling long enough for me to establish what he was truly thinking. Nevertheless, I felt his emotions churn as quickly as mine did.

"Wren, I choose you to become one of my guard members. Do you accept?" Proud my voice held, I stepped back as he knelt, keeping his eyes on mine when he answered.

"I do."

I moved closer to my mother, preparing for the words of the oath, the words that would bind them to me. Forever.

"Do you, my chosen guard, swear to protect the crown of Balmore with your life, forfeiting all outside your duties to its reigning sovereign, providing counsel, protection, and unyielding loyalty, for as long as you shall live?"

"We pledge ourselves to the crown of Balmore," they chorused together.

My heart skipped, my breath stilling for a moment, and then I signalled for my guard to stand again when my mother stepped forth.

"Rise, personal guard of Princess Rayleigh," my mother instructed. She nodded at me to continue.

"Will the four other finalists please step forward?" I said, and they each took a step from the line, looking to me. "You have been strong contenders for this role, so I am offering you the opportunity to take up immediate senior soldier positions within the palace army, working under Markin's command. Do you accept?"

All four knelt without hesitation. "We do," they replied in unison.

A whoosh of air escaped my tightening lungs. Finally. It was done. The four who didn't make it to my guard stood up and stepped away, leaving my personal guard in front of me. Holy Goddess. My. Personal. Guard.

As instructed before the ceremony, my mother and her personal guard moved off the arena grounds, and I followed with my new guard at my back. A strange surge of pride and belonging flowed through me as we walked into the small foyer area I had waited in what only felt like minutes before. My mother turned around to speak to us all.

"Welcome to the elite protection of the crown, and congratulations on making it to the personal guard," she said. "Tomorrow, you will report to the palace with your belongings and begin shadowing my guard to learn. Tonight is one for celebrating—especially as you shall be busy over the coming months and years. I wish you a great night, and I shall see you bright and early tomorrow."

My mother left with Loch and Abe. Derril and Markin stayed behind with Markin taking me to one side.

"Your mother has given you permission to go down to the tavern tonight to be a part of the informal celebrations. However, there *will* be an experienced senior soldier watching you the entire time," Markin whispered. I heard Derril speak to my guard, laughing at some joke Bo made.

"That's fine! Thank you!" I squealed, excited I'd get to see Fox.

Shar looked over at me inquisitively, so I smiled back, hoping to distract her from my mini outburst.

"You chose well. I'm proud of you."

Markin's words sent a deep needed sense of acceptance and gratitude coursing through me. Eager to always earn his approval, this meant a lot.

"I couldn't have done it without you," I replied.

"You would have. You're a strong, capable…woman." He pressed his lips together and forced a smile, and he looked at me, really looked at me. "Sometimes, I still see you as that small child running through the palace without shoes, mud trailing her behind, and leaping onto me to tell me about her latest discovery in the gardens. Usually some ugly toad," he mused. "I'm so very proud of you." A lump formed in my throat. I hugged him, not caring the others would see. My guard would find out how close I am to my mother's guard as they shadowed them anyway.

I turned to face my guard, blinking back my suddenly very wet eyes. They all talked to one another, laughing with Derril and getting along. Their essences mingled and mixed until they surrounded me with something akin to peace—I think. Soaking in the feeling, excited butterflies danced at the thought of one last night with Fox and Sadie while my guard celebrated their oaths. I sent a quick 'have fun' over my shoulder at my guard, who then looked at their retreating princess in confusion.

I was free for one more night.

TWENTY-SIX

I'D ALREADY SCALED DOWN the ivy against the wall under my window, crossed the grounds, and was by the walled gate when I noticed the shadow. I squealed and jumped back before recognising the face. Dark clothing had disguised him. Putting a hand to my racing heart, I shook my head in annoyance at my overreaction.

"Fuck! You scared me, Mahds! Wait, don't tell my mother I cursed."

The senior soldier chuckled softly. "Sorry, Rayleigh. I've been instructed to follow you."

I swallowed a brief lump of panic. *Markin trusted him. Markin trusted him. Markin trusted him.*

"I guessed as much. Any chance you could do it from not so close? I don't mean to be rude. But—"

"Don't want an escort cramping your style?" he answered

while smiling.

"Mmm, yeah. Also, I'd still like to be incognito. Would rather people not recognise me as the princess."

"Gotcha, Rayleigh, it's why I'm in civilian clothes."

We walked together for some of the way until he said he'd hang back, watch me from a distance.

I approached the door of the tavern and turned back to double check Mahds was still there. He waited some distance away, ready to enter after me. Inside, my guard celebrated. It would be weird to see them outside of all the trials.

Warmth hit me when I pushed open the old oak door; sounds of laughter and scents of drink mingled with Sadie's stew as welcome as a friend. Speaking of, I glanced around looking for the scraggly blonde I called my best friend. He had no idea I was back down here tonight, and I practically bounced on my toes in my excitement. He was going to combust when he saw me.

Fox was over by the bar, wiping it down and chatting with some patrons. I recognised some contestants within the trials. His wide smile filled me with warmth as he laughed at something one guy said, placing a hand on the guy's upper arm to brace himself. I started weaving around tables to move over to him, but before I could surprise him, he glanced over and froze. His eyes widened a fraction before he beamed.

"Ray!" he hollered, taking two long strides towards me and lifting me off my feet to spin us round. "You're here!" He set me down, laughing as much as me.

"I know! I've been given the night."

"Boy, am I glad to see you! You were amazing earlier!" My eyes darted around us, but everyone was too engrossed in celebrations.

I jerked my head towards the corner of the room where a couple were just leaving an empty booth. "Sure thing," Fox said and placed his hands on my shoulders to steer me through the cheerful crowd. Why I was the one being used as the battering ram, I didn't know. I giggled at the audacity as Fox shouted over his shoulder to the creepy bartender, "I'm taking a break!"

We navigated the bodies of the tavern and finally sat at the table. I always loved that the patrons here would rather stand by the bar than sit in the cosy booths—it worked in my favour for sure.

"You really think I did okay?"

Fox rolled his eyes. "More than okay. I got shivers! It was like you were the queen!"

"I kinda will be one day." I grimaced.

"And it will be a fine day for me."

I smiled at him, relieved to see him in such a good mood. "You look happy, made new friends?" I glanced over at the guys by the bar, the ones who had been talking with Fox, and found the one who'd made him laugh watching us. When he saw me looking, he spun back to face the bar.

"Um, yeah," Fox mumbled, scratching at his neck. "Moving on to you. How did you manage to swing getting here? With every-thing going on, I would have thought things would be tighter for you?"

"Markin said I could come down tonight as my new guard are having their last night of freedom. I have a senior soldier covering me, though. He's in here somewhere."

Fox peered around me. "Where?"

"He's being discreet!" I laughed, but then something Fox said filtered through my head. "Wait. What did you mean by 'with everything going on'? You mean the trials, right?"

"Have you not been told?" Fox asked, his brows suddenly drawing together.

"Told what?"

Fox sighed. "Don't yell at me for not knowing, okay? But the Dydairians attacked one of the nearby villages, ransacked it, the lot. They took a few people but killed everyone else."

I covered my face with my hands to hide my disgust, my shock. "Everyone? Children?" Fox nodded. "Why did I not know of this?"

Fox shrugged. "The final ceremony and choosing of the guard are taking everyone's mind off it here, hence why I think everyone is so cheery."

"But why haven't I been told from within the palace? From my mother's guard? I don't even know if anything is being done about this!" I watched Fox's face change to unease. "What do you know?"

"They sent a group of palace officers to the village to investigate. I don't know more than that. Not even sure if they're back yet because the ceremony took over."

I slumped back, mad that I didn't know. Embarrassed, almost. Why would Markin and my mother keep this from me? Again? The need to find Mahds and demand to know what he did slammed into my thoughts, but it promptly left my mind, along with most other coherent thinking, when Wren came into view.

"What are you doing here?" he hissed, his voice low as he looked around him for any signs someone recognised me.

"I'm having a drink with my friend," I replied, trying to sound like I belonged here, although his presence always made my insides quiver. I was, however, enjoying the slightly flustered look from him.

Wren turned to Fox and smiled tightly. Fox beamed back, enjoying the interaction. I kicked him lightly in the shins under the table.

"Yes, but," Wren said, flicking his eyes towards Fox and then looking at me pointedly.

I knew my smile was super sweet, and I knew it affected Wren when a muscle ticked in his jaw. For some reason, some very misguided reason I'm sure, I loved this side of him.

"Fox is fine."

"But..."

Fox laughed. "C'mon, Ray, let's not let the poor guy stress out his first night as your guard."

Wren's eyes widened a fraction before narrowing on me as I tried to control the smile threatening to show up.

"Wait, what?"

"Fox knows who I am. Always has," I said softly, sensing a change in the surrounding air. Wren closed his eyes and slowly breathed out before crossing his arms over his chest.

"He knew. Did everyone know who you were but me?"

"Wren, look, I'm sorry. It's just—" I stopped when he put his hand up. If I'm being honest, I was glad. I wasn't sure what I was going to say, probably something that got me into more trouble.

"Let's not. I need to get you back to the palace," Wren commanded. Fox whistled and then looked at me, waiting for my reaction and looked to all the world like he was enjoying himself.

"I don't think so. I get you're probably annoyed with me right now, but this is all of our last nights of freedom."

"She's right. She needs some time just as much as you do, and she's perfectly safe with me," Fox added, with what I knew was him trying to be helpful, but this only added to Wren's agitation at seeing me out here. "She can look after herself, too, you know."

"Are you mad?" Wren began loudly and then lowered his voice so he wouldn't be heard. "The whole point of these trials was so that she has dedicated warriors to protect her. How on earth is..."

"Some lowly serving commoner," Fox supplied sarcastically.

"How on earth is a 'non-warrior' meant to protect her?"

"She's done a pretty good job on her own so far I'd say."

"By getting attacked the other day?"

Fox snapped his head to me, his eyes accusing. "Oh Ray, sweetheart, what is the moody, overbearing, muscly guy referring to?" His smile sweet. Too sweet.

"Er..." I inwardly slapped a hand to my forehead. I'd forgotten I hadn't told him about that. "Nothing, just some random man who ran away when he saw I could protect myself. I was fine." I flashed a sheepish smile, trying to show Fox I was good.

"Yes, a random Dydairian," Wren interjected. I rolled my eyes.

"Not helping, Wren."

Fox tutted at me in mock disdain, but I knew he could never keep up the fake attitude.

"So, as you can see, she needs to be escorted back to the palace," Wren finished, a bit too smug.

"Markin said I could be here. I have a member of the senior officers here watching me, probably wondering what you're doing."

"Point him out, then, because we need to have a little chat."

I narrowed my eyes. He narrowed his. Our eyes never wavered as they locked in a battle of wills. Somewhere in the distance, Fox blew out an annoyed breath.

"Shall I just leave you guys to it?" he mumbled more to himself.

"Actually, I think Wren and I need to have a quick discussion outside," I replied. Fox nodded in agreement, and I stood up with Wren. "I'll see you in a few minutes, Fox."

"You stay safe, all right? Safe from everything." As he spoke, he waved his hand over his chest, leaving it over his heart. I rolled my eyes but nodded and then followed my stiff, broad-shouldered warrior-guard out of the tavern.

TWENTY-SEVEN

I SMILED WHEN WE stepped out the back but dropped it quickly when Wren spun to face me, hands on his hips, studying me wordlessly. The muscle in his jaw continued to tick while he ground his teeth.

"Wren, you're going to have to get used to this, working with me and dealing with everything I am. You'll have a heart attack if you don't." I spoke gently but was fed up with the overbearingness, fed up with people trying to control me. We both had a lot to learn if we were going to be anything close to successful.

"My job is to protect you, but you being here seems very counterproductive to that given everything going on with the Dydairians."

"Yeah, well, you'd probably know more about that than me," I muttered.

Wren frowned. "What are you implying?"

"Let's just say something is happening with the Dydairians, and my mother and her guards are doing whatever it takes to keep me away from it."

"Oh."

I looked up, surprised to hear only the one word from him. "What do you mean, 'oh'? What exactly is that supposed to mean?"

Wren crossed his arms, and I reminded myself to keep focused on his face, not his muscular forearms.

"I feel like you're more annoyed you're being kept in the dark than anything else."

"What? How can you say that? I'm meant to take over one day. I need to learn!"

"I need to learn from your guard, but I'm not expecting to be in on all matters straight away."

I threw my hands up in frustration. "Why are you being so difficult? You weren't like this before."

"Really? Before, I thought you were just someone who lived in the city. Now you're the princess who I've been chosen to protect. I plan to uphold that duty, Rayleigh. Not a lot is going to stop me."

I softened my frustrated eyes, trying to communicate that I understood where he was coming from, but I couldn't let him think he'd be able to 'boss' me around—I was to rule one day, not him.

"Your dedication is part of the reason I chose you."

"*You* chose me?"

My face heated under his scrutiny. "Yes."

"I'm surprised."

"You are?"

"Well, yes. Considering how we…" he trailed off.

"How we what?"

Wren coughed, hiding what I'm confident was a blush. Wren blushed!

"Nothing. Guess I didn't realise you had a hand in the final decision."

"Well, I did say in the ceremony 'I choose you to be my personal guard' and all that."

"I thought that was just part of the wording. I didn't think it was literal." Wren's eyes sparked with some of the humour and nature I'd gotten to know.

"I don't like us bickering, Wren. I want us to work together as a team. My mother and her personal guard are friends, confidants, and allies. That's what I want between us. That's what I knew we could have. A partnership."

Wren grew serious, his smile dropping a fraction, and my palms started sweating—not a good look. "Why *did* you choose me?" he asked quietly, and I frowned. "Why me, specifically?"

My hand inched up to my plait, pulling on the ends, winding the strands around a finger. Why did he always make me so nervous?

"Because you make me feel safe," I answered first, because despite the nervous stomach every time I laid eyes on him, I knew I was safe. "I know you'll support me and eventually come to my way of thinking," I looked up at him under my lashes, letting him know that while my tone was playful, we would be working *together*, not me blindly following his commands.

He smiled. "Okay, I get it. I hold my hands up to

you...princess." He gave a playful smirk when he said 'princess', and I pursed my lips in an attempt to be offended by his tone.

"Am I interrupting?" another voice chimed, and I jumped. Wren turned a fraction, allowing me to see behind him. Shar carried some armour over one shoulder. When she saw me, her eyes widened, but instead of chastising me like Wren had done, she barked out a throaty laugh. "You snuck out? Great!" she continued to chuckle as she moved closer to us.

"Just to be clear, I am allowed to be here. Markin made sure a senior soldier followed me to the tavern."

"Yes, our princess here has a fancying for adventures and escapism," Wren added in a dry tone.

"So it would seem," Shar replied, looking me over, no doubt trying to mesh the two images she'd seen of me together. "If Markin is allowing it, who are we to judge? Thank you again, princess, for letting me continue in the trials," Shar said, her face softening for a moment, a short display of vulnerability on show.

"No problem. I couldn't let one of the best fighters go, could I? Plus, a female guard? That has got to be handy in the years to come!" We both giggled, but Wren looked at us in confusion.

"Suck it up. Wren, you can't help being the inferior gender!" Shar joked, knocking her elbow into his crossed arms. He drew his brows even closer together for a moment.

"Fine," he huffed. "The guard were going to meet for a drink. Would you care to join us? Maybe getting to know each other in a less formal setting would be better after all."

I beamed at him. "Fox, too."

"Wouldn't expect otherwise."

Shar pulled a face. "A Fox?"

I pulled her along with me, her tall body tense as I held her arm. Wren followed behind. On the way inside the tavern, I grabbed Fox and then let Wren lead us to a small table where the other two already sat: Bo and Essiah. They each pulled the same confused face Wren had made outside, Bo comically so and Essiah reining in the surprise quickly.

"Hi!" I announced, pulling an extra chair for Fox to sit at. He sat stiffly and then leaned towards me, his eyes on the four guards.

"Um, Ray?" he started in a mock whisper. "I think you blew your cover."

I rolled my eyes playfully. "This is Fox, my best friend. He works a lot of the events at the palace, so expect to see me talking with him when I can. Fox, this is my guard," I said and gestured around the table.

"Kinda gathered that," he mumbled playfully.

"You know Wren, this is Shar, Bo, and Essiah." I pointed to each in turn who smiled or nodded at Fox.

Bo leaned forward on the table. "So, princess, you gonna tell us why you've sneaked yourself down here? Is this something we're going to have to expect?" His cheeks dimpled from grinning at me.

"I'd like to say I'll behave, but I can't make that promise." The truth left my mouth before I had time to filter it.

Bo's bark of laughter almost made me jump. "Aye, you'll be a live one. I can't wait to work with you, princess."

"Call me, Rayleigh, or Ray when we're outside the palace."

"Is this a secret trial or something?" Essiah asked seriously. Fox turned to study him as I did. He sat stiffly, a complete contrast to the relaxed, slouched nature of Bo.

"No, don't worry. I used to come down here to see Fox. I thought my days were over, but Markin said I could come down for the night while you were all having your celebrations, as long as I was shadowed by one of the senior officers."

Essiah nodded rigidly, eyes darting around the room. Perhaps he was trying to ascertain who the senior soldier was? I put it to the back of my mind that it was Mahds who was here. Markin trusted him, so I had to trust him. Maybe I could talk with him on the way back and ask what he'd been doing for Markin to find the traitor.

Bo laughed at something Shar said, and I pushed the thoughts and questions I had about a traitor amongst us away. Tonight was not the night for that. I was here to enjoy myself.

One by one, they relaxed. Even Wren lost some of the tight-ness across his shoulders as conversation flowed. It was probably pointless, but I was glad to see Fox getting on well with my guard. He especially got on with Bo and Shar as they battered jokes back and forth, attempting to discover the funniest of them. I rolled my eyes just as a loud bell rang.

I looked over at Sadie standing by the counter, her hand resting around a thick rope attached to the service bell on the wall.

"Last orders!" she croaked out. It's a miracle anyone could even hear her. I smiled at her, suddenly realising what the bell meant.

"Shoot!" I startled Fox, and the others stared at me wide-eyed as I wrapped my cloak around my shoulders, preparing the hood for when I left the building.

"What's wrong?" Wren demanded, tracking my movements. Essiah immediately went on alert, scanning the tavern. Only Fox carried on drinking his beverage in an unconcerned manner.

"Last orders mean I'm to go meet Mahds outside."

"Mahds the one Markin had follow you?" Shar questioned, and I nodded in answer. "We'll escort you out," she said. She picked up her discarded armour from earlier.

"No, honestly, it's fine!"

Wren stood, too. "Shar and I will escort you out. Bo, Essiah? You good here till we get back?"

"Sure thing!" Bo replied. Essiah pursed his lips and frowned at Fox downing the rest of his drink. Fox slammed the cup on the table when he finished the contents.

"I'll get us the last round!" he announced, kissing me on the cheek before sauntering off to the counter. He slid over it and helped himself—much to the annoyance of some of the waiting patrons. "Yeah, yeah, yeah, wait your turn!"

I faced Wren and huffed. "Fine, okay, let's go!" I ushered them both out, figuring I'd get nowhere with asking them to stay put.

Cold, dark air greeted me in an icy shock when we walked outside; I threw my hood up and wrapped my arms around myself, lightly bouncing on my toes to keep the blood flowing even as it turned to ice.

"It's freezing! When did it get so cold?" I moaned.

Shar shivered. "Who knows? Let's find this Mahds and get you back quickly. I've got a warm bed waiting for me I'd like to use."

We walked three abreast to the corner where I expected to see Mahds, except no one was there. I looked behind me, brows creased together, in case I passed him already, but the streets were uncharacteristically empty.

"He must be late?" I mumbled more to myself, but as I looked up at Wren, his alert green eyes scanning the path, concern burrowed in my mind. "What is it?" I whispered, more through being cold than a need to be quiet, but something told me I wasn't wrong to lower my voice.

Wren shook his head, listening to something, his lips turning down in concentration. Shar straightened, sensing Wren's caution, and scanned the surrounding area, too. I saw nothing but buildings and shapes in the darkness.

"We'll escort you back and double back to find Mahds. C'mon," Wren said, his voice low. For once, I didn't feel the need to argue.

This time Wren walked ahead of me and Shar behind, sandwiching me between them. I really wanted to ask what they thought was wrong, but the tension in Wren's shoulders suggested deep concentration, so I stayed quiet. I knew Dydairians had attacked in the city before and now a big part of me feared they would attack again.

A groan from our left halted our feet; we froze in our tracks. Wren's arm swung out in front of me, meeting my middle to stop me. I wasn't sure my hormones understood the contact was because of potential danger. Both my guards instinctively laid their hands over the weapons fastened to their belts.

I peered into the darkened alleyway, gulping down the lump of residual fear, remembering the attack here not too long ago. That felt like an opportunistic encounter. This ominous feeling pressing down on my chest felt...planned. Coordinated.

"Rayleigh," a hoarse voice whispered.

My feet took an instinctual step forward, but Wren's iron arm kept me back close to him. I clutched at his arm.

"Let me go! I think that's—" I didn't finish. Mahds stumbled from the darkness, his clothes ripped, his face bloody. He looked to Wren.

"Get her out of here," he wheezed. Wren didn't need telling twice. He grabbed my arm and marched us towards the castle. Shar stayed tight to our backs. My feet moved of their own accord to follow, but I tried prying my arm away. It wasn't right leaving Mahds to the wolves.

"Wren, stop. That's Mahds. We need to help him!"

"Not now."

"Shar?" I pleaded.

"No can do. Our priority is you, as is his."

I followed uselessly, tears burning my eyes at the image of a bloody Mahds, staining my vision.

My ears barely recognised the chatter up ahead when Wren yanked me into the nearest alley, holding my back tight against his front. Shar stood in front of us, facing the street entrance. Against my back, Wren's heart thundered, but his even breathing was so unlike my own chest which rose and fell quickly. I closed my eyes and greedily inhaled Wren's woodsy scent, leaning heavily against his body. His hand pressed flat against my stomach and his thumb stroked up and down, up and down, sending waves of comfort. I didn't even think he knew he was doing it.

The noise passed us and then faded away, so we moved back to the path, moving faster than before. I took Wren's hand and felt Shar on my heels. The feeling of being pursued weighed heavy. We all felt it.

The first tingles of relief warmed my numb body as we neared the palace gates, still too far to alert the soldiers, but close enough.

That was until a man's shadow appeared abruptly before us. We slammed to a halt and two other silhouettes joined the first.

"Six o'clock," Shar whispered. I looked behind me and counted three more bodies. Six in total. Both Shar and Wren drew their swords making sure I was between them still.

The first man stepped out of the shadows, and I knew without a doubt he was a Dydairian from the tight black armour he wore. The one in front of us twirled a dull sword in one hand.

"We've been looking for you," he said, his voice a lot smoother than I expected. His friends slowly came into view, all similarly dressed with swords and knives in hand. Even so, there were six. We had a chance.

Just as soon as the thought entered my head, it was crushed. From the side streets, the alleyways, at least five more men piled out, surrounding us. Our chances of fighting our way out immediately plummeted, especially given as I had no weapon of use on me. Something flicked in my core, tensing, and pain pulsed at the back of my head.

"Are you going to make this difficult for us?" the first man sneered, coming closer. Wren raised his sword into a ready position, making it known he'd attack. The man stopped and drew his eyes up and down the length of Wren's prone posture. The man's appraisal moved over to Shar's body and did the same, a quick glint of male appreciation lighting them up before he whistled. "You're no soldier."

"Try me and find out," Shar retorted. He raised his eyebrows but didn't comment; some of the other men surrounding us shared quick, dirty laughs.

"We mean no harm. Let us pass," Wren demanded, his voice deep and authoritative.

"No can do, kiddo. No can do. Grab them!" the man ordered.

Several men lurched forward, but Wren and Shar sprang into action. They kept their fighting spaces tight to me, but it opened them up to more attacks as both had no option but to go on the defensive. Fighting for me, I realised. And it was going to get them killed.

"I need a sword!" I shouted and knew Wren heard me, but neither he nor Shar could stop to hand me one. With the men all geared up, I had no choice but to stay in the middle of Shar and Wren as they fought to keep the attackers at bay.

My mind whirled, throbbing, trying to find a solution, a way out of this mess. Make a break for it and leg it back to the palace to alert the soldiers of the attack? I'd never make it through the line of men.

I growled in frustration, but it snapped into fear when the remaining men charged forward all at once. Wren and Shar were both exceptional fighters, but neither had trained together, and their coordination was slightly off because of it. They left an opening, and one man ran straight for me. Shar turned to me, realising her mistake, but still left herself open to the attack instead of me. She took the force of a blade against what little armour she wore. She fell to her knees on a short cry.

Distracted, I moved in to help her when a sword kissed the hollow of my neck, holding me immobile.

"Stop, or I cut her throat right now," the man holding me against his blade commanded to Wren. He was almost a carbon copy of the first guy who spoke—brothers?

Wren slowly lowered his sword and raised his arms, not once taking his dark eyes off the man holding the sword against me.

The first speaker clapped his brother on the shoulder.

"Well done, Lin! Bind them," he instructed to the others.

Shar gritted her teeth when hauled up. They pulled her arms behind her back to tie together. Wren's eyes stormed with fury and contempt while his hands were bound. I faced him as my arms were roughly yanked behind me, too, my wrists bound in rope. Fear warred underneath the surface of his stormy green eyes.

TWENTY-EIGHT

M Y HEAD THROBBED AND my body ached, cold from the hard surface beneath me. Instead of the crackling fire in my bedroom, something dripped.

Whispers from a conversation drifted into my ears. The soft timbre of Wren's voice mixed with Shar's.

"Should we wake her?" Shar asked.

"No, let her sleep."

"What about..."

"Nothing we can do now."

I couldn't figure out why they talked in hushed tones, and in my bedroom no less. Did Markin send them in to watch me or something?

A shiver tore through my body so violently that I reached down for my covers, only for the roughly woven material of a jacket to greet my fingers. I opened my eyes, and the brown material of a dark jacket was draped over my waist. I pushed up on cold concrete, momentarily surprised to see Wren and Shar before the memory hit me: the Dydairians. They captured us. I spun my head to the left, and bars swam into my view; I barely held onto the whimper.

We'd been thrown into a small cage, three sides made of stone and one side barred. A small window opposite the bars let in bright daylight, bringing in some much-needed form of warmth for my stiff body, but it wasn't enough to stop the hairs on my arms from standing alert. Nighttime in this cage would be a different matter; another shiver danced over my body. I slipped my hands into my hair, which had mostly come loose from its plait.

"That wasn't a dream?" I asked to no one in particular.

"No, sorry," Shar answered. Both of my guards looked at me apologetically, the weight of responsibility heavy on them.

"Don't look at me like that, guys, this was hardly your fault," I tried reassuring them. Wren drew his knees up, leaning back against the stone wall. I rearranged the jacket over me, and a woodsy scent floated up around me, calming my nerves slightly. I started handing the jacket back over to him, worried he was now too cold without it. "Thank you for your jacket."

"Keep it. It's the least I can do to ease your discomfort."

The small space we sat in returned to silence except for the drip, drip, drip, rhythmically drumming away.

"Where are we?" My mind tried to catch up with reality; I had no idea how we ended up here—I must have passed out. I went to run my fingers over my bracelet but sagged when I found bare skin, remembering I'd taken it off before I'd even left the palace like I always do. Missing even just that small touch of comfort nearly had tears spilling, and I had to furiously blink them back.

"We're not sure, but not too far out from the city, so definitely in Balmore still," Shar replied, and her answer soothed me somewhat.

"Do we have a plan?"

Wren and Shar exchanged a look before Shar said, "We need to see what they want, and while we suspect they know you're...you, we don't want to alert them to this."

"And what about Mahds? Is he here, too?"

Shar shook her head. "Haven't seen him."

I slumped over my crossed legs wondering how I managed to get in such a place, left a senior officer injured, and dragged my two new guards into being kidnapped with me. But before I could glide deeper into my pity party, a door beyond our bars creaked open. Three men I recognised from last night appeared, smiling like they'd won a jackpot.

I jumped to a standing position, crushing Wren's jacket between my hands as Wren and Shar stood either side of me. Even though I expected their weapons to have been taken off them, I still hopefully looked to their sides. Wren's hands tightened into fists next to his empty belt.

One man held up a dirty hand, finger pointing at us.

"No funny business, you hear?" he rasped, and another unlocked the barred door to our cell. They ushered us out, and we fell into what was fast becoming a standard formation: Wren, then me, and lastly Shar.

My voice screamed to be heard, demanded answers, but I kept my mouth firmly shut, following the lead from my two guards.

We walked down a long, cold corridor, not furnished or decorated. The walls were the same stone our cells were made from. A door at the end of the corridor opened, and we were quickly steered into a wide room, one of the accompanying kidnappers pushed Shar in the shoulder even though she was right behind me.

"Move it!" he sneered at her.

The room opened into a wide space with low ceilings, dark stone walls, and no furniture. An empty hall. Except for the group of Dydairians in the middle. They parted, and in the middle of them I recognised the man from Madame El's, the man Mahds had been meeting with: Lucien. He clicked his fingers, and from the other side of the room, two of his men dragged a half-conscious body between them.

"Mahds!" I breathed, but as I stepped forward, Wren pulled me back behind him. I glanced around the room, trying to figure out the numbers we were against. The faces of eight, no ten, men—all Dydairians, watched us.

Lucien smirked as his men tossed Mahds to the floor, who then groaned, pushing up to his knees. Blood stained the front of his shirt, dripping from his nose and mouth. His left eye was swollen and already a deep purple colour.

Mahds spat blood from his mouth at the base of Lucien's feet.

"Traitor," he wheezed. So Lucien had been the leak, not Mahds. Why hadn't I looked into this Lucien more?

"I see our guests are here," a man said from behind the other Dydairians. The others parted to allow him through, and I gasped. Over his black armour, he wore a long tailored black jacket, open down the middle where a sword and dagger glinted at either side of his hips. But it wasn't his clothing I fixated on. His hair. Long, past his shoulders and straight. The colour...the same colour as mine:

an icy-blonde with light grey streaked through it.

He met my stare. Icy-blue eyes locked onto mine, but whereas my eyes were wide with shock, his were hooded and controlled. He'd been expecting someone to bear a resemblance to him. I'd never met anyone on my father's side, orphaned before he married my mother. Or so I had thought. But he must be...this man must be related to my father. Related to me. He couldn't be. He was Dydairian—there was no way I was Dydairian, as that would mean my father had been. Just—it couldn't be. I stepped back in line with Wren, needing his stability, glancing quickly at him to see him frowning in confusion.

The man smiled, the skin around his eyes crinkling, just like Markin's did.

"Our wonderful guests. Welcome." His smooth voice crooned, his accent similar to the other men who had spoken to us in the cell, but more structured, whole, refined.

The men behind ushered us closer, and my legs jerked stiffly, but as we moved, I found courage coming back to me. My mother's lessons on decorum ran through my mind. I squared my shoulders, standing between Wren and Shar, their positioning not an accident, and met the older man's stare.

"What do you want with us?" I asked calmly, confidently. My mother would be proud. A quivering spasm in my already shaking stomach passed through me when I thought of her. I pushed it to one side, instead choosing to focus on her teachings—the ones she allowed me to be part of. I took a calming breath and channelled her, studying the man without blinking, without showing fear. He tilted his head to watch me and stepped closer.

"I see it. Your mother..." he mumbled quietly to himself. I

stuffed his words down and ignored it, the surprise.

"I asked you what you wanted with us," I repeated sternly, clasping my hands in front of me much like my mother would have, were she here, about to negotiate with the enemy. Again, I pushed to one side the fear at who this man was, what he might be to me. My mother could have lied about there being no family left on my father's side. It wasn't like she was ever honest with me...but this? Could she really have lied to me about this? My hands stopped shaking when I clutched them together, but I had to work on smoothing the wrinkle that wanted to crease between my brows. Did this man know I was the queen's daughter? Did he know my father? If he did, this attack wasn't unplanned at all. My mind raced through all the ways they wanted to use us. A ransom? To kill me?

The man stroked his beardless chin. "You, of course."

"And what can I help you with?" I quickly asked when Wren stiffened beside me, and Shar stood a little straighter.

"Do you know who I am, girl?" He moved one arm behind his back and held the other up in a questioning gesture. I shook my head. "I'm a leader. Like your mother is queen of Balmore, I rule the Dydairians."

I let the frown show on my face then, truly confused with what little I knew of Dydair. "No one rules Dydair, they're a lawless land."

"Yes, that *was* the case many years ago, but then we started getting your people and that other kingdom bordering us, pestering us constantly about resources and the cursed and then they erected that godforsaken wall...it got rather tiresome," he added, flashing me a quick smile.

"There's no way the druids would let you rule over them. You're lying."

"These men are certainly following me."

"Humans, yes. We won't negotiate with anyone from Dydair, let alone someone falsely claiming leadership. What's your plan? To destroy the wall so the druids could come and kill us all? Did you think you could distract us enough for that?"

"We have no intention of killing *everyone*."

"Why are we here, then? Why have you taken us?" His plans were surely foolish.

Instead of answering my question, though, he asked one of his own. "Are you quite sure the wall needs to be destroyed for druids to cross over?" I opened my mouth to speak but closed it again. "I imagine you know little about the druids, hardly surprising, given your mother, but there are a select few druids who wield shadow magic—and only a true shadow-born druid could ever rule Dydair, could ever be powerful enough to tap into the energy lines that run under the earth."

I frowned. "What are you saying?"

The man smiled and raised a hand, curling it. A plume of black shadow flew from his palm and circled me. Shar gasped behind me. Even as smoke and mist, it tightened around my torso, pinning my arms to my sides, and then he tugged me closer to him. A whimper clawed up my throat, escaping in my panicked, uneven breaths.

"Rayleigh!" Wren shouted, then cursed. I turned my head to see him and Shar being restrained by Dydairians.

The man's eyes snapped to Wren. "Quiet, boy! You'd do well to remember who's in charge here."

Wren worked his jaw, his eyes glowering at him. I turned back to the man who bared my resemblance, my lungs seizing.

"How?" I breathed. "The wall...you can't..."

"Cross over? We couldn't. Not for a long time, but as with all things, time weakens. It's time to change the game. We will not be trapped within Dydair any longer, not with the cursed growing in strength and numbers, not with the power beneath the earth threatening to overwhelm everything we know—even your precious Balmore."

"You're lying," I spat.

"Am I?"

"We won't let you destroy the wall. We won't let you unleash the cursed on us. We won't let you take everything we know from us. We will stop you!"

"And who is this 'we'? You and the queen? She isn't strong enough to stop me." He smiled to himself, and a sour taste coated my mouth.

"So why bother with all of this, the attacks on this side of the wall, if you're *so powerful* enough to just destroy us?" His left eye twitched slightly.

"I wanted your mother to know it was me behind them. I wanted her to be as frustrated and infuriated as I am!" he shouted, losing some of the cool façade he had presented. His shadows tightened around my middle, and I whimpered. Wren cursed behind me, and the shadows loosened their grip slightly. I breathed as deeply as I could trying to muster any ounce of courage I had.

The man marched closer, his face contorted in a sneer. I met his angry eyes with a bland stare, refusing to let him think he could scare me with his size. His magic.

An inch away from my face he closed his eyes and took a few jarring deep breaths. When he finally reopened them, he smiled, patting me on the shoulder like a small child. I tried not to grimace.

"Where were we? Ah yes, introduction. I am Tyton, leader of the Dydairians." His voice now calm and back to its composed tone.

"And I'm Rayleigh, heir to Balmore kingdom, but you already know this, so I'll ask again. What do you actually want with us?"

"What I want is for you to deliver a message to your mother."

"And why would I do that?" I asked politely, internally glad he didn't have immediate plans to take my head. "My mother has no desire to work with Dydair, especially not after some of the most recent stunts you've pulled."

"I don't want her to 'work with Dydair'. That isn't what this is about!" he shouted, his cheeks reddening again. He took another deep breath and relaxed his shoulders. I didn't know if getting him mad was a good or bad thing.

"Okay, then, what *is* this about?"

He smiled, and not just a normal run-of-the-mill smile but one that sent true fear writhing in my gut.

"Not yet, little one. You need to relay this message first." He slid even closer and then took my face in his cold hands. I desperately willed myself to meet him in the eyes. *Do not show fear. Do not show fear.* My mother's voice instructed the words over and over in my mind. "And coming from you? Oh, it will be a sweet, sweet gift." Tyton leaned down from his tall frame, his thin lips close to my ear, his breath a whispering promise. "Tell your mother that I know *whose* she is."

I kept my face a blank mask even though confusion seeped through every pore; his message didn't even make sense.

Mahds groaned from where he lay.

"If I pass on that message, will you let us go? He needs help," I asked, gesturing to Mahds with my head as my arms were still clamped to my side with his magic.

"Who? The senior officer in your so-called army who was meant to protect you? What an excellent job he did."

"It's hardly fair when you're ambushed by a bunch of spineless men," I argued back.

Tyton's smile was tight. "Well, either way, I think the queen needs to know what useless protection her daughter has."

A lump formed in my throat and fear spiked rapidly through my body. Tyton walked away from me, towards Mahds. He bent over him and grabbed a fistful of his hair to yank his head up with. Mahds's red and swollen eyes tried to find me, his face a purple and blue mess.

"Tyton, what are you doing? I'll deliver your message if you let us all leave," I ground out, struggling against the magic he had me in. He laughed.

"Did you hear that, boys?" Tyton raised his voice to his men in the room. "She thinks she can order me about? Who does she think she is?" The room filled with deep laughter from his men. "Tut-tut, Rayleigh. You should know that what happens next is entirely on you."

"Honour," Mahds croaked as his better eye finally met mine.

Tyton rolled his eyes, and at first, confusion as to what Tyton meant with it being entirely on me clouded my mind. But then his eyes gleamed, chilling me to my bones. He yanked Mahds's head back in an uncomfortable position.

They say time slows down at certain life events, but with this, everything happened so fast. Tyton pulled a long dagger from his belt and swiped it across Mahds's neck in one quick fluid motion that my brain barely registered.

Mahd's one good eye widened as he continued to watch me. Realisation stormed through me when bright red blood spurted from his open neck. I gasped, a scream lodged in my throat. My chest heaved, desperate for oxygen, but no air entered my lungs. Mahds's life slowly drained away right before me.

Tyton let go of Mahds's head, and his body thumped to the floor. He wiped the blade on Mahd's body before standing back up.

"You killed him," I whispered, my voice strangely hoarse despite the fact I didn't scream out loud. "You killed him!" I screamed. I lunged forward, but his magic tightened once again. To my right, Wren and Shar struggled against their captors, too.

"Yes, I did, and it would be worth knowing that I don't need three people to deliver this message. Only you." His words froze my body, my eyes darting to Shar and then Wren. Shar focused on Mahds's body, but Wren focused on me. When our eyes met, my fear and anger reflected in his. "These two must be part of your new guard," he stated, not guessed.

Wren lifted his chin. "Why don't you let us do our job, then, or are you that afraid of us you need us physically restrained?" he goaded, his muscles bunching even as they were pinned behind him.

"No, don't," I whispered, and Tyton's head twisted toward me.

"Don't? Don't what? Kill them? Are these your...friends?" He lifted a lock of my hair, running his fingers over the ends and then dropped it, looking at me expectantly. I pressed my lips together, not wanting to give anything else away. "Very well," Tyton sighed. "Kill that one." He pointed at Shar. Her eyes widened, but she squared her shoulders even as the man behind her pushed her to her knees.

"No! Wait!" I shouted, and Tyton smirked.

Wren struggled against the hands holding him. "You bastard!"

A deafening boom ripped through the room a split second before stone and plaster tore through the air, flying in all directions. My frayed hair whipped round my head as I brought my arms up in front of my face. Pain speared my side, my leg, my arm.

"Rayleigh!" Wren shouted.

TWENTY-NINE

A LARGE BODY COLLIDED with my back, and we fell in a heap on the floor, my body no longer bound in Tyton's shadows. Wren's large frame shielded most of mine as rubble rained down on us both. Face down, I could barely take a breath between the weight on my back and the swirling dust in the air. I turned my head. Daylight streamed through one wall—what remained of it. Metallic clangs and shouts roared to life around us.

Wren's weight lifted off mine with sudden force, a grunt hitting my ears. I had no time to see where he had gone or what was happening: the bottom of a boot headed towards my face. Instinctively, I rolled to my side, my back screaming as more stone cut into my already split and bleeding skin.

"Fucking bitch," Lucien spat, rearing his leg back, about to swing for me again. I scrambled to all fours and scurried out of reach, but he stormed forward and grabbed my hair, yanking me up to my knees. I hissed, sharp pain pricking over my scalp. I reached up and grabbed the hands that held my hair. "Do you have any idea how long I've had to put up with your fucking kingdom? Listen to you whine and moan—you didn't even know who I was, stupid girl. You're coming with me."

He dragged me backwards, and my feet flailed as I held onto my hair fisted in his hands, my head screaming in agony.

"Let go of me!" I screamed at him, my heart painfully beating against my ribs. Dust still settled in the air, blinding me from what was going on. I couldn't see Wren or Shar. Had no clue if they were dead or alive. No other magic flared around, so I had to hope the only druid here was Tyton.

Another explosion reverberated through the room. Stone crashed into us, and Lucien fell forward, jerking me with him. A loud ring punctured my ears, dulling the cries, the shouts, the distinct metallic clang of sword on sword.

I was underwater, sounds muffled save for the piercing, persistent ringing. The pain across my scalp lessened as Lucien's hold fell away. I tried to get to my knees, but my arms shook. My vision wavered, and I swallowed coppery blood, the wetness easing my dry mouth. I frowned. I didn't know why that observation was important.

A hand clamped down on my calf. I kicked back, my foot connecting with Lucien. He grunted. He grabbed me again and pulled me towards him. I was disoriented enough to allow it. He grabbed a fistful of my tunic, pulling the top half of my body off the floor and close to his face.

"Stop it!" he spat at me. He wiped dust away from his eyes, and

I used the opportunity. I brought my knee up between his thighs, hitting as hard as I could from this position, and when he grunted, folding over me slightly, I used my right fist and swung towards his face, connecting with his jaw. Blood oozed from split skin along his chin. He snapped his head back to mine, his eyes narrowed, teeth clenched.

Figures emerged from the swirling chaotic mist, two men grappling with each other. One man got punched in the stomach and crashed to the floor, closer to me. I recognised him instantly.

"Wren!" I croaked. Wren twisted at the sound of my voice, his eyes flashing with a wild emotion. The man above him slammed his fist into the side of Wren's face in his distraction and blood flew from his mouth.

"Got the fucker!" Wren's attacker shouted to Lucien, who let out a sinister chuckle; my skin crawled with the sound.

Wren blocked another attempt at his face. "What do you want with her?!" he roared, but another man ran out from the mist, another one of Tyton's men.

Lucien dropped me, pain flaring across my back when I hit the floor. He pressed his large, callused hand against my cheek to force it towards Wren and then leaned over me, the other side of my face biting into shards of stone beneath me. I scratched at his arm pinning my face, trying to buck my hips from where he straddled me.

Wren garbled a moan when the two over him each took their turns to punch and kick him, totally ignoring their weapons of steel. My breathing quickened: they weren't after a clean death, they were going to kill him, slowly.

"Gotta make it look good!" One of them grinned, chuckling

as he kicked Wren again.

"C'mon, *princess*," Lucien mocked close to my ear. "Show us what you're made of."

I didn't have a clue what he wanted me to show them. My next-to-useless fighting skills? My terrified thoughts? My lack of leadership qualities? There was plenty to choose from.

Wren cried out, blood pouring from his mouth. He curved in on himself, covering his stomach as one arm raised above his head in a hopeless attempt to get them to stop. Tears tracked down my face.

I was powerless.

Useless.

"They're hungry for blood. They won't stop until he's still, and even then, they'll continue beating on his cold, broken body. Is that what you want, *princess*?" I couldn't see him, but the venom, the hate in his voice speared me sharper than any knife could have.

I had to do something. I wouldn't just lie here, forced to watch Wren die in front of me. It wasn't fair. He didn't deserve to die like this. Balmore needed Wren. I needed Wren.

Anger churned in my middle, fire raced through my veins. I forced my head against Lucien's hand and slowly turned towards the man hovering above me. His eyes widened, and he sucked in air through his teeth.

I reached up and clasped his jaw between my hand, my nails biting into his skin, squeezing. Blood dribbled down his chin from the wound I'd inflicted earlier. Lucien tried to jerk out of my grasp, but my newfound strength held on with ease. A low growl whispered near us, but I didn't focus on it. Couldn't.

"No," he gasped, strained. Black lines spread on his skin from where my hand held his face, veins of something evil.

This is wrong.

I ignored the voice. Whoever's it was. The Dydairian let go of me and tried to push my hand away. I let him, and took a jarring breath in, staring at the blackened mark I'd left on his skin.

Lucien scrambled back off me, struggling to breathe, and then he collapsed, wheezing. I staggered to my feet, panting heavily. Something glinted by my foot. I stooped to pick up the dagger and stepped over him, straddling him as he had me, rage blinding.

I heard nothing, only the sound of my heavy breathing and his strained wheezes.

I saw nothing, only darkness clouding the edges of my vision. The only clear thing was this man. This man who had kidnapped us. Killed Mahds. Hurt Wren.

"You," I spat, my voice deeper, raw, "don't deserve...life." I plunged the dagger into his stomach, it slid into his flesh with sickening ease. His eyes widened, his mouth parted wordlessly. Twisting the blade in his gut, I watched with horrid satisfaction. Something slithered from me, from my hands where they rested on this hilt of the dagger protruding from Lucien's stomach, and soaked up his blood, my hands turning red with it.

Lucien shrieked, pain etched in the lines of his face as his body jerked violently. My palms flattened on his chest, and his wails intensified, fuelling me and whatever lurked beneath my skin, controlling my movement.

Black smoke—shadows—rose from my hands, from his wound, and the blood gushing from it turned blacker than night. From where his tunic stretched open at his neck, black lines crawled up his neck, over his chin, across his face. His eyes turned black, his screams dying on a gurgle as black blood bubbled from his mouth, choking him.

He died.

His life ended by my hands.

Whatever had slithered from me and into him snaked back into me and settled in my core. My vision brightened. The noises of a dying battle once again reached my ears.

"Rayleigh?"

I looked up at Shar, who hesitated for only a moment before dropping to her knees beside me.

"What did I do?" I whispered, lifting my hands. Red and black blood covered them. Shar blinked, pushing hair from her pale and sweaty face. "Did I do this?"

Shar lifted her head and looked behind me. "We have to go. Now." Her words burrowed through my confusion. And I reached forward, latching onto her arm. I ignored the way she flinched.

"Wren! He was being attacked!"

"I just saw him. He was being taken out by Abe." At my confused stare, she took my hands in hers. "Abe and Derril blew through this place and brought a unit of soldiers with them."

"They're here?" My lip trembled. They'd come for me. Of course they had.

Shar nodded. "But...but we can't let them see this. Nobody can see this," she said, pointing to the body I still sat over.

"That's-that's d-druid magic," I finished in a whisper, closing my eyes.

"And even the queen couldn't protect you if anyone found out about this."

"I'm evi—"

"No. Rayleigh. You need to let me help. This is a death sentence. Do you understand me? You will be executed."

I inhaled. My jaw quaking, my teeth gnashing together. "I have druid magic. I have druid magic."

Shar gripped my upper arms and lifted me off the man and then turned to go before quickly spinning back to put another blade in my hands. "I'll be back. Stay here. Use this if you have to. Tyton had more men here than we realised." She disappeared into the mist, and I frowned. It wasn't mist. It was smoke. Orange flames danced up ahead of me and heat licked against my skin.

Shar returned only moments later, holding a plank of wood, the tip on fire, and then she touched it to Lucien's body, lighting his clothes. She stood back and hauled me up, wrapping an arm around my back, taking one of my arms around her shoulders.

"Not a word, Rayleigh."

We stumbled through the chaos, my feet following her direction, but my mind stuck on a loop.

"I have druid magic. I deserve to die. I shouldn't have druid magic, *his* shadow magic."

Shar half dragged me up and over what was left of a stone wall. A group of men stood in the distance, a few men on the ground, injured and being tended to. Abe sat on his horse, scanning the surroundings. When his eyes landed on me, he shouted, jumped off his horse, and ran towards us. Shar stopped before he got close.

"You don't deserve to die. We'll deal with this. You gave me a chance when few would have. I owe you my life. I have your back. Trust me, trust me."

I hung onto her, staring at her as intently as she looked at me, her face tight. I didn't believe her about not deserving to die, but I nodded. My eyes fluttered close as Abe reached out and crushed me to his body, cradling my head against his chest.

"You're okay, princess. We have you."

THIRTY

MUCH OF THE RIDE I couldn't remember. I blinked and I was on a horse. Another blink and we were riding slowly on a dirt road, our injured lying on trailers being pulled by horses. Wren one of them. He would be okay once he got to a healer, I was assured. Shar watched me, staying close. At one point, when the horses stopped to rest, she and Derril stood close to each other, faces serious. She had promised to help me, but fear still stole my breath when they turned to look at me. I looked away.

I blinked, and we were back on the road. Wren woke and asked for me. I shook my head at Shar, and she trotted back to go check on him for me.

I heard Abe and Derril say Tyton had fled with a small band of men. Abe had tracked us, his speciality, but they had instructions from my mother that I was the focus, not Tyton.

It took the day. A whole day until we were approaching the

gates of the palace. Shouts of alarm and commands of order sailed through the sky. I sat up straighter on my horse.

As soon as the doors opened, my mother rushed towards me with a pale face and thin lips. Abe helped me down from my horse. A wagon rolled past. I caught Wren's eyes. He sat up straighter, and my eyes drew to where his bloodied hand down his side. He rounded the corner, disappearing from view to be seen by one of our medical staff. I turned my head just in time for my mother to crash into me.

It was the first sign of affection I'd received from her in years. And I stood immobile, frozen in her embrace. She pulled back, framing my face in her hands, turning my head to look for signs of injury.

"Are you okay? Are you hurt?"

I shook my head.

"I am unharmed," I answered, stepping back, out of her hold. Markin stormed down the steps towards us in the courtyard. His face relaxed when he caught sight of me.

"You absolutely gave us the scare of our lives." He grabbed me in a hug, too—he'd never once done that in front of others. "I'm so glad you're okay. I told your mother that Abe and Derril would find you."

Markin stepped back, and Derril and Abe stepped up behind me. Derril placed a hand on my shoulder, squeezing it slightly.

"Mahds didn't make it," he told Markin.

His nose flared, his eyes widening a fraction, guilt buried deep in them before they closed.

"I'll see to the arrangements. Make sure the injured are taken care of, and we'll reconvene this evening. Give everyone time to settle back in. Shar?"

She stepped out from the shadows where she had been standing, waiting behind me. "Yes, sir?"

"Check on Wrendor and then find Essiah and Bo. Meet me in my office as soon as Wrendor can move."

"Yes, sir." She quickly glanced at me, bobbing her head a fraction, and then marched away.

"I've asked Sheri to start a bath for you. Go, clean up, take a few hours and then we'll talk." Markin folded my arm in his, tenderly closing his hand over mine. I didn't speak as he shot a look at Derril and Abe over his shoulder before returning his gaze to me. "This is not your fault. Mahds did what was asked of him and more. He loved this kingdom. I can think of no greater honour for him than to die protecting its legacy. You."

I didn't look at his face, but I nodded and followed a soldier he had beckoned over up to my room where Sheri waited, wringing her hands. She gasped when I walked in.

"My lady!" She rushed over but stopped just short of hugging me. "Rayleigh?" she questioned, her brows drawing together.

"May I get in the bath?" I asked.

She stood for several moments, watching me, opening her mouth to speak and then closing it before she finally nodded. If she saw my shoulders sag in relief, she didn't say. I walked into the bathroom, steam filling the air.

"Would you like me to help you undress?"

"No. Thank you, that will be all."

I smiled vacantly at her as I closed the door. It didn't reach my eyes, but she smiled back regardless. When I heard the doors to my room close behind her, I pressed my forehead against the bathroom door and let the tears fall.

I dressed into a plain green dress and brushed my hair, my eyes vacantly staring at a space in front of me rather than the mirror on my desk. My father's bracelet sat where I'd left it before...I picked it up, holding it to my lips, closing my eyes as they threatened to spill again. A quick rap at my door startled me. I placed a hand over my racing heart and slipped the bracelet on.

I opened the door and frowned. Wren stood on the other side, yanking a sling off his arm. Still covered in muck and ash with dried blood streaking down his left temple, he looked up and stepped forward into my space. To keep a distance, I backed up. He closed the door behind him and used the now-useless sling to wipe at his temple, scrubbing some of the blood away. He hissed through his teeth but then dropped his arm by his side, staring at it as he worked his jaw. I let him work through his thoughts so I could compose my own. My arm drifted across my stomach, holding the jitters at bay.

"Are you okay?" he asked hoarsely.

"Physically, I'm in better shape than some," I whispered back.

He looked at me then, his sharp eyes assessing. "That doesn't fill me with confidence."

"How can I not be affected by what happened?"

Wren stepped forward and I stepped back. He frowned.

"I'm sorry you had to witness what you did. It's my fault, I—"

"It's not your fault. You tried to protect me. You did your job."

"Hardly. Doing my job would have meant stopping us from being taken."

"You were outnumbered, but you and Shar kept me alive. I am, after all, the heir. My life before others, right?"

"Little Shadow, I—" He stepped closer again and I stepped back. His face twisted in pain, and I wasn't sure it was his physical pain ailing him at that moment.

"Wren, I get it. I understand."

"No, you don't. I couldn't have stopped what he did to Mahds even if I'd placed his life above yours."

"He gave his life for me. That is a terrible responsibility to bear."

"If you are queen, you will have more lives on your hands."

"Don't you think I know that?" I spat.

"That's not what I meant, I—" He huffed and ran his hands through his hair. "I want you to trust me, to lean on me. I'm here for you."

My voice was barely above a whisper. "Only as a guard. Nothing more."

"What?" he breathed, stepping closer. I let him, and he searched my face with his bright green eyes. I committed his to memory, being this close to him.

"Whatever there was between us can be no more. I cannot have that burden—"

"Burden? That's not what we are to each other."

"And what are you to me, huh?" I argued, my voice rising. "You can't be anything to me other than my guard. You have a choice, and you make it now: you are in my personal guard, or you are not. But that is all you will ever be to me. I have a kingdom to put first. I have to secure our safety. That will mean marrying some prince—my mother already told me it would be someone royal. I will have to make hard choices in the future, and I will only do that on my own. I will bring no one else into this."

He searched my face, his eyes scanning me, his mouth opening to say something.

"So that's it. We're over?"

"We were never a 'we' in the first place. Are you in or are you out?"

He clamped his mouth shut, a muscle in his jaw jumping. He stepped back and braced his arms behind his back, looking above my head.

"I took an oath, Your Highness. I will honour that oath for you."

"Then please leave."

Wren stilled, breathing deeply before he closed his eyes and turned away sharply. He yanked open the door and closed it with more force than necessary.

I didn't jump, I didn't startle. Sounds washed over me as I sank to the floor and allowed the tears to fall once again. I needed to be empty by the time I faced others again. So I wept. I wept for Mahds. I wept for Wren.

I wept for me.

Hours later, when the sun had gone down again, I left my room. I'd eaten the food Sheri had brought me even though it had felt like sand in my mouth. But I wasn't a fool. I needed strength.

I found Loch at the bottom of the stairs, waiting for me. His face softened the moment I stood next to him.

"Don't," I said.

"What?"

"Don't give me that look of pity. I'm fine."

"Okay, then. I won't." He was silent for all of ten seconds as we walked. "Everyone is worried about you."

I breathed out, controlled. "Take me to my mother."

"She's in Markin's office, with your guard."

My steps faltered. Loch said nothing and neither did I.

We reached Markin's office, and Loch knocked once before stepping in. Eight pairs of eyes turned to face us. My guard, my mother's guard, and my mother.

Loch closed the door and stood with Abe behind my mother's chair. Markin sat behind his desk, hands clasped tightly together on the polished wood. Derril leaned against the wall behind Markin, arms folded. Wren, Shar, Essiah, and Bo stood on the other side of the room, behind the only other vacant chair. Wren's face was slightly paler than normal, but other than that, he stood tall, hands clasped behind his back like the others in my guard, all standing much more rigidly than my mother's guard.

Markin gestured his hand toward the chair.

"Take a seat, Rayleigh," he said softly.

I moved to the chair, briefly catching Wren's eyes. My mouth parted on a soft inhale, electric energy still buzzing between us. I ignored the sharp drop in my stomach, and the way my knees wobbled, and sat in the chair, folding one hand delicately over the other.

Markin cleared his throat. "Thank you all for coming here. I know you might think this is outside protocol, but you are now Princess Rayleigh's personal guard, and we do things differently. I'm in the process of clearing an office for you, but for now, we need to discuss what happened yesterday."

I blinked. Yesterday. Was it only yesterday all this hell started?

"Are you well enough, Wrendor?" my mother asked, shocking me further.

"Yes, Your Majesty," he answered from behind me, his deep voice causing a shiver to rush through me. My body tensed.

She smiled politely and then faced Markin.

"Can you tell us what happened?" he asked Wren.

"I found Rayleigh at the tavern, but she assured me a senior soldier was watching her. I should have forced her back—"

Derril chuckled. "We're talking about Rayleigh. Don't start putting blame on yourself there."

"Regardless, I could have done more. Eventually, we sat down with the other guard members and shared a drink."

"That is perfectly acceptable," Markin began, "we gave you the night, and I said she could leave to go to the tavern. What happened next?"

Wren paused, and I nodded at him to continue, without meeting his eyes.

"We left, Shar and I, to take Rayleigh to the rendezvous point with Mahds. He wasn't there, and something didn't—ah—feel right, so we decided to take her back. On the way to the palace, the Dydairians ambushed us. They had already taken Mahds when they found us."

"Did they take you straight to their hideout?"

"Yes, sir. They blindfolded us, but they didn't make any stops on the way. They removed our blindfolds when they put us in their cells for the night."

My mother's leg bounced up and down as she stared at a ring on her finger.

"I heard from Abe and Derril that you all were in the main hall when the blast happened. Is that true?"

"Yes, the Dydairians took us there first thing in the morning to speak to their leader."

"Tyton."

"Yes." My heart sank. They had known who Tyton was all along.

I leaned forward. "Did you know he was a druid?" Markin stilled but then nodded tensely. "Did you know the wall was weakening enough to allow druids to cross over?"

"We suspected but could never confirm, and we couldn't risk the public finding out. If they knew, there would be mass panic on a scale we have never seen before." Markin ran a hand over his face. "Were there any other druids?"

"None who attacked with magic," Wren answered for me when I leaned back into my chair again.

"And Tyton was the one who killed Mahds?"

"Yes, sir."

I stopped listening when he explained how Mahds died. I didn't need to relive the memory any more clearly than I was already replaying it in my head.

All four of my mother's personal guard looked at me expectantly until someone cleared their throat.

"The message?" Loch pushed.

"What?" I whispered, my voice caught from replaying Mahds's death again.

Shar placed her hand on my shoulder from behind me, giving it a short comforting squeeze before she spoke. "The message he gave you. We didn't hear it."

I fiddled with a spot on my dress for a moment before smoothing it down.

"I'd like to speak to my mother alone."

"We need to know," Markin said.

"And I said, I need to speak to my mother alone," I repeated, looking at my hand, pretending to be a lot stronger than I felt. She studied my face, her eyes showing an internal turmoil I did not understand. I wasn't sure I wanted to do this at all, but I knew what I shared next had to be between me and her.

"Leave us," she instructed.

Her guard got up to walk out, reluctantly, but my own stayed behind me. I stood facing them.

"I'm fine," I said, watching them as they then followed Abe out of the room. Wren shot me a pained look over his shoulder as Abe shut the door behind them all, leaving us in silence. My mother refused to look at my face.

"Tyton gave me a message," I stated. She closed her eyes, a sad sigh escaping her. "Why wasn't I told about Tyton, about druids crossing the boundary?" My voice wasn't soft, in fact, it was harsh.

"It is more complicated than you think," she began, and I slammed my fist down on Markin's desk beside me. The physical pain in my hand was a welcome break from the one in my heart, the pain I knew would only worsen.

"Then you damn well uncomplicate it!" I snapped. "He told me something that didn't really make sense at the time, but I've had a few hours to think about it, and you know what? I've got some pretty disturbing thoughts in my head."

"Please don't," my mother whispered, but I was too far gone to stop now.

"He said 'I know *whose* she is'." My mother's face paled dramatically, and she finally looked at me. Her familiar hazel eyes displayed a world of pain and turmoil that almost matched my own as I desperately clung to a shred of hope that my conclusions were wrong. That what happened had been something I'd made up to cope with killing Lucien. "What did he mean?"

"No, Rayleigh, I can't."

"I don't care. What. Did. He. Mean?!" I said through gritted teeth. She shook her head, hair flying loose. "Don't lie to me! Stop covering up whatever it is you're hiding! This concerns me. My life! Even my own thoughts terrify me right now, so you will tell me the truth."

"You have to understand that I was young, and I did a foolish thing. A truly foolish thing. I didn't think he knew. I thought the only people who knew were myself and Markin. That's it. I swear I did this to protect you!" She finally looked at me.

"Protect me? Yeah, you've done a grand job of that considering I was ambushed and taken by a group of Dydairians with no knowledge of who they really are or what they really want, and then I found out druids can cross the boundary! That left me and my guard at a major disadvantage you know. We lost Mahds."

"I know," she choked out.

"And I feel like it's my fault, but maybe it's yours because maybe if I had been told, I could have done something, negotiated better, something, anything!"

"I know, and I'm sorry you had to witness that."

"Enough now. I need the truth."

Silence. My mother stood, pacing back and forth in the small office. I let her. She finally stopped and wrapped her arms around her middle. She took a deep breath and met my eye, her next words quiet as if she didn't want to say the words out loud at all.

"Tyton is the leader of the Dydairians, as you said. He has worked tirelessly to amass a following and cut down anyone who disagreed with him, and he is powerful. So very powerful. He came into *our* kingdom, and hurt *our* people, because he wants me to know that it's him. He wants me to know that he's coming for me. To taunt me. Show me there's nothing I can do to stop him. He wants to come and use me like he believes I used him."

"Why? What's the point of all that? If he's powerful enough to just destroy what he sees fit, why doesn't he?"

"Because he always craves more power, and there's only one way he can get that right now."

"How?" I whisper.

"His bloodline. His heir. The shadow druid heir."

My breathing quickened.

A single tear ran down my mother's face. She swiped it away.

"Tyton is your father."

END OF BOOK 1

Authors thrive (and do a little squealy dance) when we get a review, so if you liked this book, consider leaving one so this particular author gets to do said squealy dance. Even a rating is incredibly appreciated!

WHAT'S NEXT?

Book Two, Throne of Lies and Ruin, is up next! I'm sorry about the ending of book one, but I have a bonus chapter from Wren's POV to help soften the blow (you know that chapter where he helps her find...ahem...a little bit of freedom?) By joining my newsletter, you'll get access to this and all future bonuses!

Click (if you're reading an ebook version) or scan the QR code to join and get your bonus chapter: https://rhianedwardsautho r.com/newsletter/

Reviews

I love hearing your thoughts on my books! With this book being my first NA one, I'm especially interested! Any ratings, reviews, blog posts, and private messages are highly encouraged and appreciated. Thank you for reading, reader bestie, can't wait to see you in the next one.

Acknowledgments

I have a whole host of people to thank who have helped me get this book to here. Gosh, at one point I thought I was a fool for taking this project on (especially after about fifty major rewrites of the whole plot), but eventually, the story came together and the world is rapidly expanding in my head. I literally cannot wait to continue.

To my alpha readers, and friends who have read a chapter here or there (and then terrible first drafts) thanks for your incredible input. I have many people who I have brainstormed with and worked with in this stage. Reign of Blood and Shadows wouldn't be what it is without that input, so thank you.

Throughout the process both readers and writers have given me support and encouragement. I can't even begin to explain how much that encouragement was vital, instrumental, in my completing this book.

From artists, to cover work, to paid beta readers and editors, thank you.

And I can't go without thanking my family. My husband who supports this dream of mine, and my kids who help me work through the toughest of times. It was a challenge with my health to get this book where it is, and my family were always there.

Finally, a massive shout out to all readers and book accounts who have given me the strength and the confidence to write this story as I wanted it to be told. I hope you loved it.

ABOUT RHIAN

I'm a NA/YA fantasy and paranormal author so you can expect romance, a dash of humour, and a lot of supernatural twists. If feisty women who find their voice, dangerous males, and epic love stories are your thing—I've got you covered.

Stories were my lifeline growing up, and not much has changed now I'm in my thirties! I've always enjoyed supernatural elements, anything romance, and of course, a happy ending. There is nothing that calms me more than having my head in other worlds.

When I'm not writing, I'm busy losing my sanity trying to raise to two littles and keep a very cute, but cheeky, golden retriever alive. Pretty sure I'm one vet bill away from swapping him for a goldfish.

CONTACT WITH RHIAN EDWARDS:
Website: https://rhianedwardsauthor.com
Instagram: @rhian.edwards.author

YouTube: www.youtube.com/c/RhianEdwardsAuthor
TikTok: @rhianedwardsauthor